THE SOUTH BINNESS MURDERS

A gripping crime thriller full of twists

PAULINE ROWSON

The Solent Murder Mysteries Book 16

D1452860

Joffe Books, London
www.joffebooks.com

First published in Great Britain in 2022

Cover art by Dee Dee Book Covers

ISBN: 978-1-80405-694-3

Dedicated to Stephen Keyte

CHAPTER ONE

Sunday 9 May

'Anything wrong, Dai?' Horton called out to the burly sergeant standing on the waiting pontoon at Southsea Marina as he eased his yacht alongside.

'A motor cruiser's been found stranded on South Binness Island.'

Hardly enough to draw the attention of the Marine Police Unit, Horton thought, silencing his engine and alighting as Sergeant Dai Elkins took the for'ard line and tied off. The small island was in the upper reaches of Langstone Harbour, one of a handful and all uninhabited — unless you counted the gull colony, which at this time of the year was vast. The islands were nature reserves owned and managed by the Royal Society for the Protection of Birds and comprised of sea grass, stones and gravel, with just North Binness Island boasting gorse, a few trees and a vague vestige of once having been inhabited. Unauthorized landings were forbidden.

'Anyone on board?' Horton asked, securing the line at the aft.

'No.'

'But?'

1

'You'll have to see for yourself, Andy. We've brought her in.' Elkins nodded in the direction of a small craft moored up just beyond the police launch. 'I was about to call it in when I saw you making for the marina. I didn't realize you were coming back today but then no reason why I should have been told.'

'It was a last-minute thing,' Horton replied. The official reason for his impromptu absence nineteen days ago was that he'd been assigned to work with the Intelligence Directorate undercover, using his yacht to trail a known criminal in the ports, bays and marinas of Northern France. In reality, he'd taken off after learning the shattering truth about the disappearance of his mother, Jennifer, when he was ten, and the identity of his father.

He was exhausted after his overnight channel crossing but curious to know what Elkins meant in his guarded response about the stranded boat. He nodded at PC Ripley, who was standing beside the fairly new small motor cruiser, *Wishful Thinking*. Essentially it was a day-cruising boat but could accommodate an overnight stay, or a couple of nights on board if the occupants weren't too fussy about their toilet arrangements. The cockpit gave onto a single seat at the helm. There was a bench seat on either side of the craft under which were storage lockers, but it was what was on the deck close to the locker on the starboard side that caused Horton to raise his eyebrows.

'Is that what I think it is?' He indicated some small blobs and a smear of dark red.

'You haven't seen anything yet. You might want to put these on.' Elkins handed Horton a pair of latex gloves.

'That bad, eh?'

'Seen worse.'

Horton climbed aboard. Elkins followed. Horton pushed open the sliding cabin door, swiftly taking in the blue vinyl horseshoe seating around a table in the narrow space, the grubby blue-and-white curtains, the small galley with a kettle on top of a gas burner, two mugs — one with a spoon standing in it, both unused — a packet of opened biscuits, a box of teabags, a jar of coffee and an opened packet of white sugar. But it was none of these that quickened his pulse and drew his full attention. It was the large pool of dark red on the deck between him and the table, along with the heavy crimson spatter up the side of the lockers on the right.

Elkins said, 'I don't think the owner cut himself shaving.'

Horton gave a tired smile.

'And that amount of blood means a serious injury, so where is he?'

'He could have staggered up on deck to get help, hence the blood and smear in the cockpit, then collapsed overboard.'

'Clutching the offending weapon in his hand, because it's not lying around here,' Elkins said. 'And there's nowhere it could have got lodged under. But there is another possible explanation.'

'You don't need to spell it out. I might be tired, but my brain is still functioning, just.'

'Glad all that sea air and salt hasn't corroded it. You look knackered, Andy.'

'So would you if you'd just battled your way across the English Channel in a force six, verging on seven, and rain-drops the size of golf balls.'

'How did the operation go?'

'Let's just say I'm glad to be back.'

And he meant it. He hadn't known when he had first taken off if he would return, and certainly not to work, but after several days of reflection he was sick of himself and his navel-gazing, and he was sick of the past. Besides, what else was there for him but the job? And, of course, his daughter, Emma, who he was going to spend the day with next Sunday. His access to her was limited enough without giving Catherine, his ex-wife, more ammunition to deprive him of her company. He couldn't and wouldn't abandon her.

Horton knew Elkins meant this could be a murder scene. He said, 'It might not be human blood.'

Elkins eyed him askance.

3

'Yes. I know. I've seen enough of the stuff to recognize it.' He sniffed the air. 'No smell of alcohol, and no discarded cans or empty bottles, so the boat owner doesn't appear to have been indulging in a drunken orgy with anyone when disaster struck. And it doesn't look as though a fight took place, not unless we have a very tidy assailant who put everything back in its place, including the spoon in the mug. Any boat keys at the helm?'

'Yes. Ripley piloted the boat back here. Jed Parkham, the RSPB ranger, reported it. He was heading out to the islands to count the morning roost. He says birds resting overnight give a better picture of the total colony size. You know as well as I do, Andy, that it's not unusual to find a stranded boat on the harbour shores given the winds we have, and craft do break their moorings. But it being the height of the breeding season for Mediterranean gulls and little terns, any boat seen landing or abandoned on any of the islands is a cause for concern. It could alarm them so much that they fly off and don't return to their clutch. Jed hailed the boat and when he got no reply he boarded her, saw the blood, quickly retreated and called us.'

'Where is he now?'

'Checking around the other islands and the oyster beds at Hayling Island. He said he'll give me a call if he finds anything suspicious, or a body. He'll also check out the trail cameras on the islands. They use them to pick up any foxes, or disturbances, and they also have a few time-lapse cameras. It could give us the time when the boat was washed up. I've told him if one of their cameras has picked up any sighting of *Wishful Thinking* anywhere in the harbour or around the islands to hold on to it as we might need it.'

'And the boat owner is?'

'Neil Spender. The harbour master, Ray Tomsett, says Spender's got one of the tidal moorings at the top of the harbour in Chalkdock Lake. He's had it for four years. He gave me Spender's mobile number. I've tried it. No answer. He lives in Portsmouth. Want me to send a unit to his address?'

'Any relatives?'

'Tomsett's never seen him with anyone and Spender's never mentioned a partner, but that doesn't signify much. Spender pays his dues with no quibbles. He works for Jeplie, the refuse collectors, as a binman.'

Horton was momentarily surprised. Spender's boat must have set him back about £10,000, not the sort of money a binman was likely to have lying around in his bank account. But he might have bought it on a marine mortgage or loan, been left a legacy, or was prudent with his money. It never paid to make assumptions and Spender's finances weren't Horton's concern, unless this turned out to be murder. Even then it would be the remit of the Major Crime Team and not a CID investigation. He wondered if Uckfield was back at work having recovered from his burst appendix.

Elkins consulted his notebook. 'I've got a description of Spender from Tomsett. About five feet nine, sparse grey hair, trim and wiry. Early sixties, maybe older. He's also got a deep scar on the right-hand side of his face from his hairline to the base of his nose. And no, Tomsett doesn't know how Spender came by it.'

'We'll hold off sending a unit to his address for a moment. I'd like to see where the boat was found, and Spender's mooring first.' Horton turned to Ripley, who was on the pontoon. 'Did you check his plotter?'

'Yes. Nothing for yesterday or today. The last time he used the navigational aid was a fortnight ago. He plotted a course to Yarmouth on the Isle of Wight.'

So no clue there as to where Spender had gone or what he was doing yesterday.

Elkins said, 'There might be a logbook but on seeing the blood we didn't search for one.'

'Who's duty CID?'

'Sergeant Cantelli.'

Horton would rather not disturb Cantelli on a Sunday even though Cantelli knew the drill and wouldn't utter a word of complaint at being summoned. He deserved to spend some time with his wife and five children. Horton also owed him a great deal, not least for the extra work burden he'd placed on him by his absence. Cantelli would have been told the same as their boss, DCI Lorraine Bliss, that he'd been rapidly deployed to assist on Operation Combine on the French coast, but the operation, its name and its remit had all been dreamt up by Ducale of the intelligence services, who was the only person other than Ducale's Whitehall bosses who knew the truth. It was Ducale who had set Horton off searching for the truth behind Jennifer's disappearance. And he'd found it on a foggy night, similar to the one when Jennifer had vanished.

Horton had been on board a yacht on the Isle of Wight with Lord Richard Ames and his brother, Gordon, when he had learned that their father, Viscount William Ames, was also his father, and that William Ames had killed Jennifer Horton to prevent her from telling the truth about his fascist connections during and after the war while working for British Intelligence, something which Richard and Gordon had known and had conspired to keep silent about. Not long after Jennifer's death, William, with the threat of being exposed, committed suicide by throwing himself off his yacht in the English Channel. And nineteen days ago, after leaving Richard and Gordon, Horton had heard a shot. He'd raced back but the yacht had sailed and he still didn't know which of the brothers was alive. He didn't wish to know. He only wanted to get on with his life and put the past behind him — for good.

Horton had telephoned Ducale three days ago to say he was returning to England and to duty, so he assumed that Bliss had also been told. He wondered how she had taken the news, both of his impromptu assignment and his return. She probably hoped he had sailed into the sunset for good. For eighteen months she'd been itching to get rid of him. But like a piece of grit lodged in the sole of her shoe he'd hung on, annoying her with his form of policing that didn't conform to her strictly by-the-book methods, and no matter how hard she scraped and tried to prise him out, he wouldn't budge.

'Ripley, call Taylor and ask him to come over with one of his scene of crime officers to examine and assess the scene. Stay with the boat and make sure nothing is disturbed. Elkins, let's take that trip up the harbour.'

CHAPTER TWO

Elkins steered the craft through the small boats moored on buoys and passed the humpbacked concrete structure of the Mulberry from the Second World War, providing an unusual seamark in the wide expanse of Langstone Harbour which stretched around them. To the west lay the Portsmouth shore, where small dinghies from the Locks Sailing Club were bobbing about. To the east, Hayling Island. A row of large houses with pontoons gave way to the natural coastline of the Hayling Billy Nature Reserve. Ahead rose the gentle slopes of Portsdown Hill straddled with housing and only a handful of fields remaining on the southern slopes.

Horton took a deep breath. Despite the fact he'd had nothing but sea air for nineteen days he never tired of it. He was, however, dead-beat from sailing and sleepless nights, and hastily suppressed a yawn before Elkins could see and comment on it. 'Coffee?' he asked, hoping the caffeine would stave off drowsiness.

'Tea, two sugars,' Elkins replied. 'And there's some custard creams.'

It was only then that Horton realized he was hungry. He helped himself to a biscuit while making their drinks, his thoughts returning to the bloodstained boat and its owner.

Two mugs had been on board, so had Spender entertained a companion? Had there been an argument that had got out of hand? One man had killed the other then taken off, after ditching the body in the sea and letting the boat drift? Or was it usual for the owner of *Wishful Thinking* to always have two mugs at the ready?

He took their drinks and the packet of biscuits across to Elkins at the helm. Soon South Binness Island lay ahead in a swarm of squawking, squealing, whirling seagulls drowning out the drone of the traffic noise from the motorway to the north. Horton took a third biscuit and tucked the packet under the helm. 'Better make sure they don't get wind of these.'

'I'll have to get Ripley to hose the boat down.'

'I hope Spender isn't on the island being pecked to pieces.' Horton had visions of Alfred Hitchcock's *The Birds*.

'Want to check?'

'No thanks, a drone can do that.'

Elkins smiled. 'Jed's already done it. I forgot to mention that. No sign of a body and even seagulls can't eat that fast. That's where the boat was found, on that small peninsula. It's called Dead Man's Head, God alone knows why.'

'Well, let's hope we don't find any dead men or their heads.' Horton swallowed some coffee and studied the low-lying island. 'For the boat to have ended up on this part of the island it must have drifted up from the south, or over from the south-east but not from the north, which is where his mooring is. Do you think he was returning from a night's fishing?'

'I didn't see any fishing tackle on the boat.'

Neither had Horton.

'And no fish either,' Elkins added. 'So if he, or they, did go fishing then they were either very unlucky not to have caught anything, or the accomplice, if there is one, took them home to eat.'

'Hope he chokes on the bones.' Horton polished off another biscuit. 'Let's see if Spender's tender is on his mooring.'

Elkins started the launch and manoeuvred it around the island. He found the mooring location, which Tomsett had given him.

'Empty,' declared Horton. 'And Spender would certainly have needed a tender to reach his mooring, which means either our injured man took it with him on board and then used it to get help — yeah, unlikely — or there was someone else on that boat who used the tender to get away after ditching the wounded, or dead, Spender in the sea.'

'Spender might have used it to make his getaway after killing his companion.'

'Possible, but I can't see him leaving his boat behind.'

'Why not? He could show up claiming it had been stolen.'

'Give us the glasses, Dai.'

Elkins handed over the binoculars and Horton trained them on the car park and launching slipway to the northeast. There were three cars but none with a trailer that could have towed a small dinghy or tender, which meant Spender must have used an inflatable one to reach his mooring. Horton focused in on the vehicle registration numbers and relayed them to Elkins, who consulted the Driver and Vehicle Licensing Agency database while Horton swivelled the binoculars around the area, wondering if anyone perhaps from the sea angling club to the north had seen Spender go out.

Elkins said, 'The blue Honda estate is registered to Neil Spender. The address checks with the one Tomsett gave me.'

Horton reached for his phone. 'I'll get a unit over there. Spender might have a partner, friend or relative living with him who can shed some light on his disappearance.'

'Unless we find him at home with his feet up and in robust health.'

'Doubtful, but in our game, anything is possible,' replied Horton, putting his phone on speaker so Elkins could hear the conversation.

'Andy! Thought you were saving Planet Earth from a bunch of ruthless continental criminals,' came Sergeant Wells's jovial tone.

'All done. I've decided to return to Portsmouth and save our own fair city from low-lifes and scum.'

'Better put your Superman underpants on then.'

'I will tomorrow.'

'That'll bring a smile to Bliss's face.'

'Don't bank on it.'

'No, probably too much to hope for. So, to what do we owe the pleasure of this little chat?'

'We've got blood, a boat and a missing boat owner.'

'Sounds like something out of Miss Marple.'

'If I see her I'll send her along to you, Wells. Meanwhile I've got to make do with Sergeant Elkins.'

'Can't have it all.'

Elkins laughed.

Horton said, 'Send a unit over to the boat owner's address and check he's not there with his feet up wondering what all the fuss is about.'

'Want a forced entry if he doesn't answer the door?'

'Not for the moment, just get officers asking around about him — name's Neil Spender. Oh, and ask Havant officers to examine Spender's car in the Broadmarsh coastal car park.'

'Are they looking for anything in particular? Machete? Sawn-off shotgun? Severed limbs?'

'Just an inflatable—'

'Doll.'

'Tender.' Horton grinned. 'Or a foot pump and any sundry boating equipment.'

'Sounds rather tedious but if you say so. What's the name of the boat?

'*Wishful Thinking.*'

'You're kidding.'

'No, why?'

'I'm doing a lot of that at the moment wishing we had treble the officers we've got, a hierarchy that doesn't believe in three miracles before breakfast, and a government that for once really does believe in being tough on crime and putting their money where their mouths are.'

'Now you're moving into the realms of fantasy. Call me when you have anything to report.'

'OK, Superman.'

Horton rang off with a smile. 'I might as well live up to the name, Elkins. Who needs sleep when you're superhuman?'

Elkins piloted the police launch back to the waiting pontoon just outside the marina, where Phil Taylor and Beth Tremaine from the scene of crime team were causing some curious looks from passing yachties as they examined Spender's boat. On Horton's request Ripley went in search of bacon rolls while Horton motored his yacht into the marina and then his own berth. As he was doing this his mobile rang, but he postponed answering it until he was securely moored. It was Sergeant Wells.

'There's no answer at that address, Andy, and no funny smells or noise coming from inside it. A resident in one of the other flats said she has no idea who Neil Spender is. She's never seen or spoken to him, but another woman said she saw him yesterday morning, early, probably going to work. The flats are let and managed by Leaders in the London Road. And Havant police have reported back on the car. It's locked but as it's an estate, the officer reported she could see a pair of wellington boots, an old coat, an empty cardboard box, a rug and a foot pump in the back. No visible signs of bloodstains.'

'That means Spender does have an inflatable tender that he uses to reach his mooring and that too is missing. I'll ask Elkins to alert the sailing and yacht clubs for it.'

'It also means someone was on board that boat with him. And that someone could have rowed back to the car park after attacking Spender, deflated the tender and taken it away in his own car.'

'Good point.'

'I do have these occasional flashes of brilliance, only don't tell anyone otherwise they'll be promoting me. I've also checked with the hospital to see if Mr Spender has been admitted, in case he injured himself and decided to use his own tender to reach the shore. Yeah, unlikely. He hasn't and neither has anyone been brought in bleeding profusely from a stab or bullet wound, or as a result of an accident on a boat over the last two days.'

'Your brain is working well, which is more than mine is at the moment. Ask Havant police to keep an eye on Spender's vehicle from time to time until we know what we've got here.'

'Still hoping he'll return?'

'You never know.' But Horton wasn't overly optimistic. He walked around to the waiting pontoon where Ripley handed him a bacon roll and a mug of coffee. He relayed what Wells had said and ate while watching Taylor examine the cockpit.

Beth emerged from the cabin. She consulted with Taylor for a moment, then both climbed off the boat. Taylor removed his mask and gloves.

'We've swabbed the blood, both in the cockpit and the cabin, and I'll get it off to the forensic service for a fast-track response,' he reported in his usual nasal, mournful manner. 'You should get it later today or first thing tomorrow morning. They'll confirm if it's human and if you've got more than one blood type present. We've also recorded the scene and documented the positioning of the blood. There are no footmarks or handprints in the blood itself, and no bloody prints elsewhere, nor any bloodstained implements on board. A blood pattern analyst could tell you if an assault has taken place and what type. PC Ripley asked us to look for a log-book — there isn't one.'

'Any fishing equipment?' Horton asked.

'No. Just some lines in the lockers, along with life vests, an anchor, and an old waterproof jacket with nothing in the pockets.'

He handed Horton the boat's keys. There were only two, one to the helm and the other to the cabin. Spender must have kept his flat and car keys on another key ring, which was normal for most boat owners. If they needed to enter Spender's flat the letting agent could give them a key.

Horton didn't think there was any great urgency because it was unlikely that Spender was lying ill or dead in his flat when all the indications suggested that he had been on his boat when injured or possibly attacked.

Taylor and Tremaine took their leave. Horton turned to Elkins. 'Not much we can do until we have the forensic results. I'll ask Eddie in the marina office to keep an eye on the boat. Just seal it off with the hazard tape rather than the crime scene tape.'

'If anything further occurs I'll call Cantelli and brief him. Get some sleep, Andy.'

Horton promised he would. He returned to his boat mulling over what he had learned. Spender sounded an ordinary sort of man who led an ordinary sort of life, so why the blood? Perhaps this was murder, or perhaps there was a straightforward explanation.

He reached for his phone. He had barely checked it during his absence and, as he had officially been undercover, he hadn't spoken to anyone — not that he had wanted to, but he wondered what Cantelli had made of his absenteeism, and the story put out to explain it, which he was certain Cantelli would know was false. Cantelli knew he had been trying to discover the truth about Jennifer's disappearance and that Lord Richard Ames was involved in it somewhere along the line, but that was all. He didn't know what Horton had discovered. Horton had confided that to no one, not even to Gaye, the forensic pathologist who had assisted him with some information connected to Jennifer's disappearance, although Horton had been very tempted to tell her all. Giving confidences didn't come naturally to him, a legacy of his days in care, when confessions were used to manipulate and bully.

There were six voicemails, three texts and twenty emails. Not as bad as he had anticipated. There was nothing from Harriet Ames, Richard's daughter, he noted with relief. He had last seen her at a fogbound Southampton airport before he'd taken off for the Isle of Wight and the Ames's family holiday home to confront her father. There was one voice message from his daughter, Emma, which brought both a smile of joy and a stab of pain.

'I hope you're having a nice time sailing, Daddy. Mummy and Peter are taking me to France for half-term. We're going on Peter's boat.'

His body tensed. Peter Jarvis was Catherine's latest and very rich boyfriend. Jarvis's luxury superyacht would look perfectly at home on the Riviera along with all the other millionaires' floating gin palaces. It wasn't jealousy of Jarvis's wealth that consumed Horton, but of the fact that Emma was spending more time with a man who wasn't her father than with him. And he was frightened she would get used to the luxurious life and then despise slumming it on his modest yacht. His fury was also directed at Catherine for whisking Emma away. For yet another school holiday he was being deprived of his daughter's company.

'Miss you, Daddy. Love you lots. See you next Sunday,' Emma finished.

He was looking forward to taking Emma sailing next week and spending an entire day with her, though he was half-afraid that Catherine would come up with some excuse to prevent him. Turning his attention to his texts, he saw that two were from one of his regular informers with a message to say he knew where certain parties were stashing the goods they'd stolen from houses in Copnor. Horton knew nothing about the robberies so that must have come in while he was away. He ignored the emails. He'd deal with them tomorrow in his office. Likewise, he'd then respond to Billy Jago, his informant. He rose and went out on deck, where he punched in Cantelli's number, who answered almost immediately.

'Andy, are you OK?' came Barney's worried tone.

'I'm fine and on English soil, well, water to be precise. I'm in the marina and will be back at work tomorrow. No doubt Bliss will be delighted to greet me.'

'She might when she pops over from the Major Crime Team. She's in charge in the Super's absence. Uckfield is still off sick and recuperating at home. Pity his poor wife. He must be the world's worst patient. I expect the hospital couldn't wait to get shot of him. And Dave Trueman's thinking of booking himself into a clinic or booking Bliss into one. She's driving him nuts, me too. I had hoped she'd have enough to do to keep her out of our hair, but she just can't break the habit of demanding to know what Walters and I are up to every five minutes,' Cantelli said with a smile in his voice.

'Knowing Walters as we do, that's easy to answer — eating.'

'He's got a new girlfriend. Penny.'

'The poor thing. The girl, that is.'

'Walters says they share the same interests.'

'Don't tell me, takeaway kebabs.'

Cantelli laughed.

Horton had missed the sound and he'd missed Cantelli. 'It'll be good to have you back on the job, Andy.'

'I'm on it now actually.' Horton told Cantelli what had occurred. 'It doesn't warrant you coming here,' he quickly added. 'Everything's been done that can be done so far. Elkins will call you if anything more crops up today. How are things your end? Family well?'

'Good thanks. We're all looking forward to our holiday in Italy. Ellen's packed her case about fifty times and we don't go until the end of the month.'

Horton smiled. Ellen was the eldest of Cantelli's five children, seventeen, and at college. 'Back to the land of your fathers, eh?' he said.

'Yes, it'll be good to see some of Dad's relatives. Most didn't get over for the funeral.'

Horton recalled it on a damp January day sixteen months ago. Toni Cantelli had been generous, gregarious, kind and an astute businessman. His death from a second heart attack while in hospital had hit Barney hard. He had been a prisoner of war, married a land girl and started a thriving ice cream company in Portsmouth, which had expanded into cafés that Cantelli's sister, Isabella, ran. She worked at the café on the seafront while Toni junior had taken over the ice cream business. Barney had followed in his maternal grandfather's footsteps and joined the police.

'Work is the usual,' Cantelli said. 'Thefts, muggings and assaults. I'll tell you all about them tomorrow.'

'Can't wait,' Horton answered. And ringing off, he meant it.

CHAPTER THREE

Monday

'Present for you.' Horton put the bag of doughnuts on Walters's desk. 'I was going to bring you back a stick of rock, but they don't go in for that sort of thing in France.'

The corpulent constable's eyes lit up. 'Glad it's not those croissant things — all air, nothing to sink your teeth into. Hope you had a nice holiday, guv.' Walters looked slyly at him. 'Got a bit of a tan there. This is just what I need, and a cup of coffee to go with it.'

'Then you can fetch me one. Where's Cantelli?' Horton called out entering his office.

'Dunno. In the bog?'

Horton felt as though he'd been away a month. It looked like it too, judging by the state of his desk. 'Half a rainforest here,' he muttered. He removed his leather biker's jacket and hung it on the hook behind his door. Placing his motorcycle helmet on the floor he crossed to his desk, where he pulled back the slatted blinds and threw open the window, letting in traffic noise and fumes on the gentle breeze. It promised to be a warm day, which was good for sailing and made him think of Spender's boat. He'd checked on it last night and earlier this morning after his run along Southsea seafront. The police tape hadn't been disturbed. Elkins hadn't called with any further information or with results of the blood analysis, although he might have telephoned Cantelli as he said he would. The sergeant's Ford was in its allotted space in the car park along with DCI Bliss's sports car. She was bound to have heard his Harley and no doubt would be phoning him to command his presence at any moment.

Walters entered the office bearing a plastic cup of vending machine coffee.

'Take a seat, and tell me what's been happening in my absence,' Horton instructed.

'Mind if I get my coffee and a doughnut?'

'Will your update take that long?'

'Nah, probably not.' Walters eased his frame onto one of the two seats across Horton's desk. 'DC Marsden had a good send-off by the Major Crime Team, his replacement is due end of next week. Bliss keeps popping in and out like a yo-yo. Hamilton is pregnant and Jameson's got the—'

'I meant on the streets of Portsmouth.'

'Oh, that. Same as usual. Another three house robberies in Copnor, making that seven, a break-in on the industrial estate at Milton, and some thefts at Oyster Quays in the restaurants, two women posing as waitresses and stealing diners' phones and bags. Also, some high-end car thefts, stolen to order by the sounds of it, and that's about it, aside from the usual muggings and assaults.'

'That's a relief, for a moment I thought the crime rate had gone down.' Horton swallowed some coffee and pulled a face. The taste never improved. 'We've also got an abandoned boat, which is currently moored up at my marina complete with bloodstains and a missing boat owner.'

Horton had just finished relaying what had happened when Cantelli walked in. He looked tired. It made Horton feel guilty at having been away. 'Have a doughnut, Sergeant,' Horton said, causing Walters's expression to fall. 'Walters, fetch him a tea.'

Walters waddled off.

'Anything new from Elkins yesterday?'

'If there is he didn't call me.'

'Me neither.'

'You're looking tanned.'

'So Walters said, and you're looking tired.'

'Probably the thought of my day in court with that scumbag Callum Dailey. He's up on that grievous bodily harm charge.'

'I had hoped he'd change his plea to guilty.'

'Me 'n all. Maybe he will when the court convenes. Knowing Dailey as we do, he'll probably try and bluff it out with that simpering angelic look on his face in the hope of convincing the jury he's as innocent as a newborn and a victim of mistaken identity or some such twaddle. When actually, he's not yet thirty-five and has got a record as long as your arm for affray, assault, theft and nearly everything else on the statute book.'

'Then let's hope the jury aren't fooled.'

Walters entered with the dishwater tea.

'This will put the blood back in your veins,' Horton said.

'I doubt it. Where's my doughnut?'

'You don't really want one do you, sarge?' Walters looked peeved. 'Just think of your waistline and those shorts you want to get into for your holiday in Italy.'

'You're so right, Walters. I'd hate to deprive you, especially when you look as though you need building up.'

Walters grinned and ambled out.

Horton said, 'Did the forensic service get in touch about the blood analysis from Spender's boat?'

Cantelli shook his head.

'Walters, has Joliffe phoned the results through?' Horton called out.

'No,' Walters shouted back, clearly with his mouth full by the sound of his monosyllabic answer.

'I'll chase him up,' Horton said. 'I've only been away a short while, but it feels like a lifetime. I'm sorry for putting an extra burden on you.'

'You didn't, the Intelligence Directorate did.'

Horton eyed him carefully.

'I hope it was successful.'

Horton could see that Barney knew the cover story was a whitewash. He wondered what Detective Superintendent Sawyer, the head of the Intelligence Directorate, had made of it. Sawyer had been itching to get Horton to work on his team to locate an international jewel thief, code-named Zeus, whom Sawyer believed Jennifer had known and run off with. Ducale said he hadn't disclosed the truth to Sawyer, and Horton believed him, but he didn't know what had actually been said. He wasn't going to ask either. He'd stick to his side of the tale and not elaborate or deviate from it, except to give Barney a coded message.

'I've had some time to think about the past, mine and my mother's, and I've decided that it's deflected me from what really matters and that's keeping in touch with my daughter, being there for her when she needs me, and making sure that I can see her more often.'

Cantelli nodded and sipped his tea. 'Have you heard from your solicitor about increasing your access to her?'

'Only that Catherine is refusing it. It looks as though I'll have to apply to the courts, which I didn't wish to do but I've got no choice. I have a feeling they'll think a boat is not a suitable place for a little girl to stay.'

'She stays on Peter Jarvis's boat.'

Horton gave a bitter laugh. 'There's no comparison. I'll have to look at renting or buying a flat or house.'

'One with a mooring for your boat would suit you.'

'I'm not sure my funds will run to that.' His divorce had cleaned him out, not that he was complaining — he had been determined to make sure Emma had a stable home. But if Catherine moved in with her millionaire boyfriend, she'd sell their house or rent it out, and take all the proceeds. That was the way it went. No point in being bitter about it.

'There are some waterside estate agents who might be able to help you find something,' Cantelli said, breaking through Horton's thoughts. 'No harm in putting out the feelers.'

'I will.'

His desk phone rang. 'Bliss.'

Before he could speak, she said, 'My office, Inspector. The major incident suite.'

'Do you mean Superintendent Uckfield's office, ma'am?'

'Yes.'

Horton rose. 'I don't think the witch in the wardrobe is very happy.'

'When is she ever?'

Horton made his way along the corridor and up the stairs. The incident suite was humming with activity. Sergeant Trueman, who was on the phone, nodded a greeting at him. He looked strung out. There was no sign of DI Dennings's fifteen-stone frame in his office.

Horton knocked on Uckfield's office door and, without waiting for a reply, strode in. Bliss was dressed in her customary black skirt, jacket and white shirt. Her light brown hair, as usual, was scraped back off her narrow face in a high ponytail. Her desk, or rather Uckfield's, was uncluttered, which was more than it was when Uckfield occupied it. She peered at him intently and without any preamble or an invitation to sit launched in. 'Assistant Chief Constable Dean informed me on Friday that you'd be returning to duty today, Inspector.'

Horton wondered if she wanted to add, 'More's the pity.'

'I trust you will get up to speed quickly on the number of outstanding cases, and that you will give them your full concentration.'

What did she think he was going to do? Sit back in his chair and sip tequilas?

'These crimes might seem petty compared to those of the Intelligence Directorate, but I can assure you they are not.'

Ah, so that was it, a stab of jealousy that he'd been chosen for the alleged undercover assignment.

'And we don't all have yachts,' she crisply added.

She made it sound as though he lived on one the size of Peter Jarvis's.

'DC Walters has already briefed me and we have a new and rather unusual case,' he said.

Her nostrils twitched. 'I haven't been notified of anything.'

'It happened yesterday.' He sat without being invited and brought her up to date.

'Have you run this man Spender through the police computer?'

'Not yet.'

'Then do so. He could be involved in criminal activity, drug smuggling or people smuggling. This could be a case of thieves falling out. Chase up the forensic service for that blood analysis. If it's human, which seems highly probable, then we could be looking at a murder investigation.'

She didn't exactly rub her hands — murder was no joyful matter — but Horton knew she was chomping at the bit to solve a case while in charge and gain extra brownie points. He rose and had reached the door before she said, 'I expect to be kept fully briefed.'

He didn't bother answering her. Exchanging a brief glimpse with Trueman, who rolled his eyes, Horton returned to his office.

'How did it go?' Cantelli asked.

'Well let's just say I didn't get a "welcome back" smile.'

'You expect miracles?' Walters scoffed good-naturedly.

Cantelli rose. 'I'm off to court.'

'Good luck. Oh, and if you can get a quick result, it would please Bliss.'

'Anything to oblige,' Cantelli called out.

Horton asked Walters to telephone Jeplie to find out if Spender had shown up for work — unlikely, he thought, given the circumstances, but best to check. He ran Spender's name through the Police National Computer and drew a blank. Spender had never been convicted of any crime. He emailed Bliss to let her know and then attempted to tackle his workload. Before he could dive into the mound of paper, he was interrupted by Walters with news that Spender had last been at work on Saturday morning. 'They've had no message from him to say he's sick. He lives alone according to the manager, Scott Tweed, who wanted to know why I was asking. I told him Spender's boat had been found without him on board and we were concerned about him.'

'Did Tweed know Spender owned a boat?'

'He'd heard him mention it.'

'Was he concerned about Spender?'

'Irritated, I'd say. He's had to call a stand-in last minute and that's delayed the crew going out. He has no idea if Spender was depressed or disturbed about anything. I doubt he knows him that well.'

His workmates might, and they might have been out on the boat with him, but there was little point in talking to them until they had good reason to step up the investigation. Horton put a call through to Joliffe to chivvy up the blood analysis. Joliffe grunted an apology saying that all their systems had gone down early that morning after some idiot had cut through an outside power cable during building works, and plunged them into the Dark Ages. They were working off-site on their laptops and should have a result for him later that day.

Horton then read the file on the house robberies in Copnor, after which he rang his informant, Billy Jago, and arranged to meet him later that day. He turned his attention to answering messages, reading reports and filling in what seemed to be endless and pointless forms. Every now and again he heard Walters answering the telephone.

Cantelli phoned during the court's lunch break to say that Callum was sticking to his plea of not guilty and that he was still waiting to be called to give evidence. PC Martins, who had been first on the scene, had given his.

Horton grabbed some sandwiches from the canteen and returned to his desk. He was tempted to eat outside, the day being so bright it seemed a shame to be stuck inside, and perhaps a re-examination of Spender's boat might throw some new light on his disappearance. But Horton knew that was just an excuse. Paperwork and routine were a major and increasing part of the job, and the part he hated the most. Although his assignment with the Intelligent Directorate had been fictitious, he wondered if he might be better suited transferring to that department altogether, or another that called for more action. Bliss would hang out the flags and probably hire a brass band to celebrate.

His mobile rang. It was just after two. He recognized the number as that of Felice Ellwood, an art expert he had met on that last major investigation which had led him to confronting Richard Ames over the truth of Jennifer's disappearance. Felice knew nothing about that. She'd been consulted to value some paintings belonging to a possible victim. They shared a love of sailing and he'd thought they might get to know each other better. That had been scotched, however, not only by his own sudden departure, but also by Felice being called away as her father, a renowned artist, was ill.

'Andy, there's been a robbery. Not at my gallery in Cowes,' she hastily added, 'but at Anther's Art Gallery in Southsea. I'm there now. Do you think you could come round?'

'Of course,' he answered, concerned. 'Are you all right?'

'Yes, I'm fine. No one's been hurt.'

'Are uniformed officers there?' Horton grabbed his sailing jacket from the coat hook.

'No. It's difficult to explain over the phone and I'd rather not call them. I thought you might help.'

It was puzzling but he postponed the questions and speculations. 'I'll be there in ten minutes. Give me the address.'

She relayed it. It was in a busy through road just off the seafront in the Southsea shopping centre.

'Walters, get your jacket. We're going to an art gallery, a robbery — and you'd better be on your best behaviour, a friend of mine has reported it.'

'Can't I finish my sandwiches?'

'Thought you'd eaten lunch ages ago.'

'I did, this is a snack.'

'One day, Walters, I'm going to have to prise you out of that chair.'

Walters stuffed the open sandwich packet in his jacket pocket as they made for the exit. 'Who is this friend?'

'Felice Ellwood.'

'The woman we called in for that log cabin death?'

'You remembered her name?' Horton was impressed. Walters had been on the investigation but had never met Felice. Neither had Cantelli.

'I'm not just a pretty face.'

'You're not even that.'

'My girlfriend wouldn't agree with you.'

'Then she must have problems with her vision.'

'Ha, ha. Good job I brought my sandwiches if we're off to the Isle of Wight.'

'We're not. Felice is in Southsea.'

'Pity, I quite fancied a boat trip. What's she doing here aside from reporting a robbery?'

'We'll find out when we get there.'

CHAPTER FOUR

'Andy, I'm so glad you could come,' Felice said anxiously, as she opened the door of the gallery to them. He could see the strain around her mouth and the fatigue and concern in her deep brown eyes. He introduced Walters as they stepped inside, and she closed and relocked the door. He had seen no evidence of a break-in on their arrival. The window was barred with a white chunky security grille. The door was intact. The robbers obviously hadn't entered by the front which meant they must have broken in at the rear. There was a service road behind these shops.

Following her through to a room beyond the gallery Horton quickly registered the paintings on the walls and on the easels, including a large boldly coloured abstract bearing a discreet 'Sold' sticker. Nothing looked to have been disturbed or stolen. And neither did anything appear to have been disturbed in the room Felice led them to, where two men in their sixties stood looking expectantly at the door. One was tall, gaunt and smartly turned out in casual trousers, a polo shirt and a designer waterproof jacket. His aquiline face was sallow but his tired, hazel eyes shone, intelligent and curious behind fashionable spectacles. The other man was small with thinning grey hair and was clearly agitated. He was fastidiously dressed in fawn slacks and a navy blazer, and sported a maroon-and-blue patterned cravat, which matched the handkerchief peeking out from his breast pocket.

Felice furnished the introductions. 'This is Detective Inspector Horton and Detective Constable Walters. Julian Anther and Maurice Linden.'

Linden was the gaunt man with spectacles, Anther the nervous one with the cravat. Horton shook hands with each in turn. Anther's was damp and fleeting while Linden's was firm and assured.

Felice continued, 'Julian owns the gallery and Maurice is my father's agent and long-time friend.'

'Let's all sit down,' Linden said in a firm, steady voice that told Horton he was a man used to commanding and being obeyed. 'There's nothing to be gained, Julian, by jigging up and down, and huffing and puffing. The Inspector will need the facts presented to him in a clear manner.'

Anther dashed a glance at Horton and opened his mouth to speak, then instead gave a sigh and fell heavily into the leather swivel chair behind his antique desk, scattered with paperwork. Linden gestured Horton and Walters into the two seats opposite Anther, while he drew up a third and placed it beside them. Horton hesitated and looked at Felice.

'I need to stand to explain what has happened,' she said, pushing a slender hand through her long, curly black hair.

Horton's curiosity grew.

She crossed to three paintings on a narrow antique table. One was of a sailing yacht in the style of a portrait, while the other two were landscape, one of a barge and the other of boats in a harbour. They were all boldly executed in bright colours and in an abstract style, and all about sixteen inches by twenty-three. There was something familiar to Horton about the sailing yacht picture, but he couldn't say why. Maybe he'd seen too many pictures of boats over the years. And what had they to do with the robbery?

Felice said, 'These two paintings — the landscape ones, the barge and harbour boats — were brought in to Julian on the twenty-first of April. I was called over to authenticate them, which I did on Friday the twenty-third of April, seventeen days ago. Then this third painting was brought in last Tuesday week, on the twenty-seventh of April. I'd seen a picture of it on my phone, but today is the first time I've seen it up close. I could see almost instantly it was a forgery, and on close examination of the first two paintings, I saw to my surprise that they too were forgeries, but they were certainly not that when I first examined them.'

Walters stared blankly at her. Horton's mind raced. He needed to be certain what they were talking about here. 'You're saying that two of the original paintings have been replaced by forgeries within the last seventeen days?'

'Yes.'

Horton's eyes swivelled to Linden, who looked sanguine, while Anther was obviously distressed. 'Someone has broken into the gallery and switched them?'

Anther answered, 'No, that's just it, no one has broken in.'

'But—' Walters began.

Anther hotly cut in. 'I can also assure you that no one has walked out with them, and I certainly haven't switched them.'

'No one is accusing you, sir,' Horton said. *Not yet anyway.*

Walters addressed Felice. 'But how can you tell they're fake?'

'Because I have considerable experience, Constable, having worked for Sotheby's in London, Sydney and Melbourne. And I know the artist's work intimately.' She exchanged a look with Horton.

Now he knew why the yacht painting looked familiar. He'd seen a larger, very similar version in Felice's gallery on the Isle of Wight, and he knew why Felice was upset. 'The paintings are by your father.'

'Yes, or rather the original two were my father's work, but these three are not his, although they are very good forgeries.'

'But how can you tell if they're supposedly that good?' insisted Walters. 'Is the signature dodgy or something?'

'Well, really!' expostulated Anther. 'I'd have thought—'

Linden stilled him with an upheld hand. 'It's a fair question, Julian, and a police officer's task is to ask questions.'

'Even stupid ones?' Anther sniped.

'Especially stupid ones,' Horton replied. 'It's often those that get us the answers that help to solve the crime.'

Felice addressed Walters. 'And it's not such a stupid question anyway. Yes, the signature is dodgy, as you put it. It's good but it lacks a certain fluidity — the Ls are too heavily concentrated on the vertical stroke, the same with the E. My father's signature is lighter. The style of painting is exactly like my father's but it's not quite right. Maurice is of the same opinion as I am, that these three are forgeries.'

Linden said, 'I've handled Michael's work ever since he returned from the States in 1993. Before that we were at school together. We go back a very long way. I know his work extremely well. Michael started out with drawings in chalk, pencil and wash, of ballet dancers and circus performers. But it wasn't until he switched to his real passion, seascapes, that his career really took off and that was in America. He has a certain style, as Felice said, and technique. He layers thick, bright paint with a palette knife to produce an almost collage effect. I'll admit these are very good but not quite good enough, even for Michael's early period.'

'Did you see the originals, sir?' asked Horton.

'No. This is the first time I've been in the gallery for some months.'

Felice said, 'I took photographs of the first two paintings and showed them to my father, hoping he could tell me when he had painted them. But he's in hospital and on heavy medication, so I didn't get anything from him. Then I had to go to Wales to undertake a valuation at a country house. The owner, who had been an avid art collector, had died and the estate was being auctioned with all belongings. There was a great deal to get through. I told Julian not to do anything with the first two paintings until I returned. Then Julian telephoned me last Tuesday, the day after the bank holiday, to say another painting had been brought in.'

'Who by?' asked Walters.

'By whom?' corrected Linden with a smile, while Walters looked baffled. 'We'll get to that later. Go on, Felice.'

'Julian sent me a photograph of the third painting, this one of the yacht. When I returned home from Wales on Thursday evening, I asked my father about it, but unfortunately, his condition had further deteriorated.' She pulled back her hair, gathering it behind her, her expression sorrowful. 'I told Julian I'd be over on Monday, today, to examine the third painting. In the meantime, I showed Maurice the photograph of the third painting when he arrived on the island on Friday evening.'

'I've been visiting Michael in hospital,' Linden added. 'I'm due back in London today so came over here on the hovercraft with Felice this morning. We all three had lunch before returning here to see the paintings. Felice made the discovery and rang you, Inspector.'

Horton nodded. His head was full of questions, some of which he hoped would be answered as Felice continued.

'Over the weekend Maurice and I went through my father's records looking for these three paintings. They're not named, but I have photographs of everything that has been sold, whether that is through a gallery, at an exhibition or privately, but we found no trace of them. That confirmed what we had both thought — that they were from my father's early career, and before Maurice was his agent. My father could easily have given them to someone or sold them himself. However, the moment I actually saw this third painting today, I knew it wasn't my father's. Then, when I re-examined the other two, I saw to my surprise, the original two paintings had been exchanged for forgeries. I can see that Detective Constable Walters is still not convinced.'

'He always looks like that,' Horton answered, lightly drawing a smile from Felice. 'Do you have any idea of who could have forged them?'

'None whatsoever.'

'Mr Linden?'

'No, and neither does Julian. We discussed it while we were waiting for you to arrive.'

Anther retrieved his handkerchief from the pocket of his blazer and mopped his forehead.

Felice continued, 'The forger might not be known to anyone within the art world. He or she could have given up painting and forging years ago. He could be dead. But that doesn't explain how two of the originals could have been swapped since my valuation.'

Walters shifted. Horton could see he was still sceptical about the whole thing. He was right to be. It was their job. There had been a robbery and yet there hadn't been. It struck him that they only had Felice's word for that. But why would she make that up? And these had to be forgeries because Linden had corroborated it, and Horton couldn't see any reason for him to lie.

Walters, obviously thinking along the same lines, said, 'Are there tests that can prove they're forgeries?'

Anther bristled. 'Are you questioning Miss Ellwood's expertise?'

'It's OK, Julian. Yes, there are. Sotheby's has a world-renowned specialist department for this kind of thing. They use technology to uncover almost undetectable mistakes in copies that appear flawless to the naked eye, spontaneous Raman spectroscopy and radiocarbon dating to help date the painting. Yes, they're big words,' she added, smiling at Walters's befuddled expression with his pen poised over his notebook.

Horton said, 'It's OK, you don't have to write this down. Go on, Felice.'

'They look at pigments, inks, materials and also the bindings in paper and other material on which a picture is produced — paper, canvas, wood or metal. They also use microscopic and macroscopic investigation, light source analysis, ultraviolet, infrared and X-ray diagnostics and technology. So, you see, they could tell us a great deal about the date of the paintings. They might even be able to give us indications of who that forger might be if they've seen something similar in the past. As I have worked for Sotheby's I could use my connections to get speedy help. Or you can consult your own forensic art experts, and probably should, to maintain impartiality.'

Walters looked up, bemused. 'But why go to all this trouble for a couple of paintings?'

'Because they are worth a great deal of money,' Anther answered tartly. 'The originals could fetch over £100,000 each.'

Linden said, 'Possibly double that.'

'No kidding!' Walters's eyes bulged.

Linden added, 'If the forged paintings could also have been passed off as genuine then the same amount of money applies.'

And that, thought Horton, was fraud on a large enough scale to warrant a thorough investigation. Losing the commission would be enough to seriously upset both Anther and Linden. They had no motive for switching the paintings or declaring these to be fakes, not unless Anther had been hoping to sell the forgeries and had the originals secreted away for another buyer, therefore benefiting twice. But if that had been his intention why would he have asked Felice for her opinion when no one would have known? Horton wondered how far Walters's thinking would take him. Silently he was asking himself who would benefit from the sale of genuine paintings: the thief, for one.

Walters, having digested and recovered from his shock of learning the value of the originals, said, 'I take it there hasn't been any sign of a break-in over the last seventeen days since Ms Ellwood authenticated the first two?'

'None.' Anther firmly asserted. 'I've already told you that.'

'And you haven't lost or mislaid your keys?' Walters asked.

'No. And I never leave anyone alone in the gallery. I am present at all times it is open and when it isn't, the windows are barred front and back and the alarm is always set. And before you ask, Detective Constable, I am the only person who has the code.'

'But you might have popped into the toilet, while someone was here,' persisted Walters.

'I wouldn't leave anyone in the gallery while I was in the toilet,' Anther replied tight-lipped.

'You might have got caught short, happens to all of us, a curry the night before, a kebab and—'

'I can assure you, Constable, I did not, as you say, get "caught short" either with or without a customer in the gallery. And I never eat curries or kebabs.'

'Each to their own,' muttered Walters.

Horton saw Linden's lips twitch in amusement.

'Then you're saying someone popped in, unseen, swapped the paintings and calmly left carrying the originals without you noticing?' Walters reiterated.

'Are you accusing me of making this up?' flashed Anther, ready to spring up.

'No,' Horton hastily interceded. 'We have to be clear about matters.' Walters had his uses. He wasn't afraid of saying what was on his mind, and being tactless was often an asset, not that he realized it. It went over his head. 'Let's establish some facts. Who else has access to the gallery, Mr Anther, when you're here, aside from customers that is — a cleaner for example?'

'Joyce Munroe. She cleans my apartment and the gallery on Wednesday and Friday mornings, and when she is in the gallery, I am *always* present. And I can assure you, Inspector, that she has never left here carrying any paintings.'

Horton wasn't so sure of that. The originals could easily have fitted inside a large bag or some similar receptacle, except that the cleaner would have needed to have had the forgeries in her possession in order to replace them. That seemed unlikely but not impossible. He'd keep an open mind. They also didn't know exactly when the two paintings had been swapped. It could have been at any time over the last seventeen days.

'Where do you keep your keys, sir?'

'Here on my key fob.' Anther reached into his trouser pocket and withdrew a bunch of keys. 'There are two gallery keys, one to the front door and one to the rear. They never leave me.'

'Not even when you go to bed?' Walters asked.

'They stay by my bedside, and seeing as I don't share my apartment or my bed with anyone, no one has had access to them.' Anther took a gulp of air as though he was struggling to breathe. Was he asthmatic? Horton wondered. Or was it a nervous mannerism, a reaction to the stress of what had happened. He noted that Anther's slim fingers were constantly playing with his handkerchief almost as though he wanted to tear it to shreds.

A car's horn tooted loudly and angrily outside. Anther gave a cry and visibly started.

Horton said, 'Do you rent or own the premises?'

'I own them.'

No landlord with keys then.

'How long have you lived here, Mr Anther?

'I can't see—'

'It's just background information, sir. We need to get a full picture,' Horton soothed.

'Since I opened the gallery, four years ago,' Anther replied somewhat stiffly. His fingers twitched and twirled. 'I live in the apartment above it. There is a separate entrance.'

Horton recalled seeing a door to the right of the gallery. 'I take it the paintings have always been kept in this room and nowhere else.'

'They have.'

To Felice, Horton said, 'Could you have been mistaken about the first two being originals?'

'No.'

'Then we'll need a list, Mr Anther, of everyone who has visited the gallery since the arrival of the first two paintings on the twenty-first of April.'

Linden said, 'Don't you mean from the twenty-third of April, after Felice had seen them?'

'No, because someone must have seen the originals in order to have returned to swap them for forgeries after Felice had examined them. I'm not saying any of these people are under suspicion,' he quickly added, as Anther looked about to explode, 'but we need to check them out.'

'I won't have you disturbing my customers,' Anther said determinedly. 'This mustn't get out. It will ruin my reputation.'

'How? You didn't acquire the forgeries. You asked for another opinion, surely that will reassure your customers.'

'They'll wonder if what they have bought from me in the past is genuine. You know how people gossip and say there's no smoke without fire. I don't want my customers grilled by the police, or made aware of the fact these paintings have been switched.'

Horton decided not to press Anther for the time being. 'Did you show or mention the paintings to anyone other than Miss Ellwood?'

Anther squirmed. He threw a nervous glance at Linden and Felice. That was a yes then. 'No,' he lied.

Horton let it go for now 'What about you, Mr Linden? As Mr Ellwood's agent have you mentioned to any known collectors there might be a couple of his paintings coming up for sale?'

'No. I wouldn't have done so, not until I was certain of Michael's wishes. He might have wanted to keep them.'

Felice said, 'The same goes for me.'

Horton nodded, then directed his next question to Anther. 'So, tell us about the person who brought them in.'

CHAPTER FIVE

'His name is Noel Catmore. I'd never met him before. He walked in off the street just before midday on the twenty-first of April. He said he had inherited the paintings from his late aunt some years ago. He'd put them in the attic and forgotten about them, only to find them again while clearing it out during a house move. Someone told him he ought to have them valued. He came here, said it was the only art gallery he'd seen. He clearly didn't know anything about art,' Anther ended with a disdainful air.

'He's not the only one,' mumbled Walters.

Anther took another gulp of air, fiddled with his handkerchief and darted anxious glances at Felice and Linden before his eyes came into contact with Horton's and flitted away again. 'I told Mr Catmore that the paintings were by Ellwood, who was an eminent artist, and the paintings would certainly be of interest to collectors. I couldn't give him a valuation, as I had to have them authenticated. I said I'd get back to him as soon as I could. He seemed perfectly happy with that and said he was in no hurry. Then he came back into the gallery on Tuesday the twenty-seventh of April with the third painting.' Anther mopped his forehead. 'I'd only just opened. It was ten o'clock. I said that my expert thought the first two were genuine Ellwoods, but we were still making enquiries. I asked him if he had any provenance, or paperwork with the paintings, but he said he didn't. I withheld telling him their worth, because now that he had brought in yet another Ellwood I said we'd need to look at the whole picture, so to speak. He made no protest, proclaimed that I was the expert and he looked forward to hearing from me.'

Walters looked up from his notebook. 'Could he have swapped the two he first brought in for two forgeries when he came back with the third painting?'

'I've already told you no one could have swapped them,' Anther cried. He sprang up and began to pace the room.

Linden tried to appease him. 'Julian, calm down, you'll give yourself a stroke. The police will do all they can.'

Anther directed his glare at Walters. 'I let Mr Catmore in. I showed him out. He wasn't carrying any paintings when he left. He wasn't alone in the gallery at any time. Satisfied?'

Walters opened his mouth to reply but Felice got in first. 'You think Mr Catmore might have been trying Julian out? He had the forgeries as well as the two originals all the time? But that doesn't make sense.' After a moment's realization, she quickly added, 'He brought the forgeries in to begin with hoping Julian would think they were originals and sell them for a tidy sum, while he could keep hold of the originals and sell them to someone else.'

Linden contradicted her. 'No, he wouldn't, because he'd have had no idea whom to sell them to or where.'

'But we don't know that for certain,' she insisted. 'He might have pretended to know nothing about art.'

Anther answered, 'Well he certainly didn't look like an art connoisseur.'

'How are they supposed to look?' asked Horton, deadpan, drawing an amused gleam from Linden.

'Not like he did,' Anther quipped. 'Besides, it's irrelevant, because you said they were genuine,' he shot at Felice. 'He'll blame me of course.' Anther flourished his handkerchief. 'He'll sue me for mislaying his originals. I can't have him blabbing to the media. No one will ever buy from me again. I might as well shut up shop now,' he wailed, throwing his arms in the air.

Felice interjected, with a quick glance at Horton, 'I'm sure Inspector Horton will ask Mr Catmore to cooperate by keeping it quiet, at least until the police can find out more about what's going on.'

Horton nodded. 'It's in his and all our interests to do so. If Mr Catmore acted innocently then whoever stole the originals might have been lured into a false sense of security believing that no one has spotted the switch. He, or she, could attempt to sell the originals privately, which is why we need to know who the collectors are, Mr Anther, in case they are approached. But we'll speak to Mr Catmore first, if you can give us his contact details. I'd also like details of your alarm company and cleaner, Ms Munroe, and any other trades-people who have visited the gallery since the twenty-first of April — window cleaners, electricians, plumbers, suppliers.'

'Only the window cleaner. I can't remember when he came,' Anther said vaguely, looking wan.

'His name?' Horton would check the date with him.

'Brights Window Cleaners. Do I need to call Mr Catmore before you see him? Only I've no idea what to say to him,' Anther asked anxiously.

'No. I'd like to gauge his reaction when I tell him, but it might be helpful, Felice, if you accompanied us. There might be specific questions you can ask him that Walters and I wouldn't think of. Or you might be able to pick up something from his answers that could help.'

'Of course,' she agreed. 'When do you want to go?'

'In a moment, if that's OK with you?'

'Certainly.'

'Will you need me, Inspector?' Linden asked. 'Only I'm due at an exhibition this evening in London, one of my art-ists, and I must be there. I need to catch the train in the next two hours if I'm going to make it on time.'

'We won't keep you, Mr Linden, but please give your contact details to DC Walters. And if anything occurs to you that might help, do get in touch with me or DC Walters.' Horton gave Linden his card. To Anther, Horton said, 'I'd like to inspect the rear of the premises. Perhaps I can do that while you give DC Walters the various contact details. Could I have your keys to unlock the back door?'

Anther practically slammed them into Horton's palm.

He stepped into a small kitchen with a toilet on the right. The windows facing the courtyard and the toilet window had heavy metal grilles on them and there were alarm sensors in the corners. The rear door was stout with bolts — and locked. Horton opened it. In the yard a new Jaguar was parked at an angle — Anther's, he presumed. To the right in the corner were the refuse bins, which made him think of Neil Spender. Was no news good news? he wondered, crossing the yard into the narrow service road. If he were dead though, and had fallen or been ditched in the sea, at this time of the year it would take anything from three to fourteen days for the body to resurface. The manner of Spender's disappearance was as puzzling as this: was it a murder or not a murder? Was this a robbery that wasn't a robbery? Despite what Anther had said, if the paintings had been switched and Anther himself hadn't done it — he'd had the opportunity — then someone had got in somehow and left again without drawing attention to him or herself.

Horton looked up at the rear of the gallery. There was no fire escape as the building was only two storeys high, although there was a small skylight in the roof. A high wall bounded either side of the courtyard. Next door to his left, looking at the rear, was an estate agency and on the right a beauty shop. He'd seen and noted both when he and Walters had arrived at the front.

The service road culminated in a large yard, which gave onto the goods delivery entrances of a number of retail units in the road that ran north to south at the junction beyond the beauty parlour. He turned to face a high brick wall across the service road, the boundary of small courtyard gardens of a row of three-storey nineteenth-century terraced houses opposite. Someone watching from the upstairs windows might have witnessed something suspicious taking place in the gallery courtyard but there were three factors against asking them. One, this didn't warrant a full house-to-house enquiry because there had been no physical break-in. Two, why would anyone think the act of someone carrying two paintings out of an art gallery suspicious, *if* they had seen the paintings. And three, they didn't know which day in particular the paintings had been switched. He silently added a fourth to his list — there was still that *if* about all this, though he couldn't see why Felice should lie. But, again, he considered it was possible that Anther had staged the switch himself knowing who he could sell the originals to without having to pay either Michael Ellwood or Linden's commission. In that case, Anther would net a very handsome sum. And it was possible that he'd had the forgeries in his collection for some time. Alternatively, he could have known someone who had them and had arranged this fraud so that both he and the collector benefited. Anther didn't look capable of doing so, but his hysteria could be feigned. Horton had met some villains who were world-class actors.

He returned to find the man in question slumped in his chair as though exhausted by the ordeal. Was he just a tad overdramatic? Perhaps he hadn't counted on Felice spotting the switch and calling in a police inspector known to her.

'Will you consult Sotheby's?' Felice asked.

'That will be up to my boss, Detective Chief Inspector Bliss. I'll report back to her after we've spoken to Mr Catmore.'

'I'll show you out.' Linden rose and they followed him through to the gallery. 'Julian's taken this very hard, as you can see, Inspector. He feels things deeply.'

'You've known him long?'

'For most of my life, it seems,' he said with a weary smile which, rather than lightening his expression, made it more drawn. Horton noted Felice's concerned glance in Linden's direction.

'Are any of your other clients' paintings here?' Horton asked.

'That large abstract is, and two more by the same artist. I've been trying to cut back but it's difficult when you've been doing it for so long. It's not so much a job as a labour of love.'

'Have you ever painted?' Walters asked.

'I dabbled years ago but learned very quickly that talent-spotting and selling others' works was my forte.' He stretched out a bony hand. 'It's been nice meeting you, Inspector, Constable — if only it would have been in a different circumstance.'

Felice kissed Linden continental style on both cheeks. 'I'll be in touch, Maurice.'

'What's wrong with Mr Linden?' Horton asked as they settled themselves in Walters's car.

'Cancer. Terminal. And yet he can still spend hours with my father in hospital when all it must do is remind him of what's in store for him. It must be torture and yet he never shows it.' She shook her head sadly.

Horton could see the strain that her father's illness and Linden's, not to mention this latest development, was telling on her. He'd have liked to ask her about her father and how she was coping, but Walters's presence prevented that, and he saw and sensed in Felice's expression that she knew this. Besides, there wasn't a great deal of time because Noel Catmore's house was just a short distance away. He was eager to meet the man and see what new light he could throw on this curious situation.

CHAPTER SIX

'The paintings were given to my wife, Beryl, by her Aunt Dorothy years ago,' Catmore said when, after a wary greeting, he had shown them into a small front room crowded with packing boxes and a sofa heaped with ornaments and books. Catmore had apologized for the mess and explained he was downsizing to one of those retirement flats now that his wife had passed away. 'I'd forgotten all about them. Neither my wife nor I liked them, but we didn't want to upset her aunt by saying so. We kept them just in case Aunt Dot decided to visit us again and we could quickly get them out, but she never did.' He ran a hand over his thinning grey hair and peered worriedly at them through his spectacles. 'You think there's something crooked about them?'

Horton answered. 'It appears that the third one you took into Mr Anther is a forgery.'

'Well, I'll be blowed. That's a shame. What about the other two?'

'They were genuine Ellwoods. However, there has been a worrying development.'

'They were stolen goods?' His eyes rounded.

'Not that we're aware, why should you think that?'

'I dunno, just you being here, I suppose. I can't see Aunt Dot being a crook but she could have been landed with them by some low-life. Hey, you don't think she knew they were stolen, which was why she dumped them on us?'

'No. The first two paintings were original Ellwoods but they have been replaced with forgeries.'

'How? I don't understand.' His florid faced creased up, bewildered.

'Neither do we at the moment, Mr Catmore, which is why we need to ask you some questions.'

'But I can't tell you anything about them,' he said, rubbing his unshaven chin.

'Let's go back to Aunt Dorothy. When did she give your wife the paintings?'

'I don't remember. Must be ten, twelve years ago.'

'Did she give you any paperwork with them?'

'Mr Anther asked me that, and the answer is no. I've no idea how she got them. I didn't know her. I met her that once and never again.'

'And you haven't corresponded with her since?'

'No.'

'Would any of your late wife's relatives know her or where we can contact her?'

'There aren't any, all dead. It was just me and Beryl and now it's only me,' he said forlornly.

Horton felt sorry for him.

Walters chipped in. 'What was Dorothy's full name?'

'Now you've got me. It was Mass-something-or-other, could have been Mason, Massman, Massey, something like that. I don't know.' He pushed up his glasses, looking wretched.

Felice said, 'What relation was Aunt Dot to your wife?'

Catmore scratched his head. 'Gawd knows, great-aunt or something like that. Beryl said Dot was the daughter of someone related to her mother, but she didn't know the exact link, and we never bothered to find out. Beryl and I were perfectly happy the way we were.'

Horton left a short pause before asking his wife's maiden name. 'We might be able to trace Dorothy via that.'

'Watkins.'

'How old would you say Dorothy was when she showed up on your doorstep?'

He rubbed the side of his nose and frowned. 'Age has never been my thing especially where women are concerned but if pushed, I'd go for seventy, maybe seventy-five, could have been older.'

Felice again. 'Did she say where the paintings came from?'

'No.'

Catmore was looking ragged.

'Did you or your wife ever hear Dorothy being spoken of as an artist or connected in some way with the art world?'

'She could have been an acrobat for all I know,' he joked nervously.

'Were there any artists in your late wife's family?' Felice asked.

'No.'

Walters said, 'Did you look the artist, Michael Ellwood, up on the internet?'

'No, why should I have?' he snapped. 'I've got more important things to do than sit on my backside trawling through the internet. Besides, my computer's given up the ghost and my phone's too ancient to cope with all that stuff. I'm not into it, you know. Mr Anther mentioned the artist was quite well known but I've never heard of him, although that's not surprising — I know nothing about art. How valuable would they have been, the originals that is?'

Felice answered. 'At auction the originals could have fetched £100,000, possibly more.'

Catmore sank heavily onto the edge of the sofa, his backside pushing the books and ornaments behind him. 'And now they'll be nothing because they're fake. But hang on — you said the first two were originals.' He looked up hopefully. 'I left them with Mr Anther in good faith. If he's insured—'

45

'I'm sure he must be, sir,' Horton quickly answered, 'and you might be able to claim on them. On the other hand, we might get the originals back for you.' Anther was not going to like this.

Catmore gave a wry smile. 'And I might win the lottery. No aspersions on the police, Inspector, but I won't hold my breath. The police have far more serious crimes to investigate what with all these muggings, drug pushers and knife crime you read about in the newspapers. You've better things to do than chase after some stolen paintings.'

'Nevertheless, it's still a crime,' Horton insisted. 'What did you do with the first two after finding them, before taking them to the gallery?'

'Eh?'

Horton could see Catmore's mind was still on the compensation, probably working out a ratio of the value Felice had given him. Horton hoped Anther's insurance would cover it otherwise the man would have that stroke Linden prophesized. He repeated his question.

'Oh, I put them in here,' Catmore answered, waving his arm around the room.

'Did anyone come in here during that time?'

'No. I was putting them out for the binmen when this man walked past and said they could be worth something. "What, this rubbish?" I said. He said, "One man's rubbish is another man's jewels, take them to a gallery and get an opinion, if they're not worth anything then you can throw them away."'

Walters looked up. 'Who was the man?'

'No idea, just some guy walking past. Never seen him before or since. Hey, you don't think he stole them? But that doesn't make sense because he'd have offered to take them off my hands for a fiver. And I'd probably have let him. And you say they've not been stolen but switched for fakes, so who could have done that? They've been buried for donkey's years in my attic. No one knew about them except me and the wife.'

'Can you describe this man?'

Catmore scratched his nose as he thought. 'About fifty, scraggly grey hair, thin, dark eyebrows, lean face, lined, wearing a dark waterproof jacket and trainers. Didn't exactly look down on his luck, more as though he didn't much care about appearances. Spoke quite well, no accent.'

'You're very observant,' said Horton, as Walters scribbled this down.

'People and places, yes. I was a bus driver for fifteen years and before that a coach driver, holidays abroad and in the UK, day trips, that sort of thing. I knew there was an art gallery in Southsea so I thought, "OK why not get an opinion from them, no skin off my nose." So I took the two along to Mr Anther. I thought he'd laugh me out of the gallery, but he was very keen on them, said he wanted to examine them properly and consult another expert, said he'd be in touch. Then I found the third painting, when I was excavating deeper in the attic, and took that along. He didn't say anything about the other two having been switched for forgeries.'

'He didn't know then,' Felice said. 'It's only just been discovered.'

Horton asked, 'Have you told anyone about the paintings? Friends, neighbours? Anyone at all?'

'Not a soul.'

'We'll start making some enquiries. Miss Ellwood is an art expert, she'll be assisting us.'

Catmore hauled himself up. 'I thought you were with the police. Ellwood, did you say? That's the name—'

'Yes, they're my father's paintings.'

Catmore flushed. 'Look, what I said about them being rubbish . . .'

'Don't worry. Each to their own, Mr Catmore.'

'Can't you ask your father about them?'

'I'm afraid he's very ill in hospital at present.'

'I'm sorry. And I'm sorry I can't give you more help. I only wish I could.'

47

'If you think of anything further about Aunt Dorothy which might help, or you see the man who advised you about taking them to the gallery, let DC Walters know. We'll keep you informed.'

Walters handed over his business card. Catmore promised he would.

As they made for the car, Walters said, 'I bet he's on the phone to Anther right now. I expect we'll find Anther prostrate. This passer-by Catmore talked about probably watches those TV programmes where someone finds out that the old jug their aunt gave them years ago, which they've been using to water the plants, is from the Ming dynasty. I'm surprised he didn't offer to take them off Catmore's hands and flog them himself.'

'An honest soul,' Felice posed.

'Don't meet many of them in our line of work,' Walters replied.

'He didn't throw much light on the matter, did he?' she added.

'A name,' Horton answered.

'But there must be thousands of Dorothys, and he's even vague about her surname and the date.'

'But we've got his wife's maiden name and we might be able to trace her family tree. It's all right, Walters, no need to look so horrified, although it would keep you glued to your chair in CID, which is your dream job.'

'Nah, that's calling on cafés, restaurants and takeaways.' He zapped open the car.

Horton said, 'I was thinking of asking a genealogist to try and trace Dorothy.'

His phone rang. He could see by the number it was Joliffe. To Felice, Horton said, 'I've got to take this.'

'It's OK, I'll walk back to Anther's gallery,' she replied. 'The fresh air will do me good. I'd like to think over what Mr Catmore said and see if anything new occurs to me. The forgeries will stay in Anther's gallery, which is as secure as anywhere can be, until you decide what to do. Goodbye, Walters.'

Horton climbed into the passenger seat. 'What have you got, Joliffe?'

'The blood on the boat is human. There are two blood groups present: Type O, rhesus positive. Eighty-five per cent of the UK is rhesus positive and about thirty-six per cent is blood group O, which isn't much good to you. The other blood group is AB rhesus negative, which is only one per cent of the population, which could be much more helpful. Do you know the blood group of the missing boat owner?'

'Not yet but we'll be able to get that from his medical records. Is it homicide?'

'No idea, I just analyse the blood. But if it is then let's hope your victim is blood group O. Then all you have to do is find the killer, test his or her blood group, find it is AB negative and bingo, you've got your man or woman.'

'If only it were that simple,' Horton replied with feeling, knowing Joliffe was being deliberately flippant. Were they looking at murder? It seemed likely and the only way to be certain was to call in a blood pattern analyst who would be able to tell them if an assault had taken place, and of what kind.

CHAPTER SEVEN

Bliss agreed. On the way back Horton had called Elkins and requested that he or Ripley take Spender's boat to the secure berth at Portsmouth International Port where it would be examined by the blood pattern analyst. He'd instructed Walters to get Spender's car taken to the police garage. If murder was confirmed, then the vehicle would need to be forensically examined. They also needed to check Spender's flat. Walters was liaising with the letting agents to see if they would release the key to them without a warrant. If Spender had been murdered the killer could have taken the flat keys off the body and ransacked the place. They'd also need to confirm Spender's blood group.

Bliss said she would draw up a statement for the press and social media asking those who knew Spender or had seen him on Saturday to come forward, but she'd hold back issuing it until they had more information from the blood pattern analyst and Horton's subsequent enquiries the next day. She made to dismiss him when Horton said, 'We've also got an art robbery to investigate and a possible art fraud.'

Swiftly he relayed the incident. 'Miss Ellwood suggested we send the paintings up to Sotheby's to be examined by their forensic experts. Although I don't doubt Miss Ellwood's opinion that they are forgeries, we should have it verified, and the Sotheby's experts could tell us something about the forger and possibly where, when and how the paintings originated, which could lead us to whoever switched them.'

Bliss looked dubious. Horton pressed on. 'Michael Ellwood is an internationally renowned artist. If this got out — I'm not saying it will — but if it did, questions might be asked as to why we didn't consult the top experts. We are talking big-time art theft here, ma'am, the originals could be worth hundreds of thousands of pounds. This thief and forger, who could be one and the same or two different people, could have forged other paintings by acclaimed artists, and could have an accomplice who switches them. This switch could be the tip of the iceberg. Art fraud on an international scale is second only to drug trafficking in international crime statistics, and it brings in huge money.'

'I know that.' Bliss pulled at her ponytail.

Horton continued. 'While this particular switch might have been perpetrated by small-time crooks or an opportunist, there's equally the chance it could be more than that and not the first time it has happened. On this occasion there just happened to be the artist's daughter handy, an expert herself. Miss Ellwood worked for Sotheby's, and she can speak to the appropriate people there. Because of her involvement we'll get it fast-tracked, and that means we could get a quick result.'

Horton had planted the seed. He could see it germinating in Bliss's mind. If she handled both of these cases well and got results it would be a feather in her promotion cap and could weigh heavily in her favour for a permanent move to the Major Crime Team.

Horton pressed home his point. 'I'd also like to consult a forensic locksmith. The MO at the art gallery is unusual, with no evidence of a break-in and Anther insists his keys haven't been used or copied. But a forensic locksmith can tell us if the locks have been expertly opened and if Anther's keys have been copied without his knowledge. This kind of trick could have been pulled before in the UK. And if we were to call in a genealogist to do the ground work on tracking down Catmore's Aunt Dorothy that would also free up Walters to work on the Spender investigation, if murder is confirmed. In addition, Cantelli's court case might be over tomorrow so he can assist on either investigation. I think if we were to utilize external resources, we'd get a rapid result on the art fraud.'

That did it, as he knew it would.

'All right, go ahead. Do you have a genealogist in mind?'

He did, a woman who had helped them on a sad case a couple of years ago — that of a young man found dead in his flat after two months with nothing to identify him, and no friends or relatives. There had been no suspicious circumstances, a case of sudden death syndrome. Nicola Bolton had eventually managed to trace a distant aunt.

Dismissed, Horton returned to CID, stopping off for a coffee from the machine outside. He was pleased to find that Cantelli was back but not so pleased when Cantelli reported that the trial was going to drag on another day. He was hopeful though that they'd get a conviction, unless the barrister pulled something out of the hat or the jury were completely stupid. Horton made to brief him on the art switch when Cantelli said, 'Walters has already told me.'

'Any views?'

'It sounds as though it was managed rather than opportunist, but I can't see how, unless Anther and Catmore are in it together.'

'Not Felice Ellwood?'

Cantelli hesitated. 'It wouldn't make sense for her to want to involve the police. Not unless . . .'

'What?'

'It's a publicity stunt designed to get her father's name in the media, raise his profile in the art world. Him being ill means he won't have been painting much and he's slipped under the radar.'

'I can't see her doing that.' Horton swallowed some coffee, but Cantelli had a point. If the thefts were made public then her gallery would become more widely known, and she had one of her father's paintings, possibly more, there.

Cantelli continued. 'Anther and Catmore could have been planning this for a while. They had both the originals and the forgeries and Anther wasn't counting on Felice spotting the switch. Because she did, he had no choice but to allow her to call the police, otherwise he and Catmore could have carried on with their scheme.'

Horton sat back thoughtfully. 'Which is?'

'To flog both the phoneys and the originals. Aunt Dot could have dropped off more than three paintings. She could have left five, two originals and three phoneys.'

Walters piped up, 'But why would Catmore wait this long to discover them?'

'Maybe Aunt Dot is the phoney. Catmore made her up. Walters says he was very vague about her.'

'So you know all Charlotte's relatives?'

'You bet I do! More than my life's worth to forget one of them,' Cantelli joked. 'But you're right, there might be a couple in the closet that even Charlotte doesn't know about. And as for my relatives, there are probably a few on both the English and Italian side we'd rather *not* know about.'

And Horton wished he'd never discovered his relatives. Probing the past wasn't always healthy. What was that line from a poem he'd learned at school? *Let the dead Past bury its dead!* He didn't remember where it originated nor the poet — he couldn't remember much poetry from his comprehensive school education — but certain phrases of certain poems had stuck in his mind, that being one of them, because he had kept wondering about his mother's past, why she had run off and who his father was.

'Catmore and Anther claim not to have known each other before they met over the paintings,' he said.

Cantelli's eyebrows shot up.

'I know,' Horton said, smiling. 'We don't always believe what we're told, or rather we rarely believe. Walters, check out Anther and Catmore tomorrow.'

Walters nodded, barely looking up from his computer, where he was typing up the interviews.

Cantelli said, 'What are the paintings like?'

Horton took his phone from his trouser pocket and showed Cantelli the photos he'd taken of them. 'I like the colours,' Cantelli said after a moment's consideration. 'Not sure they're my type of thing though.'

'That's what Catmore said, only he was more disparaging.' Horton put his phone back in his pocket. 'Felice took it in good part.'

'She must be worth a few bob, if what you say about the value of those paintings is true. Unless her father has spent all the money he's earned over the years and they're hard up, which means she could be in on the switch.'

'He might have squandered his money, I guess,' Horton said, feeling slightly uneasy. He knew nothing about Michael Ellwood save that he was an artist and ill in hospital, and he didn't even know the latter for a fact.

'What about collectors? Ellwood must have some who would be keen to get their hands on originals for a knock-down price, under the radar, so to speak.'

Walters interjected. 'Anther's coy on who they are. Doesn't want them to know his gallery's involved in an art theft, so he says.'

Horton said, 'We'll get the information from him or Felice in due course. We could also get it from Maurice Linden, Ellwood's agent.'

'He could be involved in the switch for the same reason,' Cantelli said. 'He's got collectors who will pay any price and he gets a nice juicy commission.'

'We'll keep it in mind. Meanwhile we try and trace Aunt Dorothy. Walters, telephone Nicola Bolton and ask if she's available to help us. If so, brief her.'

Horton returned to his office, where he put in a call to the Metropolitan Police Art and Antiques Unit. After a short delay he asked if they had anything on their records relating to the theft of paintings by Michael Ellwood, or a similar modus operandi to this case. They would check. Horton said DC Walters would send over the report later. Next, he called Paul Leney, a forensic locksmith they often consulted. Horton had been expecting to leave a message so was pleased when Leney answered. He explained what had occurred, adding, 'I'd like you to examine two locks, the front and rear entrances to the gallery. I'd also like to know if Mr Anther's keys could have been copied. How soon can you do it?'

'Late tomorrow morning suit you? I've got a gap in the diary, about half eleven.'

'Great. I'll call the gallery owner and tell him to expect you. He's rather touchy about it all, so I don't think you'll get a warm welcome.'

'I'm used to that.'

Before ringing Anther, Horton called Felice. Again, he expected a voicemail but she answered. He told her that the paintings could be sent to Sotheby's. 'They're small enough to be couriered but I'm reluctant to use a normal courier in this instance.'

'I could take them up myself by train tomorrow,' Felice suggested.

'No. I'd rather you didn't. Not that I think you'll lose them or be attacked and the paintings stolen, but it's not worth taking the risk.' Horton didn't know if the person who had switched the paintings was following the outcome of that act in some way. It hadn't been made public but Felice could be under surveillance by the thief, a thought that disturbed him.

'Then I'll ask Roy Macey to do it. Macey's are a very reputable specialist artworks removal and hanging company. Roy has done a lot of work for me and Julian. And, if you don't mind, I'd like to go with him.'

Horton said that was fine with him. If someone was following her, or the forgeries, then at least she wouldn't be alone.

She said, 'I'll telephone my contact in the forensic art department, Jonathan Reed. Providing Roy is available tomorrow, we'll take them up then. I'll stay in town. I'd like to be there when Jonathan conducts the examination. I might be able to put his findings with my records and provide further information about the artist,' she added eagerly.

Horton agreed. After ringing off he sat thoughtfully for a moment. It was Felice's mention of an artist that had triggered a thought. The thief could have entered the gallery as an artist touting his work. They hadn't asked Anther whether he had been approached by a painter. Horton would do so now after informing Anther of the latest information.

He got a frosty reception when he said the forensic locksmith would be with him tomorrow. Anther didn't see the necessity for such an examination. Horton avoided any further debate on that point and reassured Anther that Leney was a professional, that he was thorough, quiet and painstaking and wouldn't get in his way.

'Has Mr Catmore contacted you?' Horton asked.

'Not yet.'

Horton knew instantly that was a lie — he could detect it in Anther's voice. Catmore must have rung him, but whether Anther had taken the call was a different matter. Horton suspected Anther would delay speaking to Catmore for as long as possible. He told Anther that the paintings would be taken to Sotheby's by Roy Macey and Felice, hopefully tomorrow if Mr Macey was available to do it. Meanwhile they were to be kept safe and secure in the gallery. Horton wondered if he had made a mistake not taking the forgeries away. After all, someone had managed to switch them, but had they expertly broken into the gallery in order to do so? On the evidence to date it seemed not. Even if they had, surely they wouldn't do so again and steal the forgeries? Whoever had put them there was unlikely to replace them with originals. He asked Anther if any artists or anyone with a portfolio case had called in at the gallery after Felice had authenticated the first two paintings. Anther said categorically they hadn't. Horton wasn't sure if he believed him.

Next Horton rang Ruth Bowen, the blood pattern analyst, and left a message on her voicemail about Spender's boat. As he rang off Cantelli entered.

'Walters has spoken to Nicola Bolton, and she says she'll start on Aunt Dorothy right away.' He took the seat across Horton's desk. 'I got curious about Michael Ellwood. I looked him up on the internet. You're right, he is a big shot, a member of the Royal Academy of Arts.' Cantelli consulted his notes. 'Born 1958 in Bembridge on the Isle of Wight, the only child of May and John Ellwood, an intelligent boy with a gift for drawing, who flunked his GCSEs, left school aged seventeen and took off for the continent with a rucksack, a sketchpad, some pencils and not much else, so the story goes, but he probably took a change of socks and underpants.'

Horton smiled.

'He took any job he could while he painted and travelled around Europe, first Italy, then Spain and France, selling his paintings in the markets and to tourists. After living in Paris for eight years he left for America in 1988. It was in New York where he got his first break.'

'Which bears out what Maurice Linden said.'

'He met his wife, Lisa, also an artist, in 1989 in New York. She quickly fell pregnant with Felice, and the family returned to London in 1993, where his exhibitions in Britain began to sell out.'

'And Linden became his agent.'

'His work is still selling today and is highly sought after. That's about it. Oh, except that he was involved in a motorbike accident two years ago which left him with serious injuries, doesn't say what though. From the press coverage I read online, he was on the Military Road on the Isle of Wight.'

'Notorious for boy racers and accidents,' Horton said, recalling the undulating and curving coastal road on the east of the island.

'No other vehicle was involved.'

'I remember Felice telling me last month when we were investigating the log cabin death that she had returned from

Australia, where she was working for Sotheby's, because her father was ill. She opened the gallery in Cowes shortly after that. I'm assuming that her father is in hospital now as a legacy of the injuries incurred from that accident.'

'I guess so. There's probably more about him on the Royal Academy of Arts website. Want me to look?'

'No, I want you to go home.' Horton looked at the clock. The day had raced away. It was almost seven, and there was little more they could do that evening. Cantelli left, and Walters followed soon after.

Horton tracked down Sergeant Wells. 'Thought you'd be off duty by now.'

'I thought so too but I'm still here. Must love the place.'

Horton asked Wells to send a couple of officers round to the letting agents in the morning for the keys to Spender's flat. Any problems and they'd get a warrant. Then he set off for his meeting with Billy Jago in the amusement arcade at Clarence Pier.

Horton found Jago feeding one of the slot machines, hoping to win the jackpot. His bloodshot eyes squinted at Horton and away again with a slight nod at the machine beside him. Jago always liked to be dramatic. Still, the man had to be careful being a police informant. Even though he was an unofficial, unregistered one he still ran the risk of being exposed and earning himself a beating from those he shopped.

Horton fed the slot machine and pulled the lever. 'So who's doing the house robberies in Copnor?' he asked quietly.

'Joe Engels and his mate Derby Wallis.'

'I didn't know Wallis was out.'

'Two weeks ago.'

'He's not wasted much time.'

'Perhaps he likes it inside. I hear they've got Sky Sports, computers and can use their own phones.'

'Thinking of joining them?' Horton joked.

'Tempted. It's a darn sight more than I've got on the straight and narrow.'

Horton snorted and Jago threw him a withering glance. 'Mind you, if I was to get a raise . . .'

'In your dreams, Jago.'

'Yeah, and the way this country's going, they'll be taxing them next. I need a fag.'

Horton pulled the lever and was about to walk away when the coins came tumbling out. He scooped them up as Jago, dropping his secret agent act, grumbled, 'Some buggers have all the bleeding luck.'

'You take them. They'll only spoil the line of my leather jacket.' Horton handed over his pile of coins. 'Treat it as a bonus. Buy yourself a beer or two.'

Jago thrust them in the pocket of his dirty jeans, where they jangled as he shifted to retrieve a packet of cigarettes. 'Engels and Wallis stash the stolen stuff in an allotment shed off Moneyfields Avenue.'

'Aptly named.'

'Eh?'

'Go on.'

'The allotment belongs to Percy Maidstone but he ain't never going to use it again, too fat to get out of his chair never mind dig for bleeding victory.'

'I think you're in the wrong century.'

'The wrong bloody planet if you ask me.'

'Does Maidstone know what his shed's being used for?' Horton knew Maidstone of old, a habitual crook who had been inside more times than he'd been out, until he'd got too fat to climb through windows and squeeze through doors.

'Is the sun hot?' Jago said. 'But you won't get him to say so.'

'How are they shifting the stuff?'

'The usual way.' Jago inhaled deeply and darted anxious glances around him. The promenade was busy with evening strollers and those heading for the pubs and restaurants. 'The internet, down the pub, from the back of Engels' dirty grey van. I heard he and Wallis are branching out. Going to target the houses to the north around Hilsea.'

'Are you sure they can find them without satnav?'

'Ha bloody ha.'

'When do they plan to undertake this next expedition?'

Jago shrugged.

'You can do better than that.'

'End of the week, I heard, but I don't always hear right. Can I have me money? I've got a date.'

'Girlfriend?'

'Yeah.'

'Must be catching.'

'What?'

'Nothing.' Horton handed over Jago's fee, thinking of Walters and his Penny. Everyone seemed to be pairing off, except him. He thought of Felice but only for a moment before Gaye Clayton's face came into his vision. He hadn't pursued his promise of taking her to dinner. He'd mentioned it so many times — and she hadn't shot him down on asking — but work, either his or hers, had always prevented making it happen, so much so that it had become something of a standing joke between them.

Jago sidled off, fag in mouth, his spindly legs carrying him across the road to the public toilets, into which he disappeared. Horton returned to his Harley in the car park and made his way along the seafront back to his boat. He called Gaye but got her voicemail. *'Sorry, I'm unavailable right now. I'm in Hull, working. If your call is urgent leave a message and I'll get back to you as soon as I can.'*

'It's Andy, it's not urgent. And there's no body that I need you to examine. I thought you were in America. I'll call you again.'

He changed and went for a run.

CHAPTER EIGHT

Tuesday

Early the next morning, after giving instructions to Sergeant Wells following Jago's information, Horton diverted to the major incident suite, where he found Sergeant Trueman alone at his desk. His shirtsleeves were pushed up his hairy arms as though he'd been working all night and, judging by his five o'clock shadow, which was always heavy, Horton wondered if he had.

'No, just feels like it,' Trueman said. 'We're so short-staffed that I'm wondering if they've closed the station and no one's bothered to inform me. Operation Zebra, the armed robbery in Basingstoke, is soaking up all our resources. Dennings is there working under Superintendent Carolyn Buckley, which really gets up Bliss's nose. She thought she was going to be given the investigation and temporary promotion instead of holding the baby here until Uckfield returns.'

'When's the Super expected back?'

'Now, if he had his way. Phones up regularly just to make sure we're all still here and haven't skived off and that Bliss isn't messing up his desk.' He rubbed his chin and yawned.

'I'll buy you a coffee.'

'And fetch me some sandwiches, or toast, or something. I daren't leave here.'

'Not even to go to the toilet?'

'You must be kidding. Bliss has had me fitted with a catheter.'

Horton wouldn't have put it past her. He hastened to the canteen and bought Trueman and himself a bacon sandwich and coffee each.

'Make the most of it,' Horton said, handing it over and taking the seat next to him. 'I've heard the canteen's days might be numbered.'

Trueman was sidetracked for a moment by a ping from his computer. Horton ate and watched as he replied.

'Know anything about Julian Anther?' Horton asked when he once again had the sergeant's full attention. While Cantelli had a memory like an elephant, Trueman's was even better. Cantelli hadn't heard of Anther before.

It hardly took a minute for Trueman to reply, and that delay was only because his mouth was full. He said that Bliss had briefed him about the art switch, and he'd already delved into his memory store.

'He ran an art gallery in Emsworth some years ago, back in the early nineties. I was a very young rookie cop stationed at Havant. There was a robbery. Two youths managed to break in through the front door — it was an old building, many of them are in the centre of that harbour village. They stole a couple of paintings after slashing a couple of others and making a general mess.'

'That would account for Anther's nervousness and agitation, along with his insistence that he is shit-hot on security.

'It was before Bliss's time at Havant,' Trueman continued. 'She's younger than me. In fact, everyone's younger than me.' Trueman swallowed.

'That's not true.'

'If you say so. I remember that Anther closed the gallery soon after the robbery and went to live abroad. I didn't know he'd returned until Bliss told me about the art switch yesterday and the name Anther rang a bell.'

'Who needs computers with you around, Dave?' Horton sipped his coffee. 'Do you know which paintings they took?'

'I'm not that retentive. But I can look it up. You think it could be relevant?'

'No, just curious. Are the two thieves still active? I can't see them being involved in something so sophisticated as art forgery or theft, but then, who knows? Maybe they developed a taste for fine art after that job. And, while serving time in prison, they may have met up with a talented forger or big-time crooks who taught them a thing or two.'

'I'll find out, but if they have been criminally active, I haven't come across them here.'

Horton made his escape before Bliss hove into view. At the bottom of the stairs, he turned in the direction of the rear entrance and, standing under the shelter of the awning out of a fine drizzling rain, rang Uckfield's mobile number.

'What?' came Uckfield's customary terse reply, causing Horton to smile.

'Just wanted to see if you were still alive, Steve.'

Their friendship went right back to police college and Uckfield had been Horton's best man at his wedding. It had been sorely tested over the false rape allegation that had broken up Horton's marriage and had earned him a suspension, but the friendship had remained, despite being sometimes stretched to breaking point.

'No, this is a recording. Are you missing me?'

'Trueman is. He's got DCI Bliss and a whole host of investigations to oversee.'

'That's nice for him. Might make the lazy bastard work for a change.'

Horton knew Uckfield didn't mean that. Trueman worked like a Trojan. And, as Trueman had said, Uckfield had been on the phone to him and knew what was going down.

'When will you be fit to return to work?' Horton asked.

'Now, except the idiot doctor, who knows bugger all, says not for another week.'

'That's not long.'

'Long enough. I'm bored rigid. I heard you'd gone walkabout.'

'No, I was working for the Intelligence Directorate on an undercover assignment in France.'

'Oh yeah,' Uckfield said, his voice laced with scepticism.

Horton hastily continued. 'We've got rather an interesting investigation — two, actually — a missing sailor and a bloodstained boat is one, and art theft and forgery is the other.'

'Sounds delightful. Why are you telling me? I'm on sick leave.'

'Thought you might like something to keep the brain cells working.'

'Are they connected?'

'No.' Horton gave him a brief summary of both cases.

'Could be an art collector who switched the paintings after discovering the ones he had on his wall were forgeries.'

'Must be a magician then and lucky to have known the originals were in the gallery.'

'No such thing as luck.'

'A tip-off?'

'Yes, and Anther was counting on the fact that Miss Ellwood on her second visit wouldn't notice the switch.'

A theory Horton had already considered and which he and Cantelli had talked around. 'There was a robbery at Anther's gallery before, ten years ago.'

'There you are then. He's up to the same old tricks.'

'The stolen paintings were recovered from two yobs who wouldn't know an easel from an elbow.'

'Says who?'

'Trueman.'

'Then he should know. Keep me posted.' Uckfield rang off.

It was interesting that Uckfield, although in jest, had suggested the Emsworth robbery had been staged, because this one could have been too.

As Horton reached his office his mobile rang. It was Ruth Bowen, the blood pattern analyst. Horton told her what they had. 'I'd like to be present when you make your initial examination,' he said. 'Hopefully you'll be able to tell us whether or not Spender was attacked.'

Ruth said she'd be able to do that tomorrow, Wednesday morning, around 10.30. Horton was impatient at the delay but then he'd already deferred the investigation for two days since the boat had been found. Would another day make a difference in finding a killer, if it was murder? Possibly. Well, at least they'd gain entry to Spender's flat and could follow up on his blood group. Investigations could still proceed because, murder or not, they still had a missing man to locate.

Horton rang Sergeant Norris in CID at Newport on the Isle of Wight and asked him to verify that Michael Ellwood, born 1958, was a patient in St Mary's Hospital. He didn't like to doubt Felice — and he was ninety-nine per cent certain she was telling the truth, as was Maurice Linden — but he had to check. He also asked Norris to send over the report for the traffic incident that had left Ellwood with serious injuries.

Cantelli and Walters arrived at the same time, and while Cantelli checked his messages and made a couple of phone calls, Horton talked to Walters. 'See if you can get hold of any CCTV footage the city has for the rear and front of Anther's gallery. Look for anyone entering or leaving it carrying a briefcase or a large bag, portfolio case or a cardboard box after the twenty-first of April, including Julian Anther.'

'They won't have kept the footage that long unless there was an incident there and it's needed for evidence.'

'Well, see what they've got. Also speak to someone at the Royal Academy of Arts and get more background on Michael

Ellwood, aside from what Cantelli gleaned from the internet yesterday. And get a photograph of Ellwood and send it over to Trueman. There must be hundreds of pictures of Ellwood on the internet.' Not knowing what Ellwood looked like, Horton imagined thin, long hair, sharp eyes and an aquiline face, but then that was his preconception of an artist, and the real Ellwood could look a million light years from that. 'See if you can find any Ellwood art collectors on the magic machine, font of all information and disinformation, the internet. There must be some people who brag about their acquisitions.'

'Anything else you want me to do, guv? A handstand while I conjure a rabbit and a couple of villains out of a hat?'

'Now that you mention it, yes. Sergeant Wells has officers picking up Joe Engels, Derby Wallis and Percy Maidstone.'

'They'll need to hire a crane to lift the latter.'

'Yes, he makes you look positively lithe. All three are involved in the Copnor house robberies. Get a confession from them.'

'Sure, and while I'm about it I'll ask them what they did with Shergar.' Walters waddled off mumbling something about stocking up on food from the canteen.

Horton took a call from Felice.

'Roy's free to deliver the paintings to Sotheby's today,' she said. 'I'm meeting him at the gallery this morning. Maurice says I can stay in his apartment while I'm in town. My father seems a little better, but I've told the hospital I'll return immediately if there is any change.'

Horton asked to be informed when the paintings had been safely deposited with Jonathan Reed at Sotheby's. Next he rang his solicitor, Frances Greywell, and gave her instructions to proceed with the child arrangement order. He wasn't seeking to prevent Emma from leaving the country with Catherine and Jarvis, and neither was he requesting that Emma live with him, he simply wanted to increase his contact time with his daughter. He hoped that the issuing of the order would be enough to make Catherine discuss altering their arrangements and granting him his wish. It wasn't as though he was asking for weeks with his daughter, although he had requested at least a week in the summer holidays and two days at Christmas. Getting Catherine and the court to agree could depend on him finding a house or flat, as he'd already discussed with Cantelli. He didn't have time to look for one. Yet he had to make time.

Cantelli left for court and Gaye returned his call. It was good to hear her voice.

'So why aren't you in America as you said you would be?' Horton asked.

'It got postponed until the autumn. Instead, I got the wet and wild north of England and the smell of fish in Hull.'

'Not much different to Portsmouth then save for the weather, although it's raining here now.'

'In your message you said it was quiet on the body count front.'

'Not quite.' He explained about Spender and the blood on the boat.

She said, 'By the time I return you might have a body.'

'Depends when you're back.'

'End of next week.'

He heard a phone ringing in the background, then someone called her name.

'Was there anything else you wanted to say?' she asked.

He hesitated and heard her name being called again.

She said, 'Got to go. Happy hunting.'

Horton managed to make a few calls, reply to some emails and finish off a report before Wells informed him that PCs Allen and Johns had the keys to Spender's flat. Horton asked to be picked up outside the station.

'What did the letting agent tell you about Spender?' he asked, strapping the seat belt round him as the police car headed north towards the flat.

Johns swivelled round in the passenger seat to answer. 'The person who showed Spender the flat left the company seven months ago and no one else in the office has met Spender.

They've had no complaints about him, nor from him. His rent is paid by direct debit, no problems for the eighteen months he's had it. His bank and employment references checked out. His previous address was a flat in Farlington.'

Closer to where Spender kept his boat at the top of Langstone Harbour, thought Horton. 'Any idea why he moved?'

'None.'

'Was he working for Jeplie when he took this flat in London Road?'

'Yes.'

The traffic out of the city on the London Road, where Spender lived, was heavy. Cars were parked on either side of the busy road, but in spite of this, PC Allen still managed to find a space not far from the address. While Allen stayed with the car, Horton entered the shabby semi-detached Edwardian house with Johns, who began knocking on the ground-floor doors while Horton climbed the worn and grubby grey-carpeted stairs to the attic room. The smell of loneliness, rotting vegetables and drains hung in the air, reminding him of the small house he'd shared with his mother and another tenant not far from here before they'd been rehoused in the council tower block in the middle of the city. The thud of music from below started up as Horton unlocked Spender's door and let himself into a small sitting room with a kitchenette giving off it. To his right was a door which he suspected led into the bedroom and a bathroom. Nothing looked to have been disturbed.

His first impression was that Spender wasn't bothered where he lived just as long as he had a bed and a TV. There was no personalization in the form of photographs, posters, pictures, magazines or DVDs, but then Horton lived on a small yacht with only Emma's photograph and a picture she had painted of his boat. Did that mean he wasn't bothered where he lived? He knew he couldn't stomach living in a flat, despite the fact it didn't have to be as soulless, small and dingy as this, but the thought of being stuck within four walls with no sea to look out on caused his heart to contract. He'd feel trapped. His sense of claustrophobia was a legacy of being shut in the basement of a piss-hole of a children's home. It was years ago, another time, another place, but that didn't mean it had gone away.

He refocused on the flat. It was tidy and relatively clean on the surface and he wasn't going to poke around for dust and grime. There were no discarded takeaway foils or beer cans littering the sofa or the floor. Curtains framed the window, which looked down on to the street, where PC Allen was engaged in conversation with a short, stout woman with long black hair streaked with grey. She was leaning over a wheeled tartan shopping trolley and doing all the talking. Judging by her expression and gesticulations she was giving Allen a hard time about something. The PC's face showed no emotion though, just studied interest. Horton smiled to himself. A bus pulled up in front of a row of small shops opposite — a chemist, launderette, a second-hand furniture store, and a kebab takeaway.

His phone pinged. It was Sergeant Norris on the Isle of Wight confirming that Michael Ellwood was in hospital in a stable condition but was very poorly. He'd been admitted after taking a cocktail of drinks and painkillers. Suicide or accidental? wondered Horton, thinking it accounted a great deal for the strain etched on Felice's face if she believed her father had tried to kill himself. The subsequent emotions surrounding possible suicide, those of anger and guilt, were emotionally exhausting.

Horton returned to his perusal of the room. There was an anorak hanging on the back of the door and under it a heavy-duty raincoat. Nothing in the pockets. On the carpet beside them was a pair of trainers, well worn, size ten, and a pair of workman's boots. The kitchenette was modestly stocked with food. No washing machine, so Spender must use the launderette opposite.

In the bedroom the bed was made up, the sheets looked clean. There was a pair of patterned pyjamas under the quilt.

Again, no personal items in the room. He opened the wardrobe and did a double take. Here were two very smart designer-label suits of excellent quality and tailoring. They weren't brand new, but neither were they showing signs of wear. Their style was still fashionable as far as he could tell. Not owning many suits himself, only two, and not having bought any for three years, he wouldn't know. He only ever wore a suit and tie to court.

Once more, there was nothing in the pockets. There were also three handmade shirts from a bespoke tailor in London, two pairs of casual designer trousers, some T-shirts, an expensive brand of sailing jacket, a pair of designer trainers and high-quality leather lace-up shoes. Alongside these were the average chain-store jeans, T-shirts, jumpers and trainers and, in the drawers, ordinary underpants and socks save for a handful of silk and Egyptian cotton socks. Spender liked his clothes. Interesting, yes. Significant? Every man was entitled to dress how he pleased but the question forming in Horton's mind was how a refuse collector could afford a boat and some extremely expensive clothes? Perhaps they earned a great deal these days, although the flat contradicted that. It looked as though Spender had once been well off but had fallen on hard times. Maybe he'd been determined to keep hold of the boat and the clothes but had sold a house or a higher-end apartment, or had moved from a larger, more prestigious rented place, which could have been the flat the agent said he'd come from in Farlington. Perhaps a divorce had cleaned him out, or his business had gone bankrupt. Or both.

There were no bank statements or chequebooks, nor a computer or laptop. Spender must have conducted his finances online via his mobile phone. No personal correspondence, no mementos of his childhood, nothing to say who his parents were or had been or if he had any relatives. Perhaps he had been orphaned like him, Horton thought, examining the contents of the bathroom cabinet. He lifted out a packet, which, from the pharmacy label, had been prescribed by a doctor. Good, he could call in at the pharmacy and obtain the doctor's name and address. He wondered what the drugs were for. Sumatriptan. He popped the packet into an evidence bag. Despite the fact they had no confirmation they were investigating a murder, he thought it best to be on the safe side.

There was nothing here to tell him more about Spender, not even a photograph. Maybe Spender kept a picture of a loved one under his pillow, Horton thought with a cynical smile, stretching his hand under the pillows of the single bed. Surprisingly his fingers connected with something. Withdrawing it, he found it was a key with a simple metal ring through the hole at the top, an X-shaped profile, about three and a half inches long, and the name *Kale* on it. It wasn't the spare key to a car or a boat, and it was neither the right size nor shape to be a key to a standard padlock. Which door did it open? Not Spender's original door lock, Horton thought, but he tried it anyway.

It didn't fit. The key to a lover's place, perhaps, hence the sleeping with it under the pillow? A bit whimsical, he thought, putting it into an evidence bag. Why didn't Spender keep it on him? It must mean something to him to have hidden it, although stuffing it under his pillow wasn't exactly putting it in a secret place. Maybe this was a spare and he had the duplicate on his key fob — which was where? On him in the sea? If Spender had been attacked and murdered then the killer hadn't bothered to take his keys and search this flat, not unless he had been very neat, which was possible but unlikely. Horton knew he would have spotted evidence of that.

He searched under the mattress but found nothing. Looking out of the bedroom window into a concrete back-yard, there was no shed or outbuilding of any kind, so the key wasn't for that. There was also, Horton thought, as he locked up, no record of the purchase of the boat, no birth certificate or any other official papers. He must have his driver's licence on him.

Horton found PC Johns talking to a young woman with black hair, dark eye make-up and several rings in her nose and ears. Johns, seeing him, thanked her and they descended the stairs to the ground floor. 'Ms Rachel Marlington last saw Spender on Saturday morning. He was going to work, she was just coming home. She works the night shift at a supermarket. She sometimes hears Spender moving around upstairs and his television but that's about it. I can't get any answer from the other flat on the middle floor or the basement flat — probably at work. The other two occupants on the ground floor don't even know who lives in the attic.'

'What do you make of this?' Horton said.

'It's a key.'

'Well done, Johns, we'll make a copper of you yet.'

Johns grinned.

'I found it under his pillow.'

Johns raised his eyebrows. 'It could be the key to a lover's house or flat where he spends most of his time.'

'My initial thoughts, but why not keep it on him? And if he has a lover then why hasn't he or she reported him missing?'

'Because he or she killed him. Could have been a lover's tiff on board that boat, Spender got injured and fell, or was pushed overboard while lover boy or girl took off.'

'Even more reason to come forward and act the innocent.'

'Not if no one knows about this lover. She, or he, could be married.'

Was Spender secretive? Perhaps. Horton thought of the expensive clothes. 'I want to call in at the pharmacy and find out what these tablets are for.' He showed Johns the packet.

'Never heard of them.'

'I'll get Spender's doctor's name from the chemist and call on them.' There was that blood group to get too. 'I'll leave you to assist Allen, he looks as though he needs rescuing.' The woman with the shopping trolley and long grey-streaked hair was still monopolizing the constable. 'When you can extricate yourself from her, call in at the shops along here, especially the kebab place over the road. Spender could have the same taste for gourmet delights as Walters. He also probably uses that launderette. See if there is an assistant or manager who might know him. Also ask at the convenience store in the petrol station on the corner — he probably buys his petrol there as well as milk and bread. Oh, and check the nearest pub.' The Green Post was further north but certainly within walking distance. 'Call me if you discover anything significant. I'll make my own way back to the station.'

Horton waited for a gap in the traffic then dashed across to the small pharmacy.

CHAPTER NINE

'Yes, I dispensed those,' Ms Decuba said. Horton was seated in a small consulting room with an elegant woman in her mid-thirties in a brightly coloured long floral dress. He had explained he was making enquiries about Neil Spender who was missing and, on searching his flat across the road, had found a packet of prescription tablets. 'They're for severe migraine attacks and cluster headaches.'

Horton rapidly considered this. Spender could have been incapacitated by a migraine attack on board his boat, but that wouldn't have caused bleeding, not unless he'd stumbled, hit his head when falling, then crawled on deck and fallen overboard. It sounded a bit incredible, and a migraine attack didn't account for the other blood group being present, although this other person could have cut him or herself, panicked and scarpered, not wanting to get involved.

'Would the migraine have caused him to faint?' he asked.

'The pain can be severe, and people have different pain thresholds, so it is possible. He could also experience migraine with aura — that's where a recurring headache strikes after or at the same time as sensory disturbances, such as flashes of light, blind spots and other vision changes or tingling in your hands or face.'

74

'So, it is possible that this sensory disturbance could have made him stumble?'

'Yes.'

Again Horton considered if Spender could have struck himself, perhaps against the table, but Taylor and Beth Tremaine hadn't found blood spatters there, only at the bottom of the table leg. 'How long have you been dispensing this drug for him?'

'For the last year at least, since I've been working here, but he could have been prescribed them for many years. I don't have access to his medical records.'

Horton could ask the doctor, although he didn't see that the length of time Spender had suffered from these debilitating headaches mattered. 'Does he say much?'

'No. He just collects his prescription and leaves, as do many of our customers.'

Horton asked for the name of the surgery that had prescribed the drug and after interrogating the computer, the pharmacist revealed it was the Derby Road Practice, which was only a ten-minute brisk walk south, just off the London Road. The letting agents were also close by so he could return Spender's flat key at the same time. He thanked her and headed for both, losing count of the number of takeaway food shops en route — pizza places, hamburger joints, kebab houses, fish and chip shops. If he sent Walters out to enquire at them, he wouldn't see the constable for a fortnight. Walters probably knew each of these gastronomes. Perhaps he'd take Penny on a tour of them, or maybe she was already familiar with them.

Horton's phone rang. He was pleased to see it was the Metropolitan Art and Antiques Unit.

'DC Joe Trillby,' came the crisp announcement. 'I hear you've got an unusual MO.'

Horton explained what had happened as he walked on.

Trillby said, 'Everyone thinks that art theft is some guy in a dark suit scaling the walls like the Milk Tray advert but it's usually a trusted friend or business associate of the victim.

Or it could be art insurance fraud. The company pay out and Anther splits the money between himself, Catmore and Ms Ellwood. And I'm not sure I believe it when your art gallery owner says he *always* sets the alarm. I've very rarely found a gallery owner who *always* does. He can't have been present in the gallery or the back room every second someone was there. Maybe a friend slipped out the back and switched the paintings while Anther was elsewhere or otherwise occupied. But replacing the originals with forgeries has to be an inside job, someone who already had the forgeries ready. Catmore could have had both originals and forged paintings, or commissioned the forgeries once he realized the original two were in his possession.'

Horton's mind spun back to the elderly man with the liver-spotted skin, paunch and spectacles in the small terraced house with the detritus of his life scattered around him in the front room. 'I wouldn't have said he had the specialist knowledge to do so, but Anther has. It's a theory we've discussed.' He didn't like the thought of Felice being in on it though. From her manner, Horton would have said she wasn't. 'Why not fake the provenance?'

'Maybe they're not as clever as they thought. Or perhaps the artist baulked at the idea of faking provenance, or didn't see it as his or her job. He or she might not have been asked. Catmore and his accomplice, this Anther or someone else, were hoping to get away with it. They switched the first two paintings too quickly — pressure was being put on them to do so by someone behind the fraud — and they hoped that Ellwood's daughter wouldn't spot the third one was a phoney.'

'But she did.'

'Yes. That would have been a blow to them.'

Which was why Anther was so edgy. 'Anther called her in — would he have done that if he is involved?'

'Double bluff. Or he was testing her out. Or, I should say, testing out the paintings. If they fooled the daughter on that third one, herself an art expert, then they could fool the collectors. If Anther's not involved, he could have been targeted or chosen specifically. Has he a dubious past?'

'Not that we're aware of. However, there was a theft from his previous gallery. Nothing like this, some youths intent on vandalism.'

'But he'll have claimed on his insurance.'

And Horton recalled that Trueman had said Anther had then taken himself off abroad. Perhaps this was an insurance scam.

Trillby said, 'Let me know how you get on at Sotheby's. When we get the full report it'll be logged. If anything further comes to mind I'll contact you.'

Horton shelved the art theft as he drew level with the letting agents. He introduced himself to a woman in her early thirties with long dark hair and eyelashes to match, who announced she was the manager. She confirmed she had spoken earlier to PC Johns. Horton returned Spender's flat key but asked if they had a spare that he could have to save bothering them again. He'd obviously give her a receipt.

'I don't see why not. The owner lives abroad. I don't need to ask his permission.'

'Could you tell me if you issued this key?' Horton produced the one he'd found under Spender's pillow.

Her long, multicolour-varnished fingernails tapped the keyboard. 'We issued three keys to Mr Spender — one to the front door, one to his flat door and one to the back door. I've no idea what that other key is for. It's not one of ours.'

Horton asked her to contact him if she heard from Mr Spender, or if anyone else enquired about him, then made his way to the surgery just a short distance off the busy London Road. There he asked to speak to the practice manager and was requested to wait. He wasn't a fan of doctors' surgeries — they always made him feel uneasy, much as Cantelli didn't like visiting dentists.

Half an hour later he was outside with the knowledge that Spender didn't have a next of kin named on his medical records and he was blood type O positive. He had last seen the doctor a month ago and the tablets were a regular prescription. Aside from that the practice manager couldn't give him any further information without a warrant or the patient's permission, and seeing as he was missing, Horton was unlikely to get the latter. Not that it was relevant — obtaining Spender's blood group had been the primary objective. It didn't help them catch the killer though, if there was one.

He began walking along the busy thoroughfare towards the police station. Those expensive suits niggled at him, that and the key in his pocket. And there was someone who was an expert on keys who was at this moment examining locks on the art theft investigation. Horton called Leney.

'I'm at the art gallery now. Miss Ellwood and Roy Macey are here.' Horton had expected them to already have left for London seeing as it was just after one. 'I'll be along shortly, I'm just going back to the station to collect my Harley.'

His phone rang before he reached there. Expecting it to be PC Johns or Allen he was pleased to see it was Cantelli and even more delighted when Cantelli triumphantly declared that the jury had taken less than fifteen minutes to declare Callum Dailey guilty.

'Thank the Lord for sensible citizens,' Cantelli added. 'He'll be sentenced in a fortnight.'

'Let's hope he gets a long custodial one. One less lunatic on the streets.'

'For a while,' Cantelli said. 'I'm just about to head back to the station.'

'Your timing is perfect, Barney. Pick me up on the corner of Kingston Crescent.'

While Horton hurried there, he called PC Johns and asked if he had anything to report.

'Nothing to write home about,' was Johns's announcement. 'Spender shops at the petrol station convenience store, but never says much. I've got the name and number of the launderette manageress, so I'll call her. The kebab shop owner says he knows Mr Spender but has never really spoken to him and couldn't remember when he last saw him.'

Cantelli was waiting for Horton when he arrived. He gave the sergeant instructions to make for Anther's gallery in Southsea and updated him on the way. Like him, Cantelli found the key and the expensive clothes interesting but had no further speculation to add to what Horton and PC Johns had already discussed. Neither did he venture a different opinion on the blood group and Spender's migraine attacks to the one Horton expressed, agreeing only that it seemed unlikely Spender had been taken ill, cut himself and fallen overboard, albeit not impossible.

Their discussion had taken them to the rear of Anther's gallery. Cantelli pulled up behind a dark blue van bearing the name Macey, which was parked across the entrance. In the yard was Anther's Jaguar and Paul Leney's Land Rover. Leney was in the back room picking over the lock mechanism which he'd removed from the door and had placed on a plastic cover on the tabletop beside the kitchen sink.

'Found anything?' Horton asked the rotund man in his mid-fifties with thick short grey hair. He could hear both Felice and another man's voice in the gallery, though he couldn't make out what they were saying.

'The front door lock wasn't picked and neither was this one. There are no scratches or marks. I haven't examined the locks under a microscope, but I do have a magnifying glass and they haven't been manipulated.'

Horton extracted the small evidence bag from his inside jacket pocket and handed it across. 'Can you tell me anything about what that key might unlock?'

'Can I remove it?'

'I need to get it checked for prints first.' Horton didn't think anyone other than Spender's fingerprints would be on it, but it was best to be certain.

Leney examined it with his magnifying glass through the plastic bag. 'It's a cruciform key, the X-shaped profile gives it away. They're mainly used in industrial applications although some householders prefer them because their locks are very difficult to pick so they provide greater security.'

'Bit silly then, keeping it under your pillow.'

Leney raised his eyebrows. 'Maybe, but then without knowing where the corresponding lock is no one would be able to use it. It's got three sets of teeth that are located at ninety-degree angles to one another, as you can see. The four sides are flattened. It's easy to duplicate this type of key but as I said, very difficult to pick the lock.'

'I don't suppose you'd be able to tell me where that lock might be?'

'Not unless I happened to be psychic, but I can get in touch with the manufacturers and they might be able to tell me when the key was issued and to whom.'

'Please do.' Horton slipped it back into the pocket of his sailing jacket. 'We'll leave you to it, Paul.'

Felice looked up as they entered Anther's office. 'We're just about to leave,' she said with a cheerful greeting, but even in the short time since yesterday she seemed to have lost even more of her sparkle.

Horton could hear Anther's voice from the gallery beyond, and as his was the only one, Horton assumed he was on the phone. Horton made the introductions. Cantelli hadn't met Felice on the previous investigation on the Isle of Wight. Felice in turn introduced the broad-shouldered, muscular man in his late fifties with short, grey-peppered hair as Roy Macey. He was dressed in jeans and a navy-blue T-shirt sporting his company name and logo. Macey stretched out a strong hand. Horton returned his firm handshake and candid eye contact.

'I've explained to Roy what's happened,' Felice said.

'If you wouldn't mind keeping it confidential, Mr Macey.'

'That's the norm in my line of business, Inspector. We collect and deliver some extremely valuable artworks as well as hang them for both private and corporate clients. Felice said it was a delicate and confidential matter and, as it concerns Michael's paintings, I'm only too happy to help.'

'You know Mr Ellwood?'

'Yes, and his work. I've hung his paintings for clients, and for his exhibitions in London and elsewhere around the country before his accident.'

Then Macey could tell him who those clients were if Anther wasn't forthcoming. 'Have you ever seen paintings like these by Mr Ellwood or any other artist?'

'Felice asked me that and I haven't. I'd have said they were originals but then I'm not an art expert. I just move paintings and hang them, and other collectibles, musical instruments, vinyl record covers, photographs, even stuffed animal heads.'

Cantelli said, 'I wouldn't have thought there was much call for that in these politically correct days.'

'Dwindling, but you'd be staggered at what some people collect. Or perhaps not. Being a copper, you must have seen some sights.'

Horton agreed they had. Flats and houses crammed with what most would call junk, people who collected tinfoil cartons, plastic bags, newspapers, spoons — you name it, he'd seen it. He told Macey and Felice that he had reported the theft to the Metropolitan Art and Antiques Unit, who would let him know if they picked up anything on the forgeries or if it matched with any other art thefts.

Felice said, 'Can you tell Julian I'll call him as soon as the paintings are safely at Sotheby's? I'll also call you. Nice to have met you, Sergeant.'

'And you.'

'Still think she might be involved?' Horton said quietly after she and Macey had left.

Cantelli shrugged. 'Something's bugging her but that could be her dad's illness.'

Anther spun round as they entered and rapidly ended his call. If Horton thought Felice had looked fraught it was nothing compared to the change in Anther. In just a day the gallery owner looked as though he'd shed half a stone and been deprived of light for hours on end, not to mention sleep.

Horton introduced Cantelli but Anther wasn't listening. His eye contact was all over the place and his hands continually twitching. He was dressed with the same fastidiousness as yesterday but on closer examination Horton noted the breast pocket handkerchief in the blazer was missing today and his yellow-and-blue cravat was awry.

'Has Mr Catmore been on the phone to you?' Horton asked, thinking about what DC Trillby had said earlier.

'He has. Twice.' Anther began to pace the gallery, touching a painting here, straightening one on the wall there. 'He's looking to claim the value of the originals from me. I've just been on to the insurers. My God, you'd think I was asking them to pay off the national debt.' He swung round, almost knocking over a large abstract on an easel to the right of the gallery. It was taking up a lot of space and marked 'Sold'.

'I pointed out to them that my insurance policy covers me for fraudulent artwork and for theft, so what's the problem? But insurance companies like to find something in the print so small that it's practically a microdot to prevent them from coughing up.' Anther made to remove his handkerchief, then scowled as he found it missing. 'I told Mr Catmore he'll get some compensation for the third fraudulent painting but the first two weren't officially verified as originals and authenticated, aside from my opinion and Felice's, so I'm not sure how he or I stand. Is there any hope of you finding them?' he asked with desperation. Then, without bothering to wait for an answer, he continued agitatedly, 'The insurance company asked for the crime reference number.'

'I'll get DC Walters to give it to you.' Horton once again asked for the names of customers who had been inside the gallery during the critical time, and again got the same negative answer. He also pressed for names of collectors of Ellwood's paintings but drew a blank. Walters might have found some through his interrogation of the internet, but if not, then Horton would get them from one of the others, Felice, Linden or Macey.

Taking their leave of both Anther and Leney, Horton said to Cantelli, 'Well?'

'Anther's very twitchy.'

'Too twitchy?'

'Maybe. His little fraud scheme's gone wrong and someone's putting pressure on him. Where to now? Back to the station? If Bliss hears the court case is over, she'll think I've skived off home.'

'I'm surprised she hasn't been chasing me up by phone.' He hadn't reported to her about the blood group or the finding of the key. 'Make for Jeplie. I'd like to get some background on Neil Spender and a photograph if they have one on their personnel files. Bliss can then issue it to the media. I'd better phone Walters and tell him you're not playing truant.'

The phone rang for some time before it was answered. 'Where were you?'

'Answering the other phone. I can't be in two places at the same time,' Walters grouched. 'Trueman's taken over the background research on Michael Ellwood. I don't think Bliss trusts me to do it properly. Still, I'm not grumbling.'

'That will make a change. That gives you more time to work on Spender. Trace his former addresses. He must have registered on the electoral roll and paid rates in Portsmouth. Cantelli's with me. His court case finished with a result.'

Walters expressed his satisfaction with that. 'And we've got a result with the search of Maidstone's allotment shed. Uniform found it crammed with the stuff stolen from houses in Copnor. They've brought in Engels, Wallis and Maidstone, who are all keeping their mouths shut as you'd expect, and I certainly haven't got time to interview them.'

'Won't do any harm to let them stew in the cells for a while. And Maidstone might talk if we don't feed him.'

'Not sure we can do that under the Human Rights Act.'

'Then we won't tell anyone.'

They stopped off for a bite to eat at McDonald's on the way to Jeplie's offices, situated next to the incinerator on the north-eastern edge of the city. Not the healthiest of meals, Horton thought biting into his hamburger, but it was better than nothing and would keep them going. On an investigation you never knew when you would get to eat. They ate outside the car on Cantelli's insistence because he didn't want the smell to linger.

'Charlotte can sniff out a burger and chips from a hundred yards. She'll punish me by putting me on a regime of lettuce.'

'Better waft your jacket around in the fresh air, in case she sniffs it on your clothes.'

'I think the smell of the bin yard might be enough to banish it.'

CHAPTER TEN

Cantelli was right. Some minutes later the sickly-sweet smell from the yard below wafted in through the open window of Scott Tweed's poky and untidy office along with the noise of the trucks entering and the bleeping and auto-announcement of them reversing.

Tweed was a harassed, slight, balding man in his late thirties with a craggy face, large ears, sharp bloodshot eyes and a pointed nose. His tension emanated throughout the office. Horton thought if he didn't take it more steadily, he wouldn't reach forty.

'If you've come to ask me if Spender has shown up for work or been in touch, the answer is no,' Tweed said curtly. He fidgeted in his seat, his eye contact flicking to them, his phone and his computer screen.

'We can see that you're under pressure, Mr Tweed, so we won't take up much of your time,' Horton soothed. 'We're very concerned for Mr Spender's welfare.'

'Yeah, that copper on the phone said his boat had been found and that he was missing, but I've got no idea why or where he is. In fact, I can't tell you much about him. He's quiet, gets on with the job and until now was pretty reliable, just the odd day sick, migraines.'

'We'd like a photograph of Mr Spender if you have one on file. I'm assuming you would have taken one for his official identification.'

'I can email or send it to your phone.'

Horton gave him the number and a few seconds later it came through. It fitted the description Elkins had got from Tomsett, the harbour master. Spender had a lean, lived-in face, with a scar on the right-hand side, penetrating, protruding eyes and narrow lips. 'How long has he worked for Jeplie?'

'Eighteen months.'

'And before that?'

'He was unemployed.'

Not running a business that had gone bust then. 'For how long?'

'Don't know. A couple of years, I think.'

Which didn't tally with the expensive suits and the boat. Not unless during those two years he'd won the lottery or the football pools, or had come into an inheritance and blown it. Or he had bought the clothes and boat over two years ago. If that was so, though, he'd have sold the boat at least to help supplement his unemployment benefit.

Cantelli said, 'Don't you have the details on his job application?'

'I expect so. You'll have to ask human resources for that at head office. I've only got the basics and the photo for his lanyard.'

'A name and number would be helpful.'

Tweed tutted but relayed it.

Horton said, 'Can you give us Mr Spender's National Insurance number?'

'What do you want that for?'

'Just routine,' Horton answered slickly. They'd be able to check back on Spender's employment record if it became necessary.

Tweed's eyes flicked to his phone as it pinged and then to his computer. 'Human resources will give you that too.'

Horton was sure Tweed could supply it but he didn't want to be bothered by the police more than was necessary. He was probably thinking, 'Let the mandarins in head office deal with that, it's what they're there for.' Horton didn't press him. He asked if the crew had come in.

'They have, they'll be in the yard.' Tweed took them down there, checking his phone as he went. The traffic trundled past on the road beyond, and the sun beat down harder on the enclosed space making it hot and increasing the stench from the empty bin lorries. They headed across to a building on the right, where four men stood in a small kitchenette drinking from mugs and talking. Despite having discarded their high-visibility workwear, the smell of rotting fruit seemed to hang over them and in the fetid humid air. Tweed curtly furnished the introductions and then abruptly left.

Horton didn't think that either he or Cantelli had shown any reaction to the smell, but the older man — grey-haired with gaps in his teeth, who Tweed had introduced as Ken Morecombe — said, 'You get used to it after a while.'

'Is the boss always like that?' Cantelli asked pleasantly. 'Seems under a lot of pressure.'

'He panics,' Morecombe answered. 'He said you want to talk about Neil. Has anything happened to him?'

Tweed hadn't told them about Walters's telephone call yesterday then, which wasn't surprising given the manager's harassed manner.

Horton said, 'Mr Spender is missing. His boat was found abandoned in Langstone Harbour. There was no one on board, but there was blood.'

'Blood! Neil's?' Morecombe said, shocked.

'We believe so.'

There was a stunned silence broken by a man of about forty, sturdily built, with a tanned balding head, small toffee-coloured eyes, a lined forehead and a large tattoo of a spider up the side of his neck. Tweed had introduced him as Sam Farrell. 'He's had an accident and fallen overboard?'

Morecombe chipped in. 'No, the police being here must mean there's more to it than that.'

Horton answered, 'There's the possibility of foul play.'

'Someone bumped him off! No, never,' Farrell declared.

'Why do you say that?'

'Well, why should they?'

'That's what we're trying to establish. How well did you know him, Mr Farrell?'

'Me? Hardly at all. I don't work with him regularly. I'm just the stand-in.' Farrell reached into his trouser pocket and drew out a packet of cigarettes. He removed one but didn't light it. There were large 'No Smoking' signs all around the hut and in the yard. Horton gazed around at the others. Cantelli was taking notes.

'Neil's quiet,' Morecombe added. 'Doesn't say much. Thinks he's a bit above us. Says he won't be on the bins for long. But we've been hearing that ever since he started so we don't take no notice of it.'

'He was glad enough to have the job when he first came,' chipped in a slim, fit man called Colin Reams, who had a long, mournful face and looked to be in his early thirties.

Farrell said, 'I was amazed they took him on, a man of that age. Must be sixty-five if he's a day.'

'Can't discriminate against age now,' Morecombe replied.

Reams continued, 'He can't stomach the job, not that you can blame him for that, no one does it for the love of it or the money.'

Morecombe interjected, 'It beats the shit out of sitting in a factory.'

'It's all right for you, all you have to do is sit on your arse in the cabin, not run around like a loony collecting people's rubbish and taking a lot of stick from them.'

Another of the men piped up, Richard Crompton, who was in his late twenties. 'It keeps you fit though and as Ken says, I'd rather be outside than stuck indoors.'

'Each to their own,' Farrell said cockily.

Horton saw the men's expressions harden. It didn't take an expert on human relations to see that Farrell was not popular among them. The unlit cigarette remained in Farrell's nicotine-stained fingers as he continued, 'He told me he only took the job because it was all he was offered, and it's better than living on the pittance of Universal Credit. I hope I'm not chasing shit when I'm in my sixties. Bit of a comedown, if you ask me.'

Nobody looked as though they were going to nor wanted to ask him. For someone who professed not to know Spender that well, Farrell seemed to be particularly verbal.

Cantelli said, 'Did Neil say what he did before he came here?'

'Not to me,' Farrell airily declared.

'To any of you?' Cantelli asked.

They shook their heads. Morecombe again was the spokesman. 'We don't get much time to chat, we're always on the move save when we stop for our breaks. Then we're too busy eating to spend time talking.'

'Has Mr Spender spoken to any of you about his boat?' asked Horton. They all looked blank with the exception of Farrell. Horton saw a slight narrowing of his eyes before he studiously averted his gaze. 'To you, Mr Farrell?'

His lips twitched. 'Yeah, but only briefly 'cos I used to have a small boat. Did a bit of sea angling from it in the past. Neil said he goes out in the Solent to blow away the smell of crap.'

'Do you go with him?'

'Course not. Like I said, I don't know him that well.'

'Have any of you been on Mr Spender's boat?'

They shook their heads.

'Has he mentioned going out sailing with anyone?'

Again there was silence and head shaking. Farrell fiddled with his cigarette, obviously in need of a nicotine fix.

'Has he spoken of any relatives or friends?'

Morecombe looked around at the others and answered for them. 'No.'

'Has he mentioned being in a relationship?' Horton got blank looks. 'Did you work with Mr Spender last Saturday?'

Morecombe replied, 'Yes.'

'I didn't,' Farrell broke in.

'We knocked off at one,' Morecombe continued.

'Did Mr Spender say what he was doing Saturday afternoon and evening?'

'No.'

But Horton wasn't so sure about Farrell, who put the cigarette in his mouth, scratched his nose and seemed to find the design of his trainers fascinating.

It seemed that Spender was a private person. Was it really the case that these men never talked about anything personal? Perhaps it was. After all, he never spouted off about his personal life and problems around the station.

Horton had a few more questions to ask. 'Did he speak of how he got the scar?'

Reams answered, 'We joked about it, asked him if he'd been in a gang fight. We made light of it. He didn't get upset, just joked back and said, "You should have seen the other guy." Car accident, we think. That and his hands.'

'Hands? What's wrong with them?'

'Arthritis, most probably,' Morecombe volunteered.

Farrell scratched the tattoo of the spider on his neck. 'That was another reason why he shouldn't have been on the bins, but he said, "We don't have to lift the bloody things onto our shoulders and lob them into the truck, we just load them onto the automatic tailgate lift and wheel them back." Nothing wrong with his legs, not that I've ever seen them.' He beamed, showing a row of unhealthy teeth. The others remained impervious to the joke.

Reams said, 'His hands are sort of misshapen, the knuckles swollen, and he has trouble moving his fingers. I've heard him curse when we've been out on the rounds, but he never says nothing about them.'

'Does he mention headaches, migraines?' Horton asked.

The youngest man, Crompton, answered, 'He goes sick with them from time to time. Says he can feel them coming on like he did just before Bank Holiday Monday, had to go off sick on Friday and Saturday. And he does look bad too. He's had to leave the round on a few occasions and get a taxi home. We can see he's not putting it on.'

'And when he's sick, I step in,' Farrell volunteered.

'Do any of you know when he had this accident resulting in his scar and mangled hands?'

They shrugged and shook their heads. Morecombe said, 'We don't talk about personal things. We hardly talk at all unless it's about football or the government or the state of the country, but that usually causes too many arguments, so we stick to reading the newspapers and eating our sandwiches.'

Cantelli said, 'Does Mr Spender volunteer his views?'

Morecombe answered. 'Only to say we're a bunch of heathens.'

'He's an educated man then?' Horton said casually.

'Maybe.'

'He has no accent?'

Crompton spoke, 'Not unless you count that time he came across that old biddy, the one who'd put all her rubbish out in plastic supermarket bags and not in her wheelie bin.'

Reams cut in, 'Yeah, she was jabbering away at us in some foreign language, probably calling us all the names under the sun and Neil just launched into her in what must have been her language. Her gobsmacked face was a picture.'

'What language was it?'

'No idea, could have been double Dutch for all I know,' Reams replied.

Morecombe said, 'It wasn't German, I know that, not because I speak it, but it was a more sing-songy language, like Spanish or French or Italian, with lots of arm waving.'

'When was this?'

'About two months ago.' Reams's mournful face lit up. 'Now the old dear comes out every Thursday we do her round just to speak to him. We tease him about her. Reckon she's sweet on him.'

'What's her address?'

Morecombe answered. 'Kent Terrace, Southsea, fourth house in.'

'Can we have all your contact details?'

'Why?' Farrell demanded somewhat aggressively.

'We might need to talk to you again as further information comes to light. We're very anxious about Mr Spender. Sergeant Cantelli will take down your details.'

They duly gave them. They all lived in the city. Would one of them know what the key was for? Had Spender confided in them? According to Morecombe it seemed not, but Spender might have made a remark about a lock-up — he had obviously spoken about owning a boat. Horton asked them but they all looked blankly at him, except for Farrell, who looked shifty. Abruptly, he said, 'Can we go? I've got an appointment.'

Yes, with a cigarette by the look of it. Horton thanked them and made his way back to the car.

As Cantelli pulled out, he said, 'Farrell's got something to hide or I'm not a policeman with over twenty years' experience.'

'I agree. And the others don't like him. He's too cocky and defensive, but has what he's hiding got anything to do with Spender or why he's disappeared? I'll run him through the computer.' Cantelli indicated right. 'There's something fishy about Spender. I can smell it even above that awful pong. Makes me appreciate those guys even more taking away all our rubbish.'

Horton thought so too and he agreed with Cantelli about something not being quite right about Spender. To add to the expensive clothes, the boat, the mysterious key and the scarred face, there were now misshapen hands and a fluently spoken foreign language.

CHAPTER ELEVEN

'None of that could have any bearing on his disappearance and possible murder,' Bliss quipped an hour later after Horton had briefed her and Sergeant Trueman, who was looking even more wrung out than he had earlier. Bliss was a great one for delegating and then had the annoying habit of checking up every hour on what she had delegated. It was always a relief when she was in meetings. Trueman had Horton's sympathy. The incident suite wasn't as busy as he had expected, an opinion he had expressed to Trueman before Bliss had come off her phone and spotted him.

'That's because most of the team and resources are in Basingstoke along with Dennings on that armed robbery investigation. Wish I was there too, or Bliss was,' Trueman had added sotto voce before she had descended on them.

'We need that report from the blood pattern analyst.' Bliss scowled at two crime boards Trueman had initiated, one for the Spender investigation, the other for the art thefts. 'We could have wasted valuable time,' she snapped, turning her beady eye on Horton.

Something he had already considered, and it was always a possibility when the evidence wasn't clear-cut to begin with. Horton could see that Bliss was looking to put the blame squarely on his shoulders if the delay meant failure. 'I'm meeting Ruth Bowen tomorrow at the port and will get her preliminary findings,' he said. 'Meanwhile we can consider the new information and the slightly conflicting picture we have of Spender.'

'Well, get on with it,' she snapped.

Perhaps the strain of scarce resources was telling on her, Horton thought, and she was frantic to get a result to show that she was as good as, if not better than Buckley, who was heading up the Basingstoke operation.

Horton said, 'On the one hand, according to his colleagues, Spender's quiet, reserved, maybe a bit aloof and superior, and on the other he's jokey and charming, so says the launderette manageress. PC Johns spoke to her, and she confirms the physical description we have of Spender.'

'A bit of a lady's man?' ventured Trueman.

'That's a possibility given how, according to his colleagues, he charmed a resident of Kent Terrace in a fluent foreign language. I've asked Sergeant Wells to get an officer round there to establish what language.'

'Is that relevant?' Bliss cut in.

'Who knows? Spender is also a bit of a snazzy dresser judging by the designer clothes in his wardrobe, so perhaps he does like to impress the ladies and he could have impressed one sufficiently to live with her on and off. I found this under his pillow.' Horton put the key on the desk in front of him. 'The letting agent knows nothing about it. I asked Leney and he says it's the type generally used in industrial settings rather than domestic, but some private householders prefer them because they provide greater security. So, Spender could have a lover somewhere who hasn't come forward, either because she, or he, is implicated, or this person doesn't yet know he's disappeared. His work colleagues have never heard him mention anyone.'

Bliss said, 'She could be married and her husband found out about the affair.'

'Possibly. Tomorrow we'll check with the Department for Work and Pensions to see if he has claimed benefit and ask Her Majesty's Revenue and Customs for his tax record. According to his manager, Scott Tweed, Spender was unemployed, possibly for a couple of years before he was taken on at Jeplie. He might have been working abroad or claiming benefit during that time. Or he could have been recovering from an injury, given the face scar and hands. I'd say he's known much better times, hence the expensive clothes and the boat. There are no papers to say when he purchased his boat. Sergeant Elkins is making enquiries with the yacht brokers in the area but Spender could have bought it privately, or elsewhere in the UK.

'Walters has checked out Spender's previous addresses. The Farlington apartment was distinctly more upmarket than his current one judging by its location. It's possible he could have been living off his savings or an inheritance, which dwindled away. He could have run a business which went bust, or he could have been involved in criminal activity that paid well and then dried up, because before that he lived in bedsits for eleven years. Prior to that the council have no address in Portsmouth for him although he could have lived close by in Fareham or Havant.'

Bliss looked thoughtful. 'So, another possible assailant other than a lover or angry husband could be someone he crossed in crime who has finally caught up with him?'

'Yes, and the key could be to a lock-up where he keeps his papers and possibly stolen goods. But if he has the latter then why not sell them and live more luxuriously? And if he was living a double life, his designer clothes would be at the alternative address. I don't think he'd be voluntarily working as a binman just for the love of it.'

'I'll put out an appeal for anyone who knows him to come forward after Bowen has confirmed we're looking at an assault. What about this art theft? Have we made any progress on that?'

Horton's eyes flicked to the relevant crime board where Trueman had placed a picture of Michael Ellwood. The artist wasn't at all how Horton had imagined. He had short-cropped grey hair on a round face, a weak chin and a hint of uneasiness — or was that shyness? — behind the eyes. Felice didn't resemble him, so she must take after her mother.

Trueman relayed what he had discovered. 'Michael Ellwood was admitted to the Royal Academy in 2004. In order to be accepted he not only had to be professionally active as an artist in the UK but nominated by an existing Academician and then have the support of eight other Royal Academicians to become a candidate. Three times a year all the Academicians meet at a general assembly to vote in new members from the list of candidates, and because the Academy laws specify that there can only be up to a maximum of eighty Royal Academicians at any one time, there are usually only one or two new members a year.'

Bliss's lips pursed. 'Then he's a very prominent artist.'

Horton knew what she was thinking. If the switch of the paintings leaked it would make big headlines. She'd either see her name in print or Assistant Chief Constable Dean would take her off the case and put someone more senior in charge. Alternatively, Dean could hand the investigation over to the Metropolitan Art and Antiques Unit.

Trueman, also reading her thoughts, said, 'I pressed upon the Royal Academy the need for secrecy at this early stage of the investigation, especially with Ellwood so ill. I believe they'll respect that.'

Bliss said, 'Catmore might go to the media.'

'He might,' Horton answered, concerned. 'And we can't stop him. But I'll call him and remind him it's in his best interest at present to keep this quiet.'

Trueman continued. 'I had some luck finding collectors via the internet but the ones I did find are based in New York, Sydney and Italy. Ellwood's work is also owned and displayed in the corporate HQs of some major companies. I don't think any of them will have travelled to Southsea to switch a couple of paintings.'

Horton said, 'And I can't see them knowing Noel Catmore.'

'Ellwood's output has never been vast, but his work is considered brilliant. However, he hasn't painted — or at least not professionally to exhibit and sell, nor has he taken any commissions — for the last three years.'

'A year before he had his motorbike accident on the Isle of Wight,' Horton said. 'Sergeant Norris is sending over the accident report. Not that I can see how that connects with this. The two originals that were switched were painted some years ago, before he became famous.'

'According to his daughter and agent,' Bliss said caustically, 'and both could be lying. If he's not painted for that length of time he could be in financial difficulties and the daughter, agent and gallery owner have all colluded to get some money and publicity.'

A thought that had occurred to Horton, and that Cantelli had already posited. 'But surely Ellwood must have amassed considerable wealth?'

Trueman said, 'He might have squandered it all on wine, women and the horses.'

Horton's eyes again flicked to the picture. Did Ellwood look that type? But that was useless speculation because you could never judge people by their looks. He'd never have thought Spender would have designer clothes and speak a foreign language. Horton didn't know anything about Ellwood save what Felice had told him and that was precious little. It was also centred on her father's health. Cantelli had said that Ellwood had chucked in school and hitched to the continent when just seventeen, so there was a daring and rebellious streak in him. Maybe he had lived the high life.

'Any hints of those extravagances in what you unearthed, Dave?' Horton asked Trueman.

'None whatsoever. Appears to be clean-cut, no scandal. His accident made big news in the art world, in the nationals and on social media. He suffered a head injury and severe injuries to his right leg, arm and hand. Lots of speculation if he'd ever paint again, and it seems he hasn't.'

Horton considered this for a moment. 'That could be the reason for his recent suicide attempt, although he still might have overdosed accidentally. The hospital told Sergeant Norris that Ellwood was admitted after taking a cocktail of drink and painkillers.'

Bliss rubbed her nose. 'Are the paintings with Sotheby's?'

'Yes. Miss Ellwood messaged me to say they'd arrived and we should hear something more about them in the next couple of days. Leney is convinced that Anther's locks haven't been picked. He's also certain that Anther's keys haven't been copied.' Leney had phoned Horton as he and Cantelli were heading back to the station.

'Which means it's looking much more like an inside job,' Trueman concluded.

Horton had to reluctantly agree. But that didn't mean Felice was involved. Anther had to be behind this.

Bliss flicked her hand through her ponytail and crossed to the board on her high heels. 'We should reinterview Catmore.'

'Why?' asked Horton.

'Isn't it obvious?' She spun round. 'Especially in the light of Leney's report. Catmore has to be involved in this, either alone, with an unknown person, or with Anther and possibly the others. Theory number one: Catmore took away the genuine paintings and replaced them with forgeries when he brought the third one in, hoping no one would notice. You've already told me the Metropolitan Art and Antiques Unit think that highly probable. He's going to sell the originals to a collector and was hoping that Anther would also sell the forgeries as genuine ones and he'd get double the money. Even now he won't mind he's been rumbled because he can claim off Anther's insurance for the originals.'

'I don't think Catmore's that astute.' Horton repeated what he'd intimated to Trillby of the Art and Antiques Unit.

'Then, as I said, he's working with someone who *is* astute and Catmore's just the frontman. This other person had both the originals and the forgeries in his possession—'

'But why choose Catmore? He's just an ordinary guy.'

'Aunt Dorothy could have left him both the originals and the forgeries, following which he consulted a mate who knows about art and they cooked this up between them.'

Horton was still dubious about that.

Bliss continued. 'Theory number two: he took both the forgeries and originals into Anther's gallery and Anther and Catmore did a deal on them. Anther would have the contacts to sell to. They hoped that Miss Ellwood wouldn't spot the switch but as she has, Anther can still make good on the originals by flogging them to collectors under the radar and by claiming insurance on the forgeries.'

Horton said, 'He seems too genuinely distraught for that.' But there was a niggle in Horton's mind about his behaviour.

'We need to search his premises,' Bliss declared. 'The originals could still be there. I'll get a warrant and you and Cantelli can go in tomorrow morning before you meet with Ruth Bowen at Spender's boat.'

The briefing broke up and Horton returned to CID. Cantelli had left for home — his youngest child, Joe, twin of Molly, and the only boy of five children — was playing football for the Baffins Boys and Cantelli was keen to support him. It had started raining steadily, so it was going to be a muddy game. The pitch wasn't far from the allotments and Maidstone's shed full of stolen goods, which, incidentally, Maidstone had changed his mind about. He'd admitted he'd given his allotment shed key to Derby Wallis because he thought he was keen on growing vegetables — yeah, pull the other one, it's got parsnips on it. Walters was reinterviewing Engels and Wallis following this development. Penny would have to forgo seeing lover boy tonight unless he got a quick result with Engels or Wallis, or both.

Horton called Catmore but got no answer. He didn't leave a message. He was about to tackle the chaos of paperwork and the tsunami of emails when he saw that Sergeant Norris had sent him the report on Ellwood's road traffic accident. Eagerly Horton opened it.

It had happened on a late sunny afternoon in September two years ago on the Military Road, a twisting coastal road on the Isle of Wight, sandwiched between fields and the downs, cliffs and the sea. Ellwood had been seen by one witness, a car driver, heading in the opposite direction, who said the motorcyclist had been speeding and driving recklessly. Another witness, a walker, had confirmed this. He also said there had been a car behind Ellwood driving at speed, as though they were in a race. That driver hadn't stopped and had never come forward, though he must have seen Ellwood come off his motorbike. However, Ellwood's bike and his injured body had been found on the opposite side of the road, the field side. So it was possible the car had overshot Ellwood somehow and had never been aware of the accident, even though the police would have advertised it and put signs up for witnesses to come forward. Ellwood had been found some hours after the incident by the farmer, who'd been checking his ditches. He'd been in a very bad way. Head injuries and a smashed leg, arm and hand. He was lucky to be alive.

Horton's mobile rang. It was Uckfield.

'The Sally Port Inn, now.'

'Are you OK to drive?'

'I've had my appendix out, not my leg amputated.'

The phone went dead.

Horton wondered what Uckfield wanted. It wouldn't be just a matey chat. An update on work? Possibly. But why not ring Trueman to get that or ACC Dean? He switched off his computer, closed his office blinds and weaved his way through the traffic to Old Portsmouth.

CHAPTER TWELVE

Uckfield was sitting in the corner of the pub nursing half a pint of bitter and a sour expression. There was a group of men at the bar and two of the tables were taken up with diners.

'Like a refill?' Horton asked, putting his crash helmet on the floor beside the chair.

'Driving.'

Horton crossed to the bar and bought himself a coke. Then, shrugging off his leather jacket and putting it on top of the helmet, he took the seat opposite. He noted that Uckfield had lost some weight, but he was still on the stout side.

'How's Operation Giraffe going?' Uckfield grunted.

Horton smiled. 'Wrong animal. You really interested in what's happening on the armed robbery in Basingstoke?'

'Yeah, because I'd have got the villains by now instead of pissing about at home.'

'Superintendent Buckley is very competent.'

'Not saying she isn't.'

'But you're bored.'

'Wouldn't you be?'

Horton would. 'So, what do you really want to know, Steve? This can't just be because you want the pleasure of my company.'

'Tell me what you've got on this art switch, and make it snappy.'

Horton did.

'Not got very far, have you?'

'You sound like Bliss.'

Uckfield grunted and swallowed some beer. 'I've been making enquiries about these Ellwoods.' He glanced at his watch.

'With whom?' Horton asked, surprised.

'I *am* a police officer. I know a lot of people.'

Yes, including those down the Lodge.

'Ah, here he is,' Uckfield declared. Horton swung round to see a trim, suntanned man about late sixties or early seventies. On seeing Uckfield, the man smiled, and yet even from a distance the gesture to Horton seemed condescending.

Uckfield made the introductions. 'This is Damien Oxley.'

Horton rose and stretched out his hand noting the curious, slightly mocking appraisal in the grey eyes as he took Oxley's firm, dry, slender hand. He wondered if he'd pass muster on Oxley's mental scale of acceptability.

'Can I get you both a drink?' Oxley asked in a well-cultured voice that made Horton wonder if he practised it into a recording device and played it back to ensure he got just the right tone and inflection. His clothes were colour coordinated in khaki and soft blue with a razor-sharp crease in his trousers, immaculate deck shoes, an expensive zip-up casual jacket and a soft blue silk polo neck designed, Horton guessed, to disguise his ageing neck. He looked to have stepped out of a gentleman's advertisement or yacht from circa the 1930s. Oxley made Anther's fastidious dress seem positively slummy.

'No, we're fine,' Uckfield answered for them both.

'Then I'll just get one myself.' He left for the bar.

Uckfield lowered his voice. 'He's an Ellwood fan.'

'How do you know that? Aside from being a detective,' Horton quickly added, anticipating Uckfield's sarcastic response.

'I asked him. I've known Damien for a while, met him through Alison. She's a friend of Damien's wife, Leanne. We've been to dinner and out on the boats together. He keeps his motor cruiser at the Camber and lives not far from here in Barley Road, Southsea.'

'Expensive address.'

'Used to be an airline pilot, then ran an air cargo business, sold it for a fortune. After you told me about the paintings, I looked up Ellwood on the internet and saw that he's a big-shot artist, so I phoned Damien, knowing him to be an art connoisseur, and asked if he'd heard of him and Julian Anther. He had indeed, both. He'll tell you.'

Oxley returned with a gin and a small bottle of tonic. He took the seat between them and addressed Horton. 'Steve said you're investigating an unusual art theft at Julian Anther's gallery, some Michael Ellwood paintings.'

'We are, sir, but we're keeping it quiet at present until we get more information so I'd appreciate it if you could treat it as confidential.'

Uckfield broke in, 'Damien's not going to go blabbing to the press.'

Oxley's lips stretched in a semblance of a smile, as though he was afraid of stretching his lips too far because it might cause more wrinkles.

'I understand you're an admirer of Michael Ellwood's work,' Horton said.

'I am, but unfortunately I don't own any. I'd like to but I've never been successful in bidding for them at auction or buying them at exhibitions. Not that there have been any of the latter for about three years. His paintings get snapped up very quickly. Even more so since he's stopped painting following his accident, but that's understandable. Although artists can paint one-handed, I believe Michael Ellwood has never tried. But I could be wrong.'

Horton was shocked. 'He lost a hand in the motorcycle accident?' The report hadn't gone into the extent of the injuries incurred.

'Lost the use of it. It was touch-and-go whether or not they'd amputate.'

Horton took a sip of his coke. No wonder the poor man was desperate and depressed and Felice so worried about her father. Oxley, though, far from speaking sympathetically, seemed to have spoken with relish. There was a sneering bitterness about him that made Horton believe that Oxley was the type who revelled in other's misfortunes. Horton said, 'Mr Ellwood is in hospital and very unwell at the moment.'

'So I heard from Anther.'

Again, that coldness about the tone. 'When was this?'

'A couple of weeks ago. I was in the gallery.'

'Did Mr Anther tell you he had two Ellwoods in his possession?' Horton studied Oxley closely while he could feel Uckfield breathing down his neck.

'No. If I had known, I'd have asked to see them.'

'Can you remember when exactly you were there?'

Oxley sipped his drink and seemed to consider this, but Horton was sure he didn't need to. 'It was Thursday the twenty-second of April,' he finally answered.

When the first two paintings were in the gallery but before Felice had authenticated them as originals the following day. Perhaps Anther had been reluctant to reveal he had them until he was certain of them. Or was Oxley lying?

'Guy Bampton was there,' Oxley continued. 'The waste rubbish king — GKB Waste and Skip Hire.'

From his tone, this was clearly someone Oxley despised. Was that because of Bampton's business or the man himself? Uckfield seemingly sensed this because he shifted and said, 'What was he doing there? Delivering a skip?'

'He might have been, or collecting one. He was certainly dressed for it,' Oxley said disdainfully. 'I never asked.'

No, Oxley wouldn't deem to speak to someone so low down in the pecking order. Horton thought the Uckfields dinner parties and boat trips with the Oxleys must be interesting, especially if Leanne Oxley was as acerbic as her husband. Or perhaps she was quiet like Alison Uckfield and they just let the men babble on. To be fair to Uckfield though, Horton wouldn't have said that Oxley was his type.

Oxley was saying, 'Bampton collects Ellwoods — yes, rather a surprise. You wouldn't think it to look at him, or by the company he runs, or the house he lives in. It's that large one on the top of Portsdown Hill with elaborate gates, lions on giant gate posts and crenelated iron balconies.'

Horton almost expected Oxley to shudder.

'Anther could have told Bampton about the paintings,' Oxley went on, 'but he would never dare to fob him off with a forgery. Anther would lose more than his business if he tried it. Bampton is not a man to mess with. No doubt you've come across him in your line of work.'

'I can't say I have,' Horton said lightly, not betraying his dislike of Oxley. Uckfield too showed no emotion but sipped his beer.

Oxley shrugged. 'He may look like a gentle giant but that's fooled many a man.'

'You have evidence—'

Uckfield irritably interrupted Horton. 'We're not here to discuss Bampton or his possible violent tendencies, but Julian Anther, his gallery and those paintings.'

Horton wondered if Oxley was deliberately pointing the finger at Bampton. Why? Because he hated him? Or was it to disguise his own guilt? Over what though? He couldn't have switched the paintings. Or could he?

Oxley took a sip of his drink. 'They can't be very good forgeries if Anther spotted the switch.'

Again, Horton heard the acidity in Oxley's tone. Did he doubt Anther's credibility as an art expert? 'Anther didn't spot the forgeries. Michael Ellwood's daughter did.'

'Felicity! But of course, I can see why Anther would have called her over to view them. She owns a gallery in Cowes.'

'You know it?' Horton noted that Oxley had used Felicity's correct name rather than her preferred choice of Felice, which she had told him she only allowed those she liked to use.

'I've bought a painting from her. Not an Ellwood.'

'But she has one of her father's in her gallery. I'd have thought you or Mr Bampton would have acquired it as soon as possible.'

'I didn't know that, and Bampton probably doesn't know either. I wonder why she didn't call me.' He frowned. 'Or Bampton.'

'Maybe she did call Bampton but it's not to his taste,' Horton said.

'Is it a seascape?'

'Yes.'

Uckfield threw Horton a look. Horton had visited the gallery during their last major murder investigation, but Horton could see that Uckfield was wondering if there was more between him and Felice than he had known. Not that it bothered Horton if Uckfield did think that. Besides, the answer was there wasn't. Why hadn't Felice contacted Oxley or Bampton? She'd have been assured of a sale. He shelved the question for now as Oxley continued.

'Then we both would have been interested. Ellwood's circus drawings and those of dancers and acrobats don't interest either of us. How were the paintings switched, Andy, or don't you know?'

Why did Horton feel uncomfortable with Oxley addressing him by his first name? Simple — he didn't like him, and he didn't trust him. He tried not to let his feelings show. 'We're trying to establish that. Do you know a Noel Catmore?'

'No. Who's he?'

'Can I ask why you were at Anther's gallery?'

Oxley's lips twitched in a smile, recognizing the fact that Horton hadn't answered his question.

'Julian had a Cecil Canning. He's one of my wife's favourite artists. Not to my taste, too abstract, but she likes his work and it's her birthday this Saturday.'

'The big painting on the easel.' Horton remembered the 'Sold' sticker.

'Yes.'

'Did Mr Anther leave you alone at any time?'

Uckfield sniffed loudly in disapproval of the question.

But Oxley gave that superior smile of his, knowing what Horton was implicating. 'He did not. He was too keen on securing the sale of the Canning. I didn't want to make it too easy for him, even though I intended to buy it even before I entered the gallery. I like to see people earn their living.'

'Like you do?' Horton said, straight-faced, even though Uckfield had told him Oxley was retired.

Oxley's eyes narrowed perceptibly, but he answered evenly. 'No need. I sold my air freight company in 2008 for an obscene amount of money and retired. Where are the Ellwood paintings now, or rather the forgeries?'

'With the experts at Sotheby's. Do you know of any artist capable of forging them?'

'Me? No idea. I'm an ex-pilot, Andy, not an art connoisseur.' He pointedly glanced at his watch, tossed back his drink, and rose. 'We've got people coming for dinner.'

Horton stood and stretched out his hand. 'Thank you for your help.'

Oxley took it. 'I hope you find the forger. I'd like to know who is that good and why he should have chosen to forge Michael's paintings.'

'It might be a she.'

'I doubt that.'

Was Oxley trying to goad him into a response? Wondered Horton. He didn't rise to it. 'Do you know Michael Ellwood personally?'

'We've met several times at exhibitions — a quiet man, weak, rather timid, I'd say. Not at all the typical artist.'

'Is there such a thing?'

'Probably not, but you expect them to be like their art: flamboyant, colourful, unpredictable. But then perhaps Ellwood is all that, and a character of contrasts. After all, he does own a motorbike.' Oxley glanced pointedly at Horton's helmet and leather jacket. 'Under that quiet exterior Michael could be both reckless and rebellious.' Oxley made to leave then turned back. 'You should ask Bampton what he thinks of Michael and this art switch. Be funny if some of his originals are forgeries.'

Horton resumed his seat. 'Is he always like that?'

'Like what?'

'You know what I mean.'

'He's a bit brittle.'

'A bit! He's arrogant, spiteful and a snob.'

'Takes all sorts.' Uckfield tossed back the remainder of his beer. As they stepped outside he continued, 'I don't think Oxley would go to the trouble of stealing the paintings or replacing them with forgeries, because I can't see how he'd have had them in the first place.'

'Easily. He could have bought the forgeries years ago, believing them to be genuine, and when he saw the paintings in Anther's gallery and was told by Anther they were originals, he did the swap.'

'And he left the gallery with them tucked under his arm without Anther noticing?'

'Someone did.'

'Bampton. He could have had the forgeries on his wall and did the swap.' Uckfield zapped open his car.

'I'll ask him when I interview him.'

'Let me know how you get on.'

Horton refrained from telling Uckfield that he was still on sick leave and rode home along the seafront. Had Oxley pointed the finger too hard and too obviously at Guy Bampton? Clearly, he despised him. Why? Was it a case of nasty snobbishness or was it more than that? To Horton's mind, behind that egotistical manner, Oxley was a bitter, jealous and frustrated man, and that, along with his vindictiveness and superiority, made him a dangerous one.

CHAPTER THIRTEEN

Wednesday

'No one at home.' Horton lifted the brass knocker of Anther's flat and rapped it again, hard.

'Perhaps he's a heavy sleeper,' Cantelli ventured.

'Lucky him,' Horton replied. He never slept well at the best of times and last night he'd had a fitful night, dreaming of Emma and a desperate search to find somewhere to live and failing. He'd watched Emma waving goodbye to him, her eyes streaming with tears. Then his dreams had turned to Ames's missing yacht, along with the peer goading him. He'd woken with a start, angry with himself for surfing the net before retiring for any news of Richard Ames, a mistake he wouldn't repeat.

Cantelli was also looking the worse for wear. There were shadows under the sergeant's dark eyes.

'You look as though you could do with a good night's sleep, Barney.'

'Molly wasn't well in the night.'

'Sorry to hear that, not serious I hope,' Horton asked, concerned.

'I think she caught a stomach bug, at school most probably. Charlotte's keeping her off today. I expect she'll be up and about and haring around as usual by the time I get home tonight.'

Horton hoped so.

'Maybe he's gone for a coffee,' Cantelli suggested, stifling a yawn.

Horton had relayed his interview with Uckfield and Oxley on the way to the gallery. He hadn't had time to tell Bliss or Trueman about it yet. Bliss wouldn't be very pleased that Uckfield had poked his nose into her case. Horton intended interviewing Bampton to see if he could rule him out of the investigation but he'd do that after he had spoken to Anther about both Oxley's and Bampton's visits to the gallery.

Horton stepped back, almost knocking over a pedestrian, who gave him a mouthful. Looking up at the windows, he said, 'The blind is up, and the curtains are open. You could be right. He could be in the gallery.'

Horton rang the art gallery doorbell. It chimed loudly. Still no response.

Cantelli said, 'Why am I getting a bad feeling about this?'

'Because you're a copper. He could be shopping.'

'Or jogging.'

'Not Anther.'

'Walking the dog then.'

'Doesn't have one. But it says here on the sign that the gallery is closed all day Monday and on Wednesday mornings, so he could have gone for a walk. I'll try his mobile.' He did so.

'No answer.' Horton consulted the time on his phone. 'His cleaner is due here in twenty minutes, and Anther claims she doesn't have a key and that he's always here to let her in, which means he'll be back by then wherever he is. Drive around to the back, Barney, we'll see if his Jaguar is there.'

A few minutes later Cantelli pulled into the yard. There was no car.

'Not sure if that's a good or bad sign.' Cantelli crossed to the shuttered windows of the back room. 'Can't see a thing inside, the door's locked. Try him again, Andy.'

Horton did and shook his head.

'Do you think he's done a bunk with the original Ellwoods?' Cantelli asked.

'I can't see why he would leave all this behind. There must be some very valuable works of art in his gallery.'

'They might have gone walkabout with him. It could be empty for all we know.'

'Damien Oxley won't like that,' Horton replied with a glint of satisfaction at imagining Oxley's expression if he had to tell him the Canning he had purchased had disappeared along with the gallery owner. But he was worried about Anther's absence. Could Oxley have telephoned Anther last night and said the police were growing more suspicious of him, thereby putting the fear of God in him? Horton wouldn't have put it past Oxley to lay it on with a trowel just to aggravate and worry Anther. Oxley could even have lied to Anther to wind him up.

'Do we force an entry?' enquired Cantelli. 'He could be ill.'

'No. We'll wait for the cleaner. Anther might have left a message with her. Would she park here or out the front?'

'I'd have thought here. It's usually a devil of a job to get a space out front and she probably brings her own cleaning equipment.'

Cantelli was correct. Within ten minutes — during which time Horton called Paul Leney and asked him if he could pick the locks to Anther's flat and gallery, immediately if needed (to which he said he could) — a small car pulled into the yard. A podgy, pleasant woman in her early thirties with white-blonde hair tied back off an open round face climbed out. Horton had expected an older woman. Her surprise at seeing them turned to bewilderment and concern as Cantelli made the introductions and she confirmed she was Mrs Joyce Munroe, Mr Anther's cleaner, and no she hadn't had a message to say Julian would be out. She also didn't have a key. Horton checked that the contact number she had for Anther was the same as his. It was. She also had the telephone number of the gallery.

Horton tried it. The answerphone kicked in after eight rings. He retried Anther's mobile, still with no response. This certainly had a worrying smell about it. If Anther's car had been here then he would have been concerned that Anther might have done something stupid inside his apartment if Oxley had really goaded him, or if Anther were involved in the switch and whoever he was in league with had put the pressure on. Then it struck Horton that Anther could still have taken a lethal way out by using his car as the method of suicide. He rang Paul Leney and asked him to come over right away. While they waited for him, Horton turned to Mrs Munroe. 'How often do you come here?'

Anther had already given him that information but it paid to check. Cantelli removed his notebook from his jacket pocket and the short stubby pencil from behind his ear.

'Twice a week. Friday to do the flat, dust round the gallery and a clean of the kitchen and toilet, and then Wednesday morning to do the gallery and then a quick tidy-up around the flat. Julian won't let me touch any of the paintings, not even in his apartment. He's afraid I'll run the disinfectant over them.' She smiled. 'Julian is very neat, except when it comes to his clothes. He wears something once then throws it on the bed or floor. His mother must have picked up after him. I make my boys put their clothes in the laundry bin and their toys away when they've finished playing with them, although they moan about it.'

'We do the same with our kids,' Cantelli said, eliciting a beaming smile from Joyce.

Horton remembered the days he had done that with Emma. It seemed a lifetime ago now instead of two and a half years. The thought of what he had missed hurt him and he was determined to make up for lost time. He had to get greater access and he had to find somewhere to live.

He said, 'I assume that by the time you've finished in his flat on Friday and are ready to clean the gallery, his office, the kitchen and toilet, Mr Anther is in the gallery.'

'Yes. I pull the flat door closed behind me, make sure it's shut and ring the gallery bell if the door isn't open, and Julian lets me in.'

'Does he go out and leave you alone?'

'Him! You must be kidding. Not that he watches over me, but he doesn't leave the gallery while I'm there. He's very fussy.' Her brow furrowed. 'This is so unlike him. I wonder where he can be.' She looked up at the rear window and her eyes widened as she flashed them a troubled look. 'You don't think he's had a heart attack or stroke?'

Cantelli answered, 'That's why we've sent for our locksmith so that we can check.'

Horton noted she hadn't made the connection that his car was missing. He had assumed the Jaguar was Anther's but he hadn't checked with the Driver and Vehicle Licensing Agency database, something he would do shortly.

'How has Mr Anther been recently?' Cantelli asked. 'Any change in his manner?'

'He's been on edge, but then he can be nervy.'

'More so than usual?'

She nodded. 'He bit my head off a couple of times last week when I asked a question. And when I made a joke and tried to jolly him along, he told me to get on with my work, which wasn't like him. Yes, he's particular and not one for humour, but he usually smiles and is polite. He pretends to understand the joke although I know he doesn't. He's very . . . how shall I say . . . artistic. Is that the word I'm looking for?'

Cantelli nodded.

'I hope nothing's happened to him.'

'I'm sure it hasn't,' Cantelli reassured.

'Then why are you here?'

Horton hesitated. Should he tell Joyce the truth? But that would risk spreading it all over the internet. Even if he told her to keep it confidential, he doubted she'd be able to. How could he elicit information from her without giving something away of what had happened? He'd need to be economical with the truth.

'Some personal items of Mr Anther's have gone missing, and he asked us to look into it.'

'He never mentioned that to me.'

'It was only discovered on Monday.'

'You're not accusing—'

'No,' Horton quickly mollified. 'We're just trying to find out who could have come in and out of the gallery aside from customers. Did you see anyone enter while you were cleaning in the office or kitchen during the last few of weeks of April?' She would have worked on the Wednesday Catmore had taken in the first two paintings, the Friday Felice had authenticated them and again on Wednesday 28 April after Catmore had brought in painting number three. Not to mention Friday 30 April before Felicity had discovered the switch had been made.

'I might have done . . . No, I don't think so. I can't remember.' She pulled at her lower lip.

A white van with music blaring from it passed the end of the yard, heading for the rear entrances of the retail units in the adjoining road.

'The window cleaner perhaps?' Horton prompted, recalling what Anther had said on his first visit.

'Oh yes, Trevor. He comes once a month. But that was last week.'

'Does he park his van here in the yard?' Horton asked.

'Only when he does the back windows. He parks out the front, on the double yellows, to do the front ones. The traffic wardens know him and don't move him on or give him a ticket.'

Horton thought she was looking a little uneasy. So too must Cantelli have, because he said, 'Did he pop inside, maybe to use the toilet or get a drink?'

'Well, yes, as a matter of fact he did, but only to say hello. He didn't go into Julian's office or the gallery, and he would *never* take anything of Julian's. You can't accuse him of that!'

She seemed overly defensive of the window cleaner. They'd check with Mr Brightman, although Horton couldn't see why a window cleaner would swap the paintings or know which ones to swap, not unless Joyce had told him after overhearing Anther talking about the originals, on the phone perhaps.

Horton didn't think either Joyce or the window cleaner were involved because how would either know who to sell the originals to? But then another idea occurred to Horton — Joyce cleaned houses and possibly offices where expensive paintings hung, and window cleaners couldn't help seeing what was inside the properties they worked on. Would they have the knowledge of art though, and in particular of Michael Ellwood's paintings?

A Land Rover pulled up at the entrance to the yard. Leney climbed out carrying a case with the tools of his trade.

Joyce looked at Leney and back at Horton with a worried frown. 'Do you want me to wait?'

Horton didn't think there was much point. Julian Anther might return, but on the other hand . . . He said not and asked her to inform them if she heard from Mr Anther. Leney moved his car out of the way so that she could reverse out and, as he began to pick the lock to the rear door, Horton telephoned Felice.

She answered promptly and sounded pleased to hear his voice. 'I'm just heading over to the Royal Academy of Arts.'

Horton could hear the rumble of London traffic in the background punctuated by the angry sounding of car horns.

'Have you spoken to Julian Anther recently?'

'I phoned him yesterday afternoon shortly after the paintings were deposited at Sotheby's and I emailed over a receipt.'

'Did he mention anything about going away?'

'No. Why?'

'He doesn't seem to be at home or in the gallery. We're there now and gaining entry to the premises to check. His car's gone.'

'Perhaps he just needed to get away for a couple of days. He's very upset about what's happened. I can ask Maurice if he's heard from Julian and call you back.'

'No, I'll do that.' Horton asked her if she knew Damien Oxley.

'I do.'

Horton heard the reservation in her voice. He wondered if her impression of Oxley was the same as his. 'I met him last night. He says he's an admirer of your father's work but has been unsuccessful in obtaining any of his paintings. He also says he's bought a painting from you at your gallery.'

'And you're wondering why he didn't buy my father's painting that I have there.'

'Yes.'

'The painting he bought from me was in February before I exhibited my father's painting, so he didn't see it. Did you tell him I had it?'

'Yes. Has he been in touch?'

'No.'

Maybe Oxley wasn't as keen to get his hands on Ellwoods as he proclaimed. 'Oxley was also in Julian's gallery when the two paintings Catmore brought in were there. He says Julian didn't mention them or show them to him.'

'That's probably correct. Julian would wait until he was given instructions to handle the sale. He was initially only giving Mr Catmore a valuation. There was no agreement between them for Julian to sell them. Once he got a valuation, Catmore would have been perfectly free to take them to Sotheby's, Christies or any other auctioneer or gallery to sell on his behalf.'

That seemed logical to Horton.

'If Mr Catmore agreed to let Julian sell them then Julian would want commission, but Maurice, as my father's agent, would also feel entitled to a cut. Maurice might have even approached Mr Catmore direct to ask to handle the sale. It's Maurice's job to know all my father's collectors, so Julian could have been cut out of the loop, so to speak.'

'Then Maurice would know both Damien Oxley and Guy Bampton. Oxley said Bampton is an avid Ellwood collector.'

'He is. Guy certainly has a collection of my father's paintings.'

'Would Maurice have mentioned the paintings to either of them or any other collectors?'

'He says he hasn't and I believe him. He'd certainly have wanted them authenticated first, and he'd have made sure there was a written agreement between himself and Julian or between himself and Catmore to sell them.'

Horton would talk to Maurice Linden.

'Was the cleaner, Joyce, or the window cleaner in Anther's office when you came to see the first two paintings?'

'No. We were alone.'

Leney had successfully opened the rear door.

'I've got to go, Felice. Speak to you later.' He rang off. 'Listen.'

Horton cupped his ear at Cantelli's instruction.

Leney smiled knowingly. 'I told you, no one *always* sets the alarm.'

CHAPTER FOURTEEN

'Maybe he left in a hurry.' Cantelli said. He stepped inside. 'Or was too upset and distracted to remember to set the alarm.'

Leney crossed through to the gallery and let himself out of the front door to start on the lock to the flat.

Cantelli added, 'Hope Paul doesn't get arrested for breaking and entering.'

'If he does, we'll bail him out.'

Horton glanced around. There were no signs of a disturbance and no gaps on the walls of the gallery or any empty easels. He examined the painting Oxley had bought for his wife's birthday. He had no idea what it was supposed to be, but he liked the colours and the formation of the squares, squiggles and circles that were daubed upon it.

Cantelli pointed to some pictures on the wall. 'Those are more to my taste.'

They were of beaches in a sunlit land, which Horton thought by no stretch of the imagination could be Britain even on a bright summer's day, or perhaps he was being uncharitable. Cornwall could look like that on a few occasions, but hadn't when he had been on holiday there with Catherine and a three-year-old Emma, staying in a small damp cottage. It had rained consistently, or his memory said it had. And Catherine had moaned the whole time, so much so that they'd come home early. The climate in the Mediterranean suited her far better.

They moved back into the middle room, Anther's office. Horton picked up the phone and dialled for the last number. Withheld. There were three messages on the answerphone, one from the insurance company asking Anther to call back, and two from customers enquiring about artworks. Not Ellwoods. Nothing from Noel Catmore. Horton hadn't tried him again. He made a mental note to do so later.

He turned his attention to the desk drawers. 'No diary, just some business papers, invoices and odds and ends.'

'A safe? There must be one.' Cantelli opened a cupboard on the wall to the left. 'Bingo! Wonder if Paul can open it.'

Leney entered. 'Open what?'

Cantelli jerked his head at the safe and Leney cracked his knuckles with a smile. 'My pleasure. It's been a while since I did one of these.' He removed a bunch of keys from his case. 'Anther's flat door is open. The alarm wasn't set.'

'That was sloppy of him. We'd better take a look around it before a burglar nips in. We'll close the gallery door behind us, Paul, in case someone decides to walk in off the road and you sell them a Picasso. I'll give three short rings on our return.'

They stepped outside and into the narrow passageway of Anther's flat. Cantelli closed the front door behind him. 'Anther must have been in one hell of hurry not to have set any alarms.'

Horton could see the infrared sensor above the door and the alarm panel on the right-hand wall. 'Or he thought, "What the heck, I'm not coming back, so why bother?"'

Suicide? Wondered Horton as he climbed the stairs. Had Anther been that traumatized by the switch? Was he about to be ruined both financially and professionally and couldn't face living? He had once thought the same on that dark August day during his suspension when he'd taken off on his small boat. But something had prevented him. Fear? The thought of leaving Emma? Cowardice? Maybe all three.

He still had dark days, including on his recent sailing trip to France, where he'd stared at his mother's final resting place, the sea, and wondered how she had felt just before Viscount William Ames, her lover and his father, had killed her. He hoped she hadn't been too afraid. Maybe she had even been unaware that death awaited her.

He took a breath and turned to Cantelli on the landing. 'You take the room ahead, Barney. I'll do the front room.'

It was a spacious, high-ceilinged sitting room with wide windows draped in luxurious floral curtains and a contrasting Roman blind. The scattering of sofas and armchairs were flamboyantly covered in colourful and complementary cloth, but then Anther would have a good eye for design. Around the room were a number of small occasional tables and lampshades. A display case held figurines, as did the mantelpiece over the coal-effect fire, upon which there was also a carriage clock that Horton recognized as being art deco from his time in the Art and Antiques Unit. There were also some stunning paintings on the walls, which was no more than he had expected. There was no sign of any disturbance, and no Ellwoods that he could see, both by the style and by peering at the signatures.

Horton opened the drawers of a large tallboy not expecting to find the original Ellwoods, and he didn't. Had Anther taken off with them? The buyer he had lined up would provide enough money for Anther to live on comfortably for some years, but this was a lot to abandon. Horton's thoughts turned to Lord Richard Ames once more, who would surely never abandon his lifestyle. Horton doubted if he were still alive. But had he killed himself or had his brother Gordon, who was also missing, killed him and then disappeared? Horton had heard a shot being fired on Ames's yacht, but by the time he had reached it, the yacht had been swallowed up by the dark and the fog. Now Harriet Ames, Richard's daughter and an agent with Europol who Horton had worked with and liked, was living with gnawing uncertainty, just as he had done for twenty-eight years. He felt no satisfaction over that. He was sorry for her.

There was very little of interest in the drawers — some linen, tablecloths, coasters and three photograph albums, which looked to date back to Anther's childhood. A flick through them confirmed this. These might be useful to look through if they couldn't locate Anther, but Horton didn't think they would tell him much, if anything. Had he gone to a relative? Were Anther's parents still living, they could possibly be in their mid-eighties or nineties. Horton knew nothing of Anther's family background. There had been no need to ask.

As he replaced the albums, he thought of Neil Spender. Did he have relatives? No one had missed him but then he could have distant family living elsewhere in the country with whom he hadn't been in touch with for years. And thinking about relatives, Horton wondered how Nicola Bolton was getting on with tracing Noel Catmore's aunt — Dorothy Mass-something-or-other.

He studied the three photographs on the top of the tallboy while Cantelli opened and closed drawers in the kitchen. One image was of a younger Julian Anther and an older woman — his mother, Horton assumed, as there was a similarity in their looks. And the others were of Anther taken at art galleries with, Horton suspected, famous artists, except he wouldn't know one from the other. None of them were Michael Ellwood.

Cantelli appeared in the doorway. 'He'd eaten a meal, but I couldn't say when. There's crockery and cutlery in the dishwasher. Just the usual circulars in a drawer — council information, some business cards, including one for Trevor Brightman's *Brights* window cleaners.' Cantelli flourished it. 'And a few other odds and ends. Want me to check the attic rooms?'

Horton said he did, while he took the middle room, which was the bedroom with the bathroom off it. Both were larger and more elegantly furnished than the last flat he had searched, Spender's. No migraine tablets in the bathroom cabinet, only over-the-counter medicines — aspirin, headache tablets, laxatives. No keys under the pillow either, he thought with a wry smile. The double bed was made up and, to Horton, looked as though it hadn't been slept in. Clothes were strewn across it and over the armchair as Joyce had described. There were some smart casual clothes in the built-in wardrobe along with a couple of suits of good quality but not as elite as Neil Spender's. There was also a suitcase and a holdall. It didn't look as though Anther had packed his bags and cleared out, not unless he travelled very lightly.

Cantelli reappeared. 'Nothing in the attic rooms except dust, some old bits and pieces of furniture, display easels, a wooden chair and two suitcases. No body parts in them. I looked.'

'I'd say that wherever Anther went he intended to come back.'

'He might still do so. He could be visiting a prospective client in Bangor or Bognor.'

'Without setting the alarms?' Horton entered the kitchen and Cantelli followed. 'And without telling his cleaner?'

'Perhaps he's getting more absent-minded as he gets older, he forgot to tell her and forgot to set the alarm.'

Horton stared down into the small backyard and the service road beyond. He could see across to the small gardens and yards of the houses opposite and into the upper windows of three of the terraced houses, although two had net curtains and the third blinds. He could also see down into the back rooms. Or rather, he could see the windows but making out what or who was inside was a little more difficult. With binoculars or a camera, he could probably zoom in and have a good enough view, if he were a voyeur or nosy parker. Maybe one of the residents was. He was about to turn away when his eye caught some activity in the goods yard of the shops that formed a right angle to the rear of this road. In it was a large yellow skip bearing the initials GKB. One of Bampton's. He hadn't seen it on his visit here on Monday, but that was because it was in the far right-hand corner and not visible from the ground.

'I haven't seen a telephone or landline up here, have you?'

'No. There isn't a mobile phone, laptop or similar device either. Must have taken them with him.'

They descended and Horton pulled the door shut behind him, making certain it was secure, while Cantelli gave the coded three rings on the gallery front door.

Leney let them in. 'The safe's open. It was a straightforward job, an off-the-shelf one, nothing spectacular. One of my keys fitted it and Anther hadn't reset the code from the factory one.'

'I'm glad you're on our side,' Cantelli said, as they went to examine its contents.

'Ah, but am I? Want me to turn out my pockets?'

'Can't see you stashing any paintings in them,' Horton answered.

'Could be miniatures. Or perhaps Anther also went in for diamond smuggling.'

'Well, he's not taken his passport.' Cantelli straightened up with it in his hand. 'No diaries or client files. Just this, his birth certificate, insurance policies and a few documents. No money, although there might have been and he's taken it with him.'

'I'll try his number again.'

There was still no answer.

'He could have called Maurice Linden. I'll try him in the car. You can lock up now, Paul.'

Leney did so, saying he was waiting to hear from the manufacturer of the key Horton had found under Spender's pillow. As Cantelli followed Leney's Land Rover down the service road, Horton rang Linden. He answered immediately.

'Mr Linden, has Julian Anther been in touch with you?'

'Not since Monday, why?'

'He's not at home, his car's gone, and he's not answering his phone.'

There was a short silence as Linden assimilated this news and its unspoken implications. 'You think he's gone on the run?' Before Horton could comment, he continued, 'I doubt that very much, Inspector. He wouldn't leave the gallery. It's his bread and butter.'

'He might have taken another slice of loaf with him — two slices, in fact.'

'The original Ellwoods? No, Julian isn't capable of theft, and he would never have the nerve to sell them on. He's rather highly strung. I'd say he's gone away for a couple of days to calm his nerves and avoid Mr Catmore's calls and demands.'

'Have you spoken to Mr Catmore?'

'I tried to but there was no answer, probably because he doesn't recognize my number and thinks it's a nuisance call. Felice told me the paintings have arrived safely at Sotheby's. I've been making enquiries with my contacts in London. I haven't told anyone about the switch. I've simply shown the photographs of the paintings I took on Monday to a few people and asked if they have seen them before. So far, no joy, but then I didn't really expect anyone to recognize them, not if I didn't.'

'Do you know Damien Oxley or Guy Bampton?'

'Yes. Both. Guy is very keen on Michael's work and has some of his paintings. But Oxley doesn't own any. He does however buy the work of some of my other clients.'

Horton asked Linden to let him know if he heard from Anther. He hesitated for a moment on ringing Catmore, then did so. He wanted to know if Anther had contacted him or vice versa but, as Linden had said, all Horton got was the automatic voicemail.

Suddenly Horton cried, 'Pull over,' but Cantelli was already doing so. A loud toot sounded from the car behind him as he slipped in behind a white van displaying the name *Brights Window Cleaning Services*, which was half-parked on the pavement along the busy road of shops and restaurants.

'It might be one of Trevor Brightman's employees.' Cantelli climbed out, nodding in the direction of a muscular man in his early forties with close-cropped dark hair, a wide mouth and craggy suntanned features and wielding a pole which was dripping water, on the end of a hose reel.

'Mr Brightman?' Cantelli retrieved his warrant card.

'Eh? Oh yes. Police? What is it?'

'Could you stop working for a moment?'

'Yeah, OK. Just let me switch that thing off, mind the hose.' He fiddled with something in the back of his van. The water ceased. 'How can I help? I don't think I've broken any laws,' he joked.

'When did you last clean the windows of Mr Anther's gallery?' Cantelli asked.

'Last Wednesday. I do them once a month, why?'

'Did you go inside the gallery?'

'No, I only do the outside windows.'

'You didn't go inside for a drink of water or to use the toilet?'

'No. Why do you ask? Has something happened?' He looked concerned.

A bus thundered past. Cantelli let it go before he resumed. 'Did you see Mrs Munroe while you were there?'

They knew he had but they always liked confirmation.

'Yes. Is she OK? Nothing's happened to her, has it?' he said alarmed.

Cantelli calmed him. 'No, she's fine. Did you see or speak to Mr Anther?'

'No, he was in the gallery.'

'How do you know that?' asked Horton.

'Because I heard him speaking on the telephone.'

'Then you did go inside the building?'

He ran a hand over his head and looked sheepish. 'Now you come to mention it, I did.'

Cantelli said, 'Was Mrs Munroe there?'

'Yes,' Brightman said uneasily. 'I called out from the kitchen, but she didn't hear me. She had the vacuum cleaner going and you know how noisy they are. I went into the middle room and tapped her on the shoulder. She jumped a mile.'

'And she switched off the vacuum cleaner and chatted?'

'Not for long.'

Horton stepped aside to make way for a young woman with a child in a pushchair.

'Why all the questions? If I knew what you were after I might be able to help you,' Brightman said, baffled.

Horton said the same as he had to Joyce Munroe. 'Some personal items of Mr Anther's have gone missing, and he's asked us to look into it.'

'Well, don't look at me!' Brightman's expression fell. 'You don't think—'

'We're not accusing anyone, Mr Brightman,' Cantelli reassured. 'We're just trying to gather facts. You park your van at the rear?'

'Only to do the back windows. I have to park out front for the front windows, so I do them early, just after rush hour and before the shops open.'

'When you were doing the back, did you see anyone in the lane?'

'Only the usual vans going to the goods delivery yard, and a skip being delivered. There was a telephone van at the entrance to the service road.'

Horton said, 'Do you know a Noel Catmore?'

'No. Who's he?' Brightman looked genuinely perplexed.

Cantelli said, 'How long were you inside the gallery?'

'Five, ten minutes at the most.' He sniffed and dropped his eye contact.

'Was there anyone else there, aside from Mrs Munroe?'

'Not that I know of.'

At a nod from Horton, Cantelli thanked Mr Brightman. Leaving him to his hose, they climbed into the car.

Horton stretched the seat belt around himself. 'What do you think?'

'Joyce lied about him not going into the building, and that's because I think he and Joyce have a bit of a thing going. Might not be a full-blown affair but they could have chanced a kiss or two with Anther on the phone in the gallery. But I can't see either of them switching the paintings.'

Neither could Horton, but perhaps Oxley or Bampton had. For now, though, they'd postpone their enquiries into the art theft because they were due at the commercial port, where Ruth Bowen was examining Spender's boat.

CHAPTER FIFTEEN

'If the victim had injured himself and fallen overboard, I would have expected to find downward spots of blood from his injuries on the deck. I would also expect his hand marks or clothing marks to be visible in the bloodstaining, as well as his own foot marks in his blood on the deck. None of that is evident,' Ruth Bowen pronounced in a pleasing Welsh lilt, after removing her mask and disposable cap and shaking out her light brown shoulder-length hair.

'So it is murder,' Horton said.

'Most definitely.'

That meant the investigation would be stepped up, and it would certainly take priority over Anther's stolen paintings, as far as the Major Crime Team were concerned.

Ruth continued. 'Given that it is homicide, one would need to establish whether the boat is simply a dump site for the body, which has subsequently been moved, or the attack site. In this case it's the latter. There is bloodstain distribution in the form of impact spatters, directional bloodstains, and spots of blood on the boat surfaces. Following the attack, the blood would be expected to flow from the injury, or injuries, into a pool. This pool of blood would, over time, congeal and solidify, which is precisely what has happened here, as you've seen in the cabin. He was certainly attacked while on board.' She pushed her hair away from her face as the wind gusted about the quayside.

'Can you tell us anything about the weapon used?' Horton asked, as Cantelli furiously scribbled notes. They'd have Ruth's full report in due course, but this would help to speed things up.

'It was a knife, but what kind I can't say. There could also have been more than one wound. I need more time to fully examine the pooled blood — there might be evidence of fabric marks from a gloved hand from the attacker because as you have no body, and the corpse couldn't have picked himself up and thrown himself overboard, someone must have moved it. There should be drag marks and hair swipes, but there isn't.'

'Eh?' said Cantelli.

'It's where the bloodstained hair of the victim is drawn across the surface as the body is dragged or moved.'

'And these are not on the boat?' asked Cantelli again to ensure it was clear.

'They are not, which means your body was lifted and carried off the boat.'

'The attacker would have had to be very strong to do that,' Horton said.

'It could be someone used to lifting heavy objects, or who has been taught how to do it. The victim could have been carried in a fireman's lift, but not necessarily by a firefighter.'

Horton was puzzled. 'But if the killer did that immediately after stabbing the victim there wouldn't have been pooling in the cabin deck and there would be more bloodstains in the cockpit.'

'Correct. Top marks, Inspector.'

Her comment reminded Horton of Gaye, who usually delivered such a remark when the light dawned on him during an investigation. 'So, either the killer returned sometime after he had killed Spender and decided he had to ditch the body, or—'

'Someone else came on board later and moved the body for him,' Cantelli interjected. 'Two people are involved in Spender's murder.'

'There are minimal signs of that on initial examination, but a more thorough one might tell me more. However, I'd say there is a definite time lag between the victim being killed and the body being carried off the boat.'

Horton wondered if that meant the victim, who in all probability was Spender, had been dumped somewhere other than in the sea, although he didn't think that made sense because the sea made a much better hiding place. The body would sink and wouldn't resurface for some time, possibly anything up to fourteen days, and by then, as he had earlier considered, it could be miles away and much of it beyond recognition. The attacker must have carried Spender and tossed his body overboard.

Into Horton's mind flashed the refuse collectors. They lifted heavy objects. Only they didn't, as one of them had said — the automatic lift did the job for them. They didn't have to be physically strong and yet Sam Farrell was broad and muscular, and he had been very jittery. He could have carried a dead weight. But why should he have done so?

Horton briefly wondered if Taylor might get some prints from Spender's car, which was being given a thorough check. But even if they did lift Farrell's prints from it, or anyone else's for that matter, it didn't mean that person was the killer.

Cantelli put away his pencil and notebook. 'Perhaps Spender was having an affair. He and his lover were having a bit of hanky-panky on the boat, something went wrong, there was a flaming row. The lover killed Spender and then got her husband to help her dispose of the body. There is that key, which we've already said could be to a lover's flat or house.'

'Then why use the boat?'

'Don't they say variety is the spice of life? Perhaps he or she got their jollies from doing it at sea.'

'I'll take your word for that,' Horton quipped, with a smile. Then, more seriously, 'If the key is to a lover's place, wouldn't Spender have had it on his key ring?' The wind whipped around them as Ruth climbed out of her scene suit to reveal trousers and a thick jumper.

'Spender might not be the victim. He could be the killer,' Cantelli answered.

'Then why not return to his car?'

'Because he has to make it look as though he's the victim.'

Somehow though Horton couldn't see Spender abandoning his expensive designer clothes and his boat, particularly as he'd hung on to both throughout eighteen months of working for Jeplie, when he could have sold the boat and funded more desirable accommodation and a different lifestyle. He said, 'Whether it's Spender the victim or Spender the killer we need to know a lot more about him. Let's get back to the station. I'll need to report to Bliss, and you might get some joy from Jeplie's human resources manager.'

Horton thanked Ruth and had only just got in the car when his mobile rang. It was Elkins.

'We've found Spender's tender. It's on the shore just past the sailing club off the Eastern Road.'

'Not far from where Spender's boat was found. Ruth has just confirmed homicide. Spender's killer could have let the boat drift and taken off in the tender.'

'There's no sign of the oars — could one have been the murder weapon?'

'No, Ruth says Spender was stabbed.'

'Must have ditched them in the sea then. There's also no outboard motor, but it's Spender's tender all right. It's got his boat's name painted on it, *Wishful Thinking*. A member of the club called me half an hour ago. He'd arrived early to do some work on his own tender and found it. He'd read the notice in the sailing club bulletin that we were looking for it.'

'Take it round to the secure berth at the port, Dai. Taylor can go over it later.'

'Will do. The secretary said he'll send an email round to all the members with a picture of it — which I've taken and sent to him — and ask if anyone else noticed it or someone alighting from it. I've asked the sea angling club secretary if any of their members saw Spender on his boat on their way in or out of Bedhampton Creek, but so far no one has. Oh, and Jed Parkham, the RSPB ranger, says there's no sign on their trail cameras of anyone illegally alighting on any of the islands in the harbour, and there's nothing to determine when Spender's boat became stranded on Dead Man's Head.'

Horton had suspected as much. He relayed the news to Cantelli as they drove back to the station, where Walters was finishing off with Engels, Wallis and Maidstone. Walters had finally got confessions out of all three.

While Horton briefed Bliss about Anther's vanishing act and the findings of Ruth Bowen, Cantelli got on to Jeplie. The investigation was stepped up and it was four hours later when Bliss called a briefing to pull together the information that he, Cantelli, Trueman and others had gleaned about Spender. His flat was sealed off, and Taylor and Tremaine and two uniformed officers were detailed to examine it. Even though it wasn't the scene of the crime it could reveal further information about Spender and his contacts. The occupants of the building were being more thoroughly questioned and details of Spender's bank account had been obtained from the managing agent. Trueman was applying to gain access to it and to Spender's mobile phone account.

Cantelli began his report. 'Before working for Jeplie there's a gap of just over two years, as Scott Tweed told us, but according to the Department for Work and Pensions, Spender wasn't claiming unemployment or sickness benefit and neither was he paying National Insurance. Prior to that he worked for Southern trains for eleven years on their train presentation team — in other words, cleaning up after passengers got off.'

'His reason for leaving?' asked Bliss.

'To travel abroad, or so his job application form says. But we know that's a lie because he was living in the flat in Farlington.'

Trueman said, 'He could have locked the flat up and gone overseas.'

'And lived on what?'

'An inheritance?'

Bliss said, 'If his scar and mangled hands were caused by an accident, he could have got compensation.'

'I'll check with the compensation database to see if he made a claim and if a payment was made,' Cantelli replied. 'His job application form details don't go back further than his Southern trains employment, so I checked with the Department for Work and Pensions. There's no record of Spender paying National Insurance or being on benefit of any kind between 1976, when he would have left school aged seventeen, and 1993, when he began claiming sickness and invalidity benefit. This stopped in 2003, and there are no tax returns for him during that period either.'

'So it's likely he was injured in 1993 and then passed as fit to work in 2003,' Bliss said.

'Yes. But that doesn't explain what he was doing for two years before going to work for Jeplie. There is no next of kin named on his job application form. I checked out his details with the Register of Births, Deaths and Marriages. No marriage certificate in his name, both parents deceased. There are two Spenders named in the telephone directory — could be relatives.'

'Get uniform to check them out,' Bliss commanded.

Trueman nodded.

It was agreed that Cantelli would visit the medical practice tomorrow and get what he could of Spender's medical history, in particular if there had been an accident, although that alone wouldn't explain why someone had killed him. It was a case of gathering as much information as possible, including sightings of Spender in the hours before his death and of his boat, of which all the harbour masters, ports and marinas had been notified.

It was just on eight when Horton left the station. Bliss had already gone and so too had Trueman. Two things among many in the Spender investigation niggled away at him — the key he'd discovered under the pillow and the fact that Spender had been fluent in a foreign language. They'd speculated that Spender could have lived abroad from 1976 until 1993. There had been no record of him having served in the armed forces, so perhaps, like Ellwood, he'd taken off for sunnier climes and foreign shores as soon as he'd left school. If so, there would be records of his employment in that country.

An officer had called on the lady Spender had conversed with in her own language but, unfortunately, she'd been out. Horton wondered if she'd be at home now. Instead of heading directly for his boat he diverted to Kent Terrace. He knew he didn't look like a copper in his leather biker's gear, and he didn't wish to alarm the occupant so, with his warrant card at the ready, he knocked on the door, only half-expecting an answer and prepared to give instructions for her to phone the station to confirm who he was. He was pleased when the door opened. After showing his ID, he asked if he could speak to the lady who conversed with a refuse collector in a foreign language.

The woman's thinly plucked, arched black eyebrows shot up her lined forehead and she scrutinized him with a coquettish glance. 'It's not often I get such a handsome caller and a police officer. Come in, Inspector, it is I who has such lovely talks with Neil.' She stepped back, allowing Horton to enter a narrow passageway.

'I won't keep you long Mrs . . . ?'

'Mademoiselle Michèle Dufrés,' she said coyly as though she were seventeen and not seventy, and that was being generous with her age. In her mind she probably was seventeen. She was neatly dressed in grey tailored trousers and a white polo neck cotton jumper. Her shoulder-length grey-blonde hair framed a face that bore the lines and complexion of a smoker, and her musky perfume couldn't quite disguise the nicotine smell lingering about her and the house. She waved a long bony hand in the direction of a room on her right and Horton entered a fussily furnished room where a gas fire flickered even though the evening was warm.

'Please sit down. Would you like a drink? Sherry? Cognac? No, you look like a whisky man to me.'

'No thank you.'

'On duty, eh? You policemen are all the same,' she teased, as though she had known many over the years. Perhaps she had.

He returned her smile. There was no need to say he didn't drink. He explained why he was there, saying they were concerned about Mr Spender, who was missing — he didn't wish to reveal he'd in all probability been murdered and alarm her. Her answer stunned him.

'Ah, but you are mistaken about Neil being missing because he told me I would no longer see him.'

'He did?' Horton said, taken aback, wondering if Cantelli had been correct in that Spender had been the killer and not the victim.

'Such a charming man. I will miss our little chats. So delightful to converse with someone in my mother tongue. You English rarely bother to learn another language. I asked him why a Frenchman was working in England on the dust-bins. He said he was undercover. For what, I said? Drugs? Prostitutes? He tapped the side of his nose and said dust-men hear and see a lot of things, many people treat them as though they are invisible and that I'd be astonished what he learned.'

She reached for the packet of cigarettes on the table in front of her and offered it across. He politely declined, his mind racing with this new information.

'Do you have any vices, Inspector?' she flirted. 'No, don't answer me. I like to leave that to my imagination.' She lit the cigarette with her immaculately manicured yet nicotine-stained fingers and inhaled. 'Neil said he was English but had lived in France for some years as a young man after leaving his English school.' She exhaled.

Horton was delighted with this new evidence, although he didn't know where or even if it helped with the investigation. 'Did he say where?'

'Paris, of course,' she answered, her tone saying, *Is there anywhere else?* 'Every time I saw him, we exchanged a joke or two. I'd ask him if he had learned any more dark secrets and he'd wink and say plenty. He said he had lots of material.'

'Material?'

'For a book, of course.'

'He was a writer?' Horton's thoughts flew to the mangled hands.

'Like Georges Simenon, eh? Crime novels. He said there are plenty of crimes around here.'

Had Spender been flirting and teasing her? Was Mademoiselle Dufrés making this up? Perhaps she wanted to appear mysterious and interesting. There was nothing in Spender's flat or background to substantiate the claim of his being a writer, although there were those mangled hands — the tools of a writer — and there was also that key under his pillow. Perhaps it was to his writer's den, where he went in his spare time to produce his manuscript.

She picked some tobacco from her yellow teeth. 'It's a pity I won't see him any longer, but you don't need to worry about him missing. He's gone away.'

'When did he tell you he was leaving?' Horton asked. None of Spender's colleagues had spoken of this and Scott Tweed certainly hadn't known it, because if Spender had handed in his notice he would have said.

'Last Thursday when he came for the rubbish. I just happened to be outside.'

I bet. Horton thought she might have been hoping to cultivate a romance with Spender. He couldn't help recalling what PC Johns had reported from the launderette manageress about Spender being charming.

'He said, "You won't be seeing me anymore after today, Michèle." I asked him why. He said, "I've hit the jackpot." I said, "What jackpot? Your book with all the secrets is going to be big success?" He said, "Yes, it will run and run."

'I asked if I was in it. He laughed and said not unless I had done something wickedly criminal. I said of course I had in my youth, but that was my secret.' She tossed back her head and laughed.

Horton smiled politely. He asked a couple more questions about Neil Spender but didn't get any further valuable material, only how she'd like to have seen him out of his smelly clothes and, although she had asked about his scar and his hands, he would never say how he had got his injuries. He liked to be mysterious, she added. He certainly seemed to have achieved that, thought Horton, extricating himself as tactfully as possible.

As he rode along Barley Road — where Uckfield said Damien Oxley lived, almost literally around the corner from Mademoiselle Dufrés — and past Anther's gallery, all shuttered and closed, he had to force himself to postpone considering the new information he'd gleaned and concentrate on the roads. It was only as he alighted in the marina car park and made his way along the pontoon to his boat that he let his mind run over the conversation with Mademoiselle Dufrés. Spender had intimated quite clearly to her that he had come into money, he'd 'hit the jackpot'. Had Spender written a book that had earned him a handsome advance? Could this be the second time he'd done so, the first being when he had resigned from his job at Southern trains, bought expensive clothes and a boat? Spender's bank account would verify if this were the case and certainly his tax returns, where any substantial sum of money would have been declared — money received legitimately, that was. But Cantelli had said that according to Her Majesty's Revenue and Customs, Spender hadn't paid tax between finishing working for Southern trains and taking the job at Jeplie.

But another reason occurred to Horton as he unlocked his boat, Mademoiselle Dufrés's words spinning round in his head. *I'd ask him if he had learned any more dark secrets . . . dustmen hear and see a lot of things, many people treat them as though they are invisible . . . I'd be astonished what he learned.* Horton didn't think that Spender was a writer, nor that his material had anything to do with a book, either fact or fiction leastways, not a book for public consumption. Spender was a blackmailer.

CHAPTER SIXTEEN

Thursday

Horton had no evidence of that save the expensive designer clothes and boat, and the fact Spender had been killed by some-one, who could have been his blackmail victim. After sleeping with the ideas and theories going around his head, which caused him to wake constantly throughout the night, he rose early and decided to see if he could track down someone on the Southern presentation team who might have worked with Spender.

As he made his way to Fratton railway station he wished, not for the first time, that he had someone he could confide in. Not the nitty gritty and gruesome elements of his inves-tigations, just the gist of them, the ideas and frustrations and the delights when they achieved a result. Catherine had never wanted to know about his cases, save initially when they were going out together and had first been married. That had worn off about the same time as his promotion prospects began to stall. He knew she had hoped he'd have a meteoric rise through the ranks. His promotion hadn't been sluggish by any means, and he'd achieved success and passed all the exams before the Lucy Richardson affair, which had halted his career and wrecked his marriage. Catherine too had her career to consider and, after taking minimum maternity leave following Emma's birth, she'd returned to her father's marine manufacturing company, where she had been promoted from marketing manager to marketing director. He wondered how her position now fitted in with her relationship with the millionaire Peter Jarvis and their numerous overseas holidays. Of course, her relationship with Jarvis might not last.

There was someone he would have liked to talk the case over with and he had considered calling Gaye. Then he'd opted not to. She too had a career and was probably up to her eyes in corpses or lecturing would-be forensic pathologists.

At the railway station he showed his ID and asked if he could speak to anyone working for Southern on the train presentation team. He was directed to the opposite platform over the bridge and told that the London Victoria train was due in. Someone from the team would be waiting at the harbour station to embark and go through the train clearing up the litter, returning to Fratton once this had been achieved.

Horton joined the train not expecting that person to have worked with Spender, but he was delighted when the man he encountered at Portsmouth Harbour Station said he had.

'I heard on the local radio station there's an appeal out for him, but I didn't think you lot would be interested in me knowing him that long ago.'

'It's probably not relevant, but we need to gather and sift lots of information at this early stage of the investigation to know what might be.'

'Mind if I carry on with the job? The train's running late and will be off again in a moment. I get off at Fratton and can give you a bit of time then, although I don't think I can help much.'

Horton agreed. Some minutes later they were standing on the platform at Fratton in the blustery damp wind, away from the body of passengers.

'I remember him on account of his scar and his mangled hands,' Spraggs, a small man with a lived-in face, said. 'He sort of stuck in my mind.'

'Did he say how he had come by the injuries?'

'Was mugged.'

Not an accident then as Spender's crew had intimated, and they'd discussed in the briefing yesterday.

'Where?' Horton didn't think the mugging had taken place in Portsmouth but then he had only checked if Spender had a criminal record, which he hadn't, and not if he had been a victim of crime.

Spraggs shrugged. 'Don't know, he never said. He told me he couldn't remember a thing about it. His memory was shot to pieces from the kicking he was given. He was ill for a long time. Said he'd been locked up in a mental ward. He joked about being mad, but he weren't.'

'Did he have a partner or girlfriend?'

'Might have done but he never spoke of one.'

'Any family?'

Spraggs again shrugged. 'Not that he mentioned. We didn't talk that much. I only worked with him for about a year before he left. I remember that he used to get these really bad headaches and had to go off sick with them.'

Just as the refuse crew had said. 'Do you know why he left?'

'Said he'd come into some money.'

'Enough to give up working?'

'I guess so.'

'How?'

'No idea. I teased him about winning the lottery, but he said it was better than that.'

Horton thanked Spraggs and considered this as he headed for the police station. It was very similar to what Spender had told Mademoiselle Dufrés, which made Horton wonder if Spender had found a blackmail victim back then and again recently.

Walters was out. He'd messaged to say there had been another couple of thefts in one of the restaurants at Oyster Quays early last night. Uniform had attended and taken details and he was going to interview the restaurant owner as it looked as though, at last, they had a strong lead on it. He didn't say what that was.

Horton also had a message from Taylor to say they had picked up several prints from Spender's vehicle. These had been sent over to the fingerprint bureau. They'd also got hair samples along with dirt and mud but no blood. Horton hadn't expected the latter. Beth Tremaine was examining Spender's tender later that day and Taylor and a couple of officers were going into Spender's flat.

Cantelli was going straight to Spender's doctor. Horton sent him a text to say he'd just discovered that one of Spender's former colleagues said his injuries had occurred as a result of an assault. Horton checked on the database to see if the mugging Spender had experienced had been in Portsmouth. It hadn't.

He relayed the information to Bliss, wrote up his report, attended to some work and again tried Julian Anther's phone. He called his gallery number and his mobile phone but got the voicemail on both. He left a message asking Anther to call him urgently. He was about to ring Catmore, who had dropped a little off his radar because of the Spender homicide, when Cantelli swept in.

Horton beckoned him into his office and gestured him into the seat across his desk. 'You looked pleased with yourself,' he said. 'Has Spender's doctor come up trumps even without a warrant?'

'She has. Dr Hamman was extremely cooperative, especially when I told her my wife was a nurse, and that Spender had in all probability been murdered. I also got your text so was able to tell her we knew that Spender had been assaulted, most probably in 1993. Seeing as we had that information already, Dr Hamman confirmed I was correct. Spender was the victim of a vicious assault in March 1993 at Newhaven in East Sussex.'

Horton told him about his interview with the Southern cleaner and with Mademoiselle Dufrés last night, including his theory that Spender might have been blackmailing someone both times, only this time his victim had taken an exception to it and killed him.

'That could also have been the case in 1993,' Horton added. 'He got a beating as a warning to lay off and lost his memory. As a result, he couldn't continue his dirty blackmail game because he had no idea who his victim had been.'

'It's possible,' Cantelli concurred. 'On the other hand, as Spender suffered multiple fractures to his hands, it could have been because he was in with a gang of crooks and put his hands too deeply into the till. Dr Hamman says he was lucky to be alive. Because of the severity of his head injury, he spent many weeks in hospital before being transferred to a specialist head injury hospital outside Wimbledon, and then the psychiatric hospital here in Portsmouth.'

'Because he came from here?'

'Yes. His birth was registered in Portsmouth. His memory was impaired, as you said, along with his coordination, and he experienced debilitating headaches.'

'The migraines.'

'Yes. He made good progress and in 2003 he was able to take up a job.'

'As a cleaner for Southern.'

'Where, from his employment record, he worked for eleven years. Dr Hamman couldn't really tell me anything about Spender's character, except that on the two occasions she has seen him he seemed intelligent and friendly.'

Horton sat back, considering Cantelli's news. 'The assault case will give us more on Spender and details of possible relatives or friends. Trueman will get the file. It might also tell us who his 1993 attacker was, and if he was found and convicted.'

'You thinking his assailant could be out of prison and out to finish what he started in 1993? If so, he's waited a long time.'

'Maybe he's been in prison a long time, not for assault but for murder. Spender might not have been alone when he was attacked.'

'Good point.' Cantelli rose. 'I'll check if Spender got any compensation.'

Before he could, Walters waltzed in. 'Got a result, guv,' he cried.

'Another one! They'll be promoting you soon,' Horton rejoined.

Waters snorted. 'Just brought in those two women pretending to be waitresses and targeting diners at Oyster Quays. One of the waiters had taken a picture of the busy restaurant last night for social media and marketing. He scrolled through them for me and guess who was in it?'

'Go on, spoil us.'

'Tina Rustingham.'

Cantelli looked startled. Horton was also astounded. They knew Tina of old. Cantelli voiced what had been running through Horton's mind. 'She would never have the brains to think up a ploy like that.'

'She didn't, but she told us who did. Marlene Denham.'

'Ah, might have known.' Cantelli nodded. 'Cocky little piece and nasty with it.'

'PCs Somerfield and Bailey have booked Rustingham and Denham into the guest suite. I'll let them stew for a while. And talking of food, I'm off to get some sandwiches.'

'While you're there fetch me some,' Horton requested. Cantelli had his own home-made ones.

He made his postponed call to Catmore. The landline was dead. Catmore had stopped it because of his move, understandably so. He tried the mobile number he had given them. That gave one ring and then cut out. Worrying. Maybe Catmore had forgotten to charge the battery, or he had damaged his phone. Horton tried to put the thought aside, but it refused to go. Like Cantelli, when they had been knocking on Anther's door, he had a funny feeling in the pit of his stomach. Something wasn't right. He had been trying Catmore for two days now without a result. He recalled what Trillby of the Metropolitan Art and Antiques Unit had said — Bliss also — that Catmore and Anther could be in on the art switch together. Although he had dismissed it, he wondered if he was wrong.

He grabbed his sailing jacket and entered the CID office just as Walters returned with a packet of sandwiches. Taking them from him and stuffing them in his pocket, he said to Cantelli, 'Better bring yours. I want to check on Catmore. He's still not answering his phone.'

Horton knew he could and should have sent a unit round to Catmore's address — it was what Bliss and Uckfield would have done — but that hollow feeling in his stomach wasn't hunger, it was instinct. On the way he called Trueman, quickly reported what he and Cantelli had learned about Spender and asked him to look up the Newhaven assault report. Trueman said the phones were going ballistic after Bliss's statement, as Horton could hear in the background, and the emails and messages were coming in from the social media coverage on Spender's disappearance. Uckfield too had been on the phone wanting an update.

Horton relayed what he and Cantelli were doing and rang off. He managed to eat a sandwich before Cantelli drew into the long narrow road of terraced houses where Catmore lived. A medium-sized removal van was blocking the road.

Cantelli pulled up behind it. A man was standing in Catmore's forecourt, another was at the door. The man turned and shook his head, looking puzzled.

Horton climbed out and made for them. 'What's wrong?' he asked, his concern deepening. He quickly showed his warrant card, which drew a startled look from both men.

'Can't get an answer,' the older of the two said. 'He's booked for this afternoon. I've thumped the door until my fists ache and rang the bell.'

'Everything's boxed up.' The younger man indicated the downstairs window, which he'd been peering through.

Cantelli addressed Horton. 'He could have had a heart attack or stroke.'

'Call up a unit.'

Cantelli stepped away to do so while Horton pressed the bell. There was still no answer. He peered through the window. In the front room where he, Walters and Felice had sat on Monday, there were two sealed boxes, a sofa, chair and sideboard. The upstairs curtains were open. There was no rear entrance to any houses in this terraced road.

'When did you last speak to Mr Catmore?' Horton asked the removal men.

'Tuesday, late afternoon,' the older one answered. 'He said all was on schedule and he'd be ready.'

'Are the new people moving in this afternoon?'

'I think so. They'll probably be here at any moment.'

In that case they would have a key and there would be no need to force the door, something the new owners wouldn't be pleased to find on arrival. And neither would they be happy when they found the previous owner hadn't moved, and that there was possibly a sick man or even a dead body in the house.

Cantelli returned. A car tooted loudly and impatiently. Behind it was the bin lorry. Horton immediately recognized the crew running along the pavements and retrieving the narrow wheelie bins.

He turned to the removal men. 'You'd better move the van, see if you can park further down the road.'

'All right.'

Cantelli said, 'I'll do the same.'

As they drove off, Farrell and Reams drew level. Horton saw Farrell do a double take. He looked as though he was about to make a bolt for it but restrained himself. 'What are you doing here?' he asked belligerently.

'Trying to get hold of Mr Catmore. Do you know him?'

'No. Not my usual round, as I told you.'

'Do you know him, Mr Reams?'

'I've seen him and nodded to him, but that's all. His bin's not out on the pavement. I'm not supposed to go into the forecourt.'

Horton lifted the lid and peered inside. It was half-full with a handful of plastic household-refuse bags tied at the neck. 'Better leave it for now.'

Reams shrugged. 'Any news on Neil? I heard it on the radio. I can't think who would want to harm him.'

'Can you, Mr Farrell?

'Me! Course not. I don't know him very well.'

As you keep saying. It was a lie. His eye contact was all over the place, as though seeking an escape route. Horton had seen that expression in many a criminal about to be apprehended. And Farrell was suffering itchy feet syndrome in preparation to scarper if need be. He knew something all right. Perhaps Spender had confided in him about a possible blackmail victim and Farrell had thought of taking over from Spender after eliminating him.

Cantelli returned, breaking the tension. Farrell took advantage of it.

'Got to go.' He darted off.

Horton watched the refuse men run down the road following the lorry. He addressed Cantelli. 'He's crooked or I'm not a copper.'

'And we haven't run him through the database. I forgot all about it. I'll do it when we get back.'

For now, they had another problem on their hands. Horton again checked the windows. They were double-glazed, as was the door, so there was no easy way in. There was a method of lifting the door up and forcing an entry, which firefighters used, but the ramrod would do the trick. First, though, he'd call the estate agent, whose name and telephone number were on the 'Sold' board.

'I've been calling Mr Catmore with no answer,' the agent said, worried. 'We should have completed, but nothing's happening.'

'Do you have a key?'

'Yes.'

'Could you get over here and open up for us?'

'Be there in ten minutes.'

The patrol unit had arrived and managed to park a short distance down the road as a car had pulled out. Horton wondered what car Catmore drove, assuming he had one. He greeted PCs Bailey and Seaton and said they would hold fire forcing an entry until the agent arrived with the key.

They didn't have long to wait. A small car drew up and a short, overweight man in his late thirties with a beard and a worried expression on his plump, pallid face jumped out and hurried towards them, leaving the car parked in the middle of the road. He handed over the key. 'I hope to God the poor man's not inside, well, you know . . . dead.'

'If you'd wait here, Mr Perry.'

'Too right I will.'

Horton detailed Bailey to stay with the estate agent while he entered the house, calling out. There was no answer. He instructed Seaton to take the stairs while he and Cantelli went through the ground-floor rooms. There was no sign of Catmore nor of a disturbance of any kind. There was also nowhere in the small back garden Catmore could be concealed. There wasn't even a shed.

'All clear upstairs,' Seaton called out. 'Just a bed and chest of drawers. No Mr Catmore.'

'Is the bed made up?'

'Yes.'

'Take a look in the attic, Seaton. I know he won't be up there but best to check.'

They could hear the ladder being pulled down. 'Nothing but dust,' came Seaton's shout.

Horton turned to Cantelli. 'This is getting infectious. First Spender, then Anther, now Catmore. At this rate we'll be accused of carelessness.'

Cantelli gave a grim smile.

'So, where the devil is he?' asked Horton.

CHAPTER SEVENTEEN

It was one of the first questions Bliss asked when they returned to the station. A more detailed search and close scrutiny of both the bathroom and kitchen had revealed no visible blood spatters or drops, but that didn't mean they wouldn't need to return and re-examine the house if Catmore turned up dead. Horton had no reason to believe that but an itch between his shoulder blades said it was possible. Catmore's disappearance alongside Anther's made him very uneasy. His instinct also told him there was a great deal more to the art switch than they had originally considered.

He had retained the key to the house and given a receipt to the agent, who had the unenviable task of informing the prospective new owners that their move would be postponed. With the exception of one box, which Cantelli had transported to his car, the rest remained in situ. Fortunately, Catmore was methodical and had labelled all his boxes, of which there were only four. The one that now was in the CID operation room was labelled 'Personal papers, photographs and books'. Horton wondered if it might give them more information about Dorothy. Cantelli was going through it while Horton updated Bliss. Horton was also keen to hear what Nicola Bolton had learned, but that wouldn't be until

Monday. She had phoned Walters to say she was hot on the trail and needed a couple more days before she could run through the information with them.

PCs Bailey and Seaton had interviewed Catmore's next-door neighbours and those living opposite and, finding a couple of people at home, had been able to establish that Catmore drove a grey Ford Fiesta, which wasn't parked along the road. No one knew the registration number, but Walters was getting that from the Driver and Vehicle Licensing Agency and would put a call out for it. Horton also reported to Bliss that the woman over the road had seen Catmore leave the house on Tuesday evening at about six thirty, but she had no idea when he had returned — she didn't spend her life looking out of the window, she had more important things to do. But Bailey had established that when she had taken her dog for a shit later that evening, just after nine, she hadn't seen any lights on.

Catmore's bed had been made up, so it was probable that he had gone missing on Tuesday night. Anther was likely to have disappeared that same night. Although they didn't know that for certain, he hadn't been there yesterday morning when they had searched his flat and gallery.

Horton hadn't believed that Catmore was involved in the art switch, but now he wasn't so sure. Bliss pointedly reminded him that she had requested Catmore to be reinterviewed, which he had failed to do, and that as a result the villains could have slipped through their fingers. Horton didn't see much point in telling Bliss he had been otherwise engaged. He started to think that maybe he had made an error in not prioritizing another interview with Noel Catmore. Perhaps he was losing his grip. The last few months had taken a toll on him mentally and even though he had vowed to put the Ames family behind him, it was easier said than done, especially when the Ames brothers and their yacht were still missing. Speculation continued in the media, and Horton dreaded a phone call or visit from Harriet Ames, as he would have to lie to her about having seen her father on that fogbound night.

Was he losing his touch? As he returned to CID, he silently acknowledged there was a sense of flatness inside him, an emptiness that he recognized was the result of coming down from the adrenaline he'd been living on for over two years while working on that surveillance operation and then undercover at Oyster Quays. Then had come the false rape charge, the break-up of his marriage, his drinking and depression, the need to find the truth behind his mother's disappearance, all of which had kept him keyed up. Now it was all over. Perhaps a fresh challenge was what he needed. He could apply to another unit or another station in Hampshire.

Bliss's words resounded in his head. He might have slipped up with Catmore, but had he also made errors of judgement with Spender by not stepping up the investigation earlier? Should he have immediately treated it as murder instead of waiting for Ruth Bowen's results? He despised self-doubt, it was a crippling emotion. And harking back at what he should or should not have done was a pointless exercise anyway.

Bliss had said there was nothing further on the forensic examination of Spender's tender. Hair samples and prints had been taken from Spender's flat but nothing of relevance had been found in the search, and the officers' questioning of the other occupants had brought the same result that he and Johns had got previously. The calls, emails and messages they had received of possible sightings of Spender were so out of the way as to be improbable, but officers in various constabularies were checking them out anyway.

He grabbed a coffee and found Cantelli, who had the contents of Catmore's box spread out on two desks.

'Anything?'

'Birth certificates for Catmore and his late wife, their marriage certificate and his wife's death certificate. Nicola's probably got all that information anyway from the Register of Births, Deaths and Marriages. No passport, no diaries, a couple of photograph albums, but I can't see Aunt Dorothy named in any of them. A handful of books on sports personalities and a couple on metal-detecting. I wonder if a metal detector is in one of the other boxes. He could have gone out with it on Tuesday night when the neighbour saw him and had an accident.'

'If he's a metal detectorist then he might have a social media profile,' Walters chipped in. 'They like to boast about their treasure finds or say where they're hunting. Could help us to locate him.'

'He told us he didn't bother with the internet,' Horton answered.

Walters tapped into his computer. 'Nothing showing up under his name on a general search. But he could be registered under another name or an avatar.'

Cantelli said, 'I'll get Ellen to look tomorrow. She's a whiz at that kind of thing.' Ellen was Cantelli's eldest and now at college studying computing.

Horton returned to his office. There was no news from Sotheby's. It was probably too early for them to have completed their examination of the paintings. He resisted the urge to ring them or Felice and tried to concentrate on his work, but his mind refused to cooperate. He had no evidence that either Anther or Catmore were involved in art theft, yet Damien Oxley's acidic words reverberated around his head. Guy Bampton, the skip hire and waste rubbish king, collected Ellwoods — had Anther or Catmore contacted him? Had Bampton acquired the originals and Anther and Catmore skipped the country with the proceeds? If they had, would Anther really leave his gallery like that, and Catmore all his belongings, not to mention the fact he'd exchanged on a retirement apartment? Perhaps that was chicken feed compared to what they had realized on the sale of the originals.

He needed that CCTV footage from Walters. He found the constable putting on his jacket in readiness to leave.

'Did you get the camera footage of Anther's gallery?'

'It's as I said, guv, they don't keep it for that long. There's nothing covering the rear, only the road and pavement along the front of the gallery, but not specifically its entrance, and that only since Tuesday when I requested it. I did a quick run-through but couldn't pick up anything suspicious.'

'Any sign of Anther or anyone entering his gallery?'

Walters shook his head.

'Ask the estate agents and beauty salon on either side of the gallery if either of them has their own CCTV or webcams covering the rear. We might pick up Anther leaving. Find out if they saw or heard his car and if so what time. See if you can establish if the gallery was open on Tuesday, and when?'

'Righty-ho. I'll do it first thing tomorrow.' And with that Walters sauntered out.

Horton addressed Cantelli. 'Anything on Farrell?'

'Yes, he's got form for receiving stolen goods, three years ago, custodial sentence. That could be why he looked so shifty when we spoke to him, he's either worried we'd pick up on that or he's up to his old tricks.'

'With Spender?'

'Maybe and they fell out.'

But that didn't fit with Horton's blackmail theory. Not unless, as he'd considered earlier, Farrell had wanted to muscle in on Spender's racket after learning about it from Spender or overhearing about it. But would he have? Farrell didn't usually work with Spender unless one of the other crew was on holiday or sick. Yes, that was possible. Farrell could have been relief then. There was also the fact that Spender had a boat and Farrell claimed to have owned one once. A shared interest could have brought them closer together.

But was Farrell capable of murder? Maybe. Or perhaps there had been an argument that had got out of control. Except the cabin hadn't suggested that. It was too neat. The mugs were clean and unbroken, the spoon standing in one. Farrell could have tidied up, but Horton didn't think he looked the type to have done that.

Cantelli left for home and Horton returned to his desk. He gazed out of the window to see Bliss marching across the car park, her laptop briefcase in hand. He watched her drive away and Cantelli followed soon after. His thoughts returned to Spender. He was becoming more of an enigma as time progressed. What had he been doing in Paris, if Mademoiselle Dufrés could be believed. The fact that Spender spoke fluent French backed that up, along with the information there were no tax records for him from 1976 to 1993. Now they had also discovered he had been assaulted in Newhaven, and if Horton's memory served him correctly, there was a ferry service from Newhaven to Dieppe. Could Spender have been returning from France when he was attacked?

Perhaps Spender had a blackmail victim in France who had died. With his financial means cut off, Spender had returned to England. Although they had the month of his assault, Horton didn't know when he had returned. It could have been earlier in 1993, or a couple of years before that. Just because Her Majesty's Revenue and Customs didn't have records for Spender it didn't mean he wasn't in England. He could just not have been working, or rather not declaring and paying any tax. So maybe Spender *had* come home earlier and found himself another victim, who after a while decided enough was enough, hence the assault, putting paid to Spender's criminal activities for some years, until Spender saw or overheard something while working on the train. That period of blackmail had also come to an end, but recently Spender had discovered a new victim and a new secret to exploit for financial gain. Had his victim killed him or had Farrell decided to take over?

Farrell didn't strike Horton as being particularly bright, and if he had killed Spender in order to muscle in on the blackmail, his days might also be numbered. Horton looked up his address, which they'd got when interviewing the crew. Interestingly he lived not far from where Spender's tender had been found abandoned on the eastern shores.

He reached for his jacket and helmet. He might have messed up on not reinterviewing Catmore, but he wasn't going to make the same mistake with Farrell.

His mobile rang. It was Uckfield. Briefly Horton hesitated before answering as he made his way out of the station.

'Have I got the plague?' Uckfield demanded.

'Not that I know of.'

'Oxley's been on to me, says he can't get hold of Julian Anther.'

'That makes two of us.'

'He's worried he won't be able to collect the painting he bought for his wife's birthday.'

'Not concerned about Anther's welfare then?' Horton said cynically, sidestepping a couple of officers talking in the corridor.

'Is he at risk?'

'Yes, at risk if he's absconded the country with the original Ellwoods, or he's done so to escape someone who has them and is threatening him. Or he's topped himself out of despair and fear that his reputation will be ruined. But he's not the only one missing aside from Neil Spender, the refuse collector.'

'I know who he is. So, who else have you mislaid?'

'Noel Catmore.'

There was a moment's silence while Uckfield assimilated this. Horton stood in the rear entrance.

'Could have run off with Anther and the paintings.'

'Possibly.'

'But you're doubtful?'

'Doesn't smell right. And there's another one who doesn't smell right — Sam Farrell, works on the bins with Spender's crew. He's edgy and defensive, knows more than he's saying, and he's got form. I'm going to reinterview him but—'

'No time like the present. Give me the address. I'll meet you there in twenty minutes. And don't tell me I'm off sick. I am not sick, and neither am I off, my brain is functioning perfectly.'

'Glad someone's is,' Horton muttered, as the line went dead.

CHAPTER EIGHTEEN

Farrell's flat was on the corner of a main road, just past the Methodist Church, the front of which was an electrical shop. The door to the flat was in the side road. There was no sign of life in the windows as Horton looked up at them, but that meant little. A fire escape at the rear of the building went out into a small yard with a wooden gate by the side of a garage door, both of which looked as though they hadn't been opened or painted in years. The road led down to another, forming a T-junction. Horton cruised down it to get his bearings. There was a block of garages to the north of the no-through road under the flyover, which ran east towards the shore, not far from the sailing club where Spender's tender had been found at Langstone Harbour.

Uckfield drew up as Horton returned. 'Shall I do the honours?'

Horton stepped back. 'Be my guest, at your rank you don't get much chance of action.'

Uckfield thumped the door and kept it up until a man's voice came from inside. 'All right, where's the fire?' Throwing open the door, he gave a start of surprise as he recognized Horton.

'What do you want?' he asked warily. His eyes shifted to the burly Uckfield beside Horton.

'This is Detective Superintendent Uckfield,' Horton said.

Farrell's jaw dropped. Then, trying to recover his equilibrium, said in a mocking voice that held the edge of fear in it, 'Blimey, what have I done? Robbed a bank?'

'No, killed a man,' Uckfield replied matter-of-factly.

It took a moment for Uckfield's phrase to sink in. 'You what? You're nuts! Who am I supposed to have killed?'

Horton said, 'Can we come in?'

'No, you bloody can't.'

But Uckfield was having none of it. Before Farrell could close the door, Uckfield slapped his hand on it and, moving forward, he pushed hard until Farrell had no choice but to step back, or else risk being squashed. Horton followed Uckfield into the dim hallway, which smelled of grease and dirt.

'Hey, you can't do this. You need a warrant,' Farrell protested.

'Know your rights, eh? But then you would, having a criminal record,' retorted Uckfield.

'I might have known you'd throw that at me.'

'Do you live alone?' Horton eyed the grubby hall with the stairs facing them and the narrow corridor leading to the back door.

'That's none of your business.'

Uckfield stepped forward, forcing Farrell to stagger back against the wall. He thrust his face into Farrell's and said quietly, 'Everything is our business where you are concerned, Mr Farrell. Now let's have some cooperation. Unless you'd prefer to talk at the station?'

Farrell's mouth tightened. 'I need a fag.' He reached into his trouser pocket for his cigarettes. 'I can't smoke in here.'

'Why not? Oh, I see, it would spoil the décor?' Uckfield said with heavy sarcasm, his gaze sweeping the soiled, threadbare carpet and mouldy beige walls.

'Yeah, it would,' Farrell snapped. But he stayed rooted to the spot. Horton could see that he dared not march out knowing that either he or Uckfield would climb the stairs and look around his flat.

'Then Inspector Horton and I will talk to you outside in the yard. After you.'

But Farrell wasn't falling for it. 'No, after you, Superintendent,' he jeered.

Uckfield suddenly capitulated. He brushed past Farrell, surprising him. Horton followed suit leaving Farrell to rush after them as Uckfield flung open the rear door and stepped into the small concrete yard beneath the fire escape.

Horton could see and hear the traffic trundling over the flyover to their left. Somewhere, someone had loud music thumping and a car was revving up, possibly in or outside the garage block at the end of the road.

Farrell lit up and inhaled deeply. 'Now what's all this crap about me being a killer?' he said lightly, a little more at ease. 'Who am I supposed to have killed?'

Horton answered. 'Neil Spender.'

'You're joking? Blimey, you think I killed Neil. Why would I want to do that?'

'That's what we'd like you to tell us.'

'But I haven't seen him since . . .'

'Yes?'

'For ages.'

That hadn't been what he had been about to say.

'I hardly knew the bloke,' Farrell added, his nostrils twitching so much they made the spider tattoo on his neck look alive.

'Knew?' Horton said sharply while Uckfield took a toothpick from the pocket of his jacket.

'Don't confuse me. I meant know. You're trying to trip me up.'

Horton again, 'No, we're trying to find out what was going on between you and Spender.'

'Nothing.'

157

'But he did talk to you about his boat.'

'Yes, I already told you that. Lots of people talk to me about boats.'

'Do they? Why should they confide in you? Are you some kind of expert?'

'I didn't mean that.' Farrell took a long drag of his cigarette and exhaled. 'There's nothing I can tell you about Neil. I just worked with him a few times, like I said before.'

'Did Spender mention where he went on his boat?'

'I've already told you, no.'

'I don't believe you.'

'That's your prerogative.'

'We think he was up to no good.'

'Stealing, you mean?' Farrell's eyes narrowed. He picked some tobacco from his teeth. A tabby cat appeared on the top of the wall, watching them.

'That or blackmail. Perhaps you thought you'd like a slice of what Spender was going to get.'

'Blackmail! Who the hell would Neil blackmail?'

'You tell us.'

'I can't because I haven't the faintest idea what you're talking about.'

Horton thought it had the ring of truth about it because Farrell had relaxed. 'Then let's talk about theft.'

There was a sudden slight tension in Farrell's body language and the spider's tentacles stretched further as Farrell's Adam's apple went up and down.

Perhaps he had been wrong about the blackmail. Thieving was Spender's racket for which he'd received a beating years ago. But that didn't ring true with what Mademoiselle Dufrés had said, or Colin Spraggs of Southern, not unless Spender had been into big-time theft, such as robbing a bank or stealing valuable items from a house, although nothing like that had been reported on their patch recently. There were the high-end car thefts, but Horton didn't see those as fitting Spender's style. He wondered if it could be drugs. Dealers were known to be active on trains and at ports. Had Spender overheard or seen a drugs deal going down at Newhaven port in 1993 and been beaten up when he tried to blackmail the gangmaster? And he'd heard or seen a deal going down on Southern, but had got out intact and with money to burn in his pocket. Intimidation and violence were drug dealers' trademarks. He'd got away with it two years ago, perhaps because this dealer had gone to prison, as Cantelli had suggested. If Farrell was hoping to pick up where Spender had left off, he would be next in line if he didn't watch out.

'You're playing a dangerous game, Farrell, if you think you can take over from Spender and blackmail a drug dealer.'

'A dealer! Rubbish. I don't know what you're talking about.'

'Then how about stolen goods.'

Bingo, Farrell was back on the alert.

'We found this key in Spender's flat.' He produced it. 'Know what it unlocks?'

'What am I, Houdini? I haven't a fucking clue.' He puffed at his cigarette. The cat jumped down from the wall and sauntered over to them.

'I think this key is where you and Spender stashed whatever you stole.'

'I know nothing about any stolen goods. Now sod off.'

But Horton had no intention of doing so, not while he sniffed that Farrell was involved in Spender's disappearance. 'You probably had a row. Spender wanted a bigger cut. You killed him, ditched his body in the sea, cast his boat adrift and then, using the tender, returned to the shore. That shore,' he pointed towards the east, 'where you left the tender and walked home.'

Farrell threw his cigarette on the ground. 'Who says?'

'I do.' Horton stepped forward.

Farrell licked his lips. The cat meowed and rubbed up against Farrell's leg but angrily he kicked it away. It screeched, snarled and cowered.

Uckfield said, 'Charge him, Inspector, with cruelty to an animal.'

'I hardly bloody touched it. I like cats.'

'Didn't look that way to me and the cat doesn't agree with you either,' Uckfield replied as the animal ran to the wall and scrambled up it.

Horton said, 'Mr Sam Farrell you are charged with inflicting—'

'All right, I did take Neil's tender, but it's not what you think.'

'Then I suggest you correct our thinking,' Horton replied. *At last!*

'Neil and I were going out fishing Saturday night. He picked me up in his car and drove to Broadmarsh car park. He inflated the tender and we rowed out to the boat.' Farrell reached for his packet of cigarettes, opened it and, finding it empty, tossed it on the ground with the other rubbish littering the courtyard. He seemed to have dried up.

Horton helped him out. 'What time?'

'About five o'clock.'

Farrell's eyes were all over the place. That was obviously a lie.

'Try again?'

'Might have been later, seven-ish. We were going to do a bit of night fishing.'

'Without fishing tackle?' quipped Horton.

'Neil said he had some on the boat and I took mine with me. We'd only just boarded when he had a phone call, and don't ask me who it was because I don't know. He said he couldn't take me fishing because he had to meet someone. He said I could take the tender back to the shore.'

'Leaving you to walk home from the car park?'

'He was very keen to get to this meeting.'

'Why didn't he give you his car keys?'

'I dunno. He didn't, and I thought sod it, I'm not going to walk from Broadmarsh all the way home. It's over five miles. So, I rowed across the harbour to the sailing club and ditched the tender there and walked home. Much closer.'

'Not caring that Spender would be stuck on his mooring.'

'Well, he didn't seem to mind. When I asked how he would get back to the shore, he said, "That's my problem."'

'And he wasn't bothered that you would just leave the tender beside his car for anyone to steal?' Horton said incredulously.

'It was dark and night-time.'

Uckfield said sharply, 'Then it must have been well after sunset at eight thirty and not seven o'clock.'

'If you say so.'

'I do, and you're a lying little shit.'

'Hey, you can't talk to me like that!'

'I can to scum like you,' Uckfield answered brusquely.

Farrell looked about to protest but must have seen something in Uckfield's eyes that changed his mind. 'I left Neil going out down the harbour in his boat and that was the last I saw or heard from him until you and that sergeant showed up in the yard and said he was missing.'

'You didn't call him?'

'No.'

'Why not?'

'I just didn't. I have no idea what he was doing or who he was going to see.'

Horton studied him. 'We found the tender.'

'Where?'

'Where you left it.'

'Then you know I'm telling the truth,' Farrell declared, victoriously.

'I doubt that,' snapped Uckfield. 'Get your coat.'

'Why? I've told you all I know.'

'Then you can come down to the station and repeat it. We'll put it in a statement for you to sign. I'll call up a unit and Inspector Horton will escort you to your flat to fetch your coat.'

'I don't need one,' Farrell gabbled.

'Then you must want another packet of fags.'

'No.'

'Given up suddenly? I wonder why that is?' Uckfield sneered. 'Is there something you don't want us to find in your flat? Like bloodstained clothes?'

'What the hell are you talking about?'

'You are the last person to see Neil Spender alive. You are probably the last person to see him dead. You went out on his boat, as you have freely admitted, you quarrelled, you killed him, ditched his body in the sea, cast his boat adrift and, in the tender, rowed back to the harbour and threw the oars in the sea because they had your fingerprints on them.'

'I've told you what happened. I've got nothing to do with Neil's death.'

'No? Then we'll see what else we can find in your flat, and I don't mean dirty underpants and dishes.'

'You can't search it without a warrant.'

'Oh, yes we can.'

Horton was calling up for a patrol car.

Farrell looked despairingly at them. 'I want the duty lawyer. I'm not having you fit me up.'

'You can call one when you get to the station. Fetch his jacket, Inspector, we don't want Mr Farrell hiding anything if we let him go upstairs alone.'

'There's one there on the back of the front door,' Farrell said.

Horton lifted it off and searched the pockets before handing it over to him.

'You won't find anything in my flat. I haven't done anything.'

'That's what they all say,' Uckfield said wearily. 'And we *never* believe it.'

The patrol car was there within minutes. Uckfield gave instructions to the uniformed officers to book Farrell in and make sure his clothes and footwear were removed for forensic examination. Farrell left, protesting loudly. They climbed the stairs, coming out on a landing. It matched the decrepit state downstairs.

Uckfield took a deep breath. 'Ah, how I missed the stench of filth and decay.'

Would he, Horton wondered, if he left the force or transferred to another unit that didn't require as much frontline action? The answer was yes. And he had missed Uckfield. He'd still like to be on that Major Crime Team with him but that would mean shifting DI Dennings, unless Dennings transferred or the Major Crime Team expanded.

'I wonder who owns the building.' Horton stepped into the room facing the front. 'Whoever it is clearly doesn't care much for their tenants.'

'Don't think Farrell cares much about his accommodation anyway. A cell is probably the height of luxury to him,' came Uckfield's reply from a rear room. Horton agreed. The place stank of cigarette smoke and stale food. The ceilings and walls were yellow with nicotine, the carpet grubby, the chairs tatty and covered with clothes and soiled takeaway foil tins. Farrell might take away other people's rubbish, but he obviously didn't believe in taking away his own.

'No stolen items in here,' Uckfield called from the kitchen. 'Just congealed food, grease, dirt and unwashed dishes.'

'There's nothing of any significance in the living room,' Horton said, entering the bedroom.

Uckfield joined him. 'Dirty underwear, a load of old bits and bobs, obviously nicked from people's dustbins, but can't charge the bugger for that. Let's see if he's stashed his bloodstained clothes and shoes.'

Uckfield searched the rickety wardrobe and cupboards while Horton flicked through the clothes lying around on the bed, floor and chairs. 'Can't see any with bloodstains.'

'Could be invisible to the naked eye or he could have washed them.'

Horton raised his eyebrows.

'Yeah, I know, doesn't look like he's washed anything for weeks.'

'Or vacuumed,' Horton replied, looking under the bed. He straightened up. 'I think Farrell might be telling the truth. Spender did go to meet someone who either killed him or he killed them. But I don't believe those two men were going fishing and nor were they going out in the Solent to look at the stars.' Horton recalled his conversation with Elkins on South Binness Island as the gulls had squealed and squawked around them. 'I think they were egg hunting.'

'He's a bit too long in the tooth for collecting birds' eggs.'

'Not if there's a lucrative market in it. And there is, according to the RSPB ranger, Jed Parkham. It's why they count the number of birds roosting and have trail cameras on the islands. The birds are protected and so are their eggs.'

'Have any been missing? Eggs, that is?'

'I don't think so. That could have been Spender and Farrell's first foray.'

'Let's ask him.'

Over an hour later Farrell, dressed in a disposable white suit in the interview room, continued to deny killing Spender but finally admitted their nocturnal jaunt had been to steal eggs from South Binness Island and other islands in the harbour with the intention of selling them to a restaurant in Southsea. One, which he reluctantly gave the name of, was a stone's throw from Anther's gallery. Spender had told Farrell that gulls' eggs were a delicacy. Posh restaurant clients liked them and some restaurants would buy them under the counter and put a big markup on them.

Horton was interested to know where Spender had acquired his culinary knowledge. Farrell seemed to think he must have read it somewhere, or overheard someone mentioning it, but Horton's mind kept harking back to the expensive clothes, the boat, the gap of two years in Spender's employment record when he wasn't claiming any benefit. Had he also been eating out in expensive restaurants? Alone or with a partner? No one had come forward, so perhaps the woman or man — if there had been one — had ditched Spender when the money ran out. Perhaps Spender had developed the taste for gulls' eggs and knowledge of their exclusivity while living in France between 1976 and 1993.

He asked Farrell if Spender knew the restaurateur personally. Farrell shrugged but ventured that he'd probably met him on the bin round. 'Not that many people speak to us,' he added. 'We're invisible most of the time unless we're blocking the road or refusing to take their rubbish away.'

Farrell had repeated what Mademoiselle Dufrés had claimed Spender had uttered to her — *Dustmen hear and see a lot of things, many people treat them as though they are invisible and that I'd be astonished what he learned.* Horton was back to the blackmail motive. Spender had gone to meet his new victim on Saturday night. But how they were going to find his intended victim on such a wide round, he didn't know. Even running all the residents through the computer wouldn't give them who Spender had decided to blackmail. Whoever it was probably wouldn't have a criminal record, and so would pay to maintain their unblemished reputation.

Over coffee in the empty incident suite, Uckfield said, 'We'll hold him until after the forensic examination of his clothes and flat. We might come up with something to make the charge of murder stick, rather than attempted theft of gulls' eggs.'

Horton doubted it.

Uckfield grinned impishly. 'Can't manage without me, eh? A killer detained and I'm not even on duty. But I will be Monday. I've been signed off the sick list as of then.'

Horton didn't think Bliss would be very pleased.

As he returned home, the interview played around his head and refused to budge. He stopped off for some fish and chips and ate them on board. He was convinced that Farrell was telling the truth. It was the sort of antic he would be up to, thieving, and although Spender didn't have a criminal record, Horton had the strong impression he was crooked. Perhaps he had a record in France. It might be worth checking out.

Why had Spender involved Farrell, though? Why not just steal the eggs himself and sell them? Perhaps he had a bird phobia. Those gulls could be pretty scary and highly protective. And why not seek a willing accomplice? Perhaps Spender wanted Farrell to do the dirty work while he remained on board.

OK, so who had telephoned Spender and caused him to change his plans? Trueman was already applying for access to Spender's mobile phone account. That would take time, if they were even permitted to see it. The phone company could withhold records as could the bank. And even if they were able to study Spender's phone records, the killer could have called him from a payphone and therefore be untraceable.

Elkins was still trying to find out who Spender had bought his boat from, which could confirm if it was paid for in cash. That would be irregular to say the least. Not many people went around with anything up to £10,000 in their pockets.

As Horton lay on his bunk there was something more that nagged away at him. It was thoughts of Spender's boat, and the curtailed excursion with Farrell — something he had missed. But he couldn't for the life of him think what it was.

CHAPTER NINETEEN

Friday

It came to him just before dawn.

'Spender's boat hook,' he announced to Bliss the next morning. 'It's missing.'

Horton produced a picture of one he'd printed off the internet earlier. 'As you can see it's got a blunt tip, which is used for pushing the boat off the buoy, and a hook when hooking up to the buoy. Spender would have had one on board because his boat is moored up to a buoy in Langstone Harbour. There wasn't one on the boat when PC Ripley brought it into the marina. When I reinterviewed Farrell earlier this morning, he said there was definitely a boat hook on board, which he used, and he swears it was still there when he left the boat after Spender had received his telephone call.'

'Which he would say if he had killed him,' Bliss grumbled, smarting from the fact that Uckfield had muscled in on the investigation, made an arrest and that he was returning to duty on Monday.

'It didn't register with me that it was missing, neither did it with Sergeant Elkins or PC Ripley. It should have done, but at that stage we weren't certain we were looking at homicide. I've also checked with Taylor and he confirms that when he and Beth Tremaine examined the craft there was no boat hook. I've also spoken to Ruth Bowen, who says it is entirely possible it was used as a murder weapon, as the blood patterns match. Ruth says that the shaft of the boat hook could have been used to strike the victim, who fell onto the deck. Then the hook, or even the blunt part of the implement, could have been used to stab the victim while down. The assailant thrust it into his chest, pulled it out and tossed it overboard.'

Bliss's nostrils tightened. When Horton had told Cantelli and Walters, the latter had muttered, 'Nasty.'

'Farrell continues to deny that he and Spender had been out on earlier occasions thieving from the islands or from boats and yards around the coast. He's adamant that Saturday was their first trip and it was to steal eggs, but I don't believe him. I looked up the list of marine-related stolen items and it indicates it's possible that is what they've been up to. There was nothing in his flat or Spender's, but the goods could be kept off the premises, much like in the case of Derby and Engels from the house robberies, who had stashed the goods in Maidstone's allotment shed. The key I found could be to a lock-up, only Farrell denies knowing anything about it, but then he would say that. The lock-up could be close to the water, somewhere Spender can get his boat into and offload the gear without anyone seeing. A boathouse or shed close to one of the lesser-known private pontoons or creeks around Portsmouth, Langstone or Chichester Harbours. Sergeant Elkins will check them out but that's a lot of ground or, I should say, water to cover.'

'Could a third party be involved, someone who owns such a place?' asked Bliss.

'It's possible. I'm hoping Leney will get some news from the key manufacturers today or Monday, which could help.' Horton would have to contact Leney to ask him once again to let him and Uckfield into Anther's Art Gallery tomorrow morning. 'But I don't think that's the motive for Spender's death. I still believe he was a blackmailer. And I don't think Farrell's our killer. If there is no forensic evidence to put him at the scene of the crime i.e., the boat, then we will have to release him. Even if we find his prints and hairs and DNA on Spender's boat that doesn't mean Farrell killed Spender. He's admitted being on board. He claims his blood group is O — Cantelli's checking that out with Farrell's doctor. I can't see Farrell lying about something so easy to check. That leaves us still searching for someone with the blood group AB negative, but we have no other suspects and even if we find someone with that rare blood group it doesn't mean that person killed Spender.'

'We don't seem to be getting very far,' Bliss said with an irritable sigh. She paced Uckfield's office, the tension showing in her angular figure. 'And none of the reports of sightings of Spender from the announcement have come to anything. Where do you suggest we go next with the investigation?'

He felt like saying, 'Why ask me when you rarely do?' but he didn't. 'There's the testimony of Mademoiselle Dufrés. We could follow that up. Spender, I'm sure, came across some information on his round that he could milk for money but, before you say it, I know checking that could take for ever and how would we know who the intended victim was? One of his crew members might have seen or overheard Spender talking to someone, which could give us a pointer, but it's very vague. We could also ask the French police if Spender has a criminal record. Mademoiselle Dufrés said Spender lived in Paris, although I think that is speculation on her part.'

'I'll contact the Préfecture de Police de Paris.' Bliss looked relieved that there was something she could do. 'What are you doing about the art thefts?'

'Walters is visiting Catmore's house to see if he's packed a metal detector, as he has books on the subject. It's possible he became ill or has had an accident while out detecting, in which case he'd have the detector on him. If we find one packed it could at least rule out that theory. I'm going to interview Guy Bampton about the Michael Ellwood paintings. He's a collector and he could tell us more about Julian Anther. I take it nothing's come in from the all-ports alert on Anther?'

'No.' She returned to her seat and glanced at her computer. 'Let me know if anything further comes to light, and hurry up the analysis on Farrell's clothes.'

Horton returned to his office, where Cantelli confirmed that Farrell was blood group O. He also said that as Ellen had a project to complete at college, he'd held off asking her to search for Catmore on internet forums and social media last night, but he would ask her that evening and she'd have the weekend to check him out.

They made their way to Bampton's office, which was a stone's throw from the refuse crew's depot on the eastern side of Portsmouth and not far from Langstone Harbour. From Oxley's description Horton could have expected someone coarse but firstly he didn't trust Oxley's opinion and secondly it never paid to think in stereotypes. Bampton, in his early sixties, was a broad man with a strong, rugged face, a powerful jaw, sparkling light blue eyes and a softly spoken voice. His office was modern and remarkably tidy, boasting pictures of skips, lorries and construction projects. Horton had anticipated something chaotic and tatty, perhaps because of the association between rubbish and skips, but again that was stereotypical thinking. They were offered refreshment, which they declined.

'Don't mind if I finish my coffee?' Bampton said brightly.

'Not at all.' Horton noted the expensive jewelled signet ring on his finger as he lifted, left-handed, a coffee cup the size of a soup bowl.

'You're here about the Michael Ellwood paintings. I saw them in the gallery.'

'Mr Anther showed them to you?' Horton said surprised, although he shouldn't have been because he had suspected Anther had lied about not showing or mentioning them to anyone.

'He didn't have to, I spotted them. I'll save you asking the questions, Inspector and tell you what happened. Every now and then I like to go out with the boys delivering and collecting skips. It keeps them on their toes, and it keeps me in touch with my customers. That way I can make sure I stay one step ahead of giving them what they want, even if they don't know what they want.'

Horton was beginning to see what had happened but there were still many questions he wanted answers to. Hopefully Bampton would provide them.

Cantelli looked up from his note-taking. 'Your company gave me a very good service when my brother and I demolished an old coal bunker.'

'Glad to hear it, Sergeant. Well, three weeks ago, on the twenty-second of April, I was riding out delivering a skip to the backyard of the retail units at the end of the service road behind the gallery, and picking up a full skip. My driver dropped me off at Anther's rear entrance. I thought, while I was in the area, I'd drop in to see if he had any new paintings I might be interested in. I thumped on the back door until Julian answered. He looked put out to see me, but I'm a good customer and he had no option but to invite me in. I spotted the two Ellwoods immediately.'

'Did you tell him?' asked Horton.

'Not then, but he saw me notice them. If Oxley hadn't been in the gallery, I would have asked about them, but I didn't want him sniffing around, even though I knew he'd never cough up enough to buy them. He's too tight-fisted, all mouth and no money unless his wife, Leanne, can prise it out of him — and she does for what she wants, which isn't always what Oxley wants. Seeing him there was a bonus, especially as I was dressed in my old work clothes.' Bampton's face broke into a broad grin and there was a malicious gleam in his eyes. Horton could see that he took great delight in winding up the supercilious, snobbish Oxley, probably hamming up his working-class act and adding an air of coarseness.

'When I returned to my office, I called Anther and asked him about the Ellwoods. He said they might be up for sale. He'd let me know.'

Anther had denied speaking to anyone about them. Horton knew that had been a lie, but it was good to have it confirmed.

'And has he been in touch since then, sir?' asked Cantelli.

'Yes. He told me a third Ellwood had surfaced but wouldn't say how. He'd asked Felice over to authenticate it and she had arranged to visit on Monday. I didn't hear from her or Julian, so on Wednesday I rang him, but there was no answer. I didn't leave a message. I rang him again yesterday, still no answer.'

'What time was this?' Cantelli asked.

'About 3 p.m. on Wednesday and yesterday just after 7 p.m.'

'His mobile or the gallery number?'

'Mobile. Then this morning, just before you arrived, I called and spoke to Felice.'

Horton noted that Bampton used the form of her name she only allowed those she liked to use. To everyone else she was Felicity, including Julian Anther and Oxley.

'She told me there had been a hitch. That the originals had been replaced with forgeries.'

Horton covered his surprise that she had relayed the information about the forgeries. They had agreed the fewer who knew about it the better. Perhaps Bampton had been very persuasive.

'I then called Maurice Linden,' Bampton continued. 'About twenty minutes ago. He confirmed what Felice had said, not that I doubted her, but I was worried that the ones I have might not be the genuine article. Maurice assured me that mine are certainly not forgeries. And, of course, I have the provenance to prove it, although I'm told that can also be faked. Maurice said that you'd told him Anther was not in the gallery or in his flat and he hadn't heard from him, which is disturbing, hence your visit here.' Bampton sat forward. 'Do you think he's got the originals and run off with them?'

'Would he do that?' Horton asked.

Bampton considered for a moment. Then sat back. 'No. He hasn't got the balls for it.'

Horton was secretly inclined to agree. It was much more likely that, upset over what had happened, Anther had needed some time and space as had been intimated by Linden and Felice.

'How long have you known him?' he asked.

'Over twenty years.'

Horton was momentarily stunned. He hadn't expected that.

'I knew him when he had the gallery in Emsworth in the early nineties. He'd just opened it, about 1993 I think it was, and I went to the opening. I've always been interested in art, and it is a very good investment. The robbery really shook him up, and he closed the gallery shortly afterwards, went to live abroad. He opened this gallery in Southsea about four years ago, which was when we resumed contact.'

Cantelli said, 'What did he do during those in-between years?'

'Lectured on art, travelled, dealt a little. He never said much about it.'

Horton said, 'Is there anyone you can think of who might purchase the Ellwood originals under the radar, so to speak?'

'No. Those sorts don't bid at auctions, and they don't boast about what they've got. As you are no doubt aware the originals usually stay in a cellar where the sad gits can sit gloating over them while sipping champagne, telling themselves how clever they are. If by any wild chance Julian has sold to someone who has paid him a great deal of money, then all I can say is he might not live long enough to spend it.'

Horton silently agreed. Bampton drained his coffee. Cantelli's pencil paused over his notebook. Outside a lorry began reversing with the message announcing it was doing so.

Horton said, 'If Mr Anther hasn't run off with the originals is there anywhere you think he might be? Would he have gone to any friends? Relatives?'

'Might have done but I've never heard him speak of any. Never seen him with any girl or boyfriend either.'

'Do you know Mr Ellwood personally?' Horton was keen to hear if Bampton agreed with the brittle, acerbic Oxley.

'Yes. We've chatted at his exhibitions and met at a couple of lunches and dinners at the Royal Academy of Arts. I'm a patron. Yes, it always surprises people that a man who has made his fortune out of shifting shit and other people's rubbish can have an eye for beauty and a knowledge of art.'

Horton knew that neither he nor Cantelli had shown any surprise — Bampton's reaction was, he thought, a defensive reflex borne from the looks other people had given him over the years. Oxley looked down his nose at the earth-shifting rubbish king, but then Oxley sneered at most people. And he didn't have the sole prerogative when it came to snobbery.

'What's Michael Ellwood like?' asked Horton, genuinely interested. He hadn't got a feel of the man and he should have done.

'Talented.'

'I meant as a man. We haven't met him and it's unlikely we will, given he is so ill in hospital.'

Bampton nodded and looked sorrowful for a moment. 'He's gentle, reflective, considerate and sensitive. He feels things deeply and that's expressed in his art. He was devastated when Lisa, his wife, died. He couldn't stomach London without her so he returned to the Isle of Wight, where he was born and raised, hoping it would help. It did to an extent, but it also isolated him further. Maurice Linden has been a tower of strength to Michael, they've been friends since school days, but he can't replace Lisa. Michael and I used to meet up for drinks a couple of times a year. But I haven't seen him for three years, not because I didn't want to, but because he wouldn't see anyone. I tried both before and after his accident, but he cut himself off from everyone, not just me. The black dog, I'm afraid. Depression. And, of course, he has been seriously ill from the accident, and now this latest.'

'You think he tried to kill himself?'

'I do. And he's been trying ever since that accident, maybe even before it. Alcohol. His liver is shot to pieces and his kidneys are shutting down. I'm taking my boat over to the island this weekend and I'm going to visit him in hospital. Felice says he's heavily sedated, so he'll probably have no idea I'm there but . . .'

He left his words hanging in the air. After a short silence, Horton said, 'Did you know Felice has one of her father's paintings in her gallery in Cowes?'

Bampton's shocked expression told Horton he didn't. 'Is it still there?' he said eagerly and then his brow puckered. 'Why didn't she tell me?'

Horton could see his mind was already working to call her the moment they left. 'Did anyone other than Mr Anther, Mr Oxley and Felice know you visited Anther's gallery on the twenty-second of April and that Julian Anther had told you he might have some Ellwood paintings coming up for sale?'

Bampton's eyes narrowed slightly. 'I told my wife. My skip driver also knew I was in the gallery.' Earnestly he said, 'I didn't switch the paintings, Inspector. I didn't substitute the originals with forgeries and take the originals away in the lorry, which is what you're thinking.'

But it would have been easy enough for him to do so, in conjunction with Anther. Alternatively, Bampton could have threatened Anther into handing over the originals. 'Do you know of an artist capable of forging those paintings?'

Bampton shook his large head.

'Do you recognize the name Dorothy Masson or Masset, or something similar?'

'No.'

'She might have been a collector,' Horton prompted.

'Means nothing to me.'

'Or Mr Noel Catmore?'

'Never heard of him.'

Was Bampton lying? Maybe.

Bampton consulted his watch and rose. 'I'm sorry, gents, but I've got a meeting and I'm already late for it. Happy to talk to you again, and I'll let you know if I hear from Julian or think of anything else that can help.'

He showed them out in a friendly manner and with a crushing handshake.

They made for the car in the visitors' space at the front of the single-storey office building. 'Want to call in at Jeplie while we're here?' Cantelli asked.

Horton looked to where the smoke from the incinerator was curling westward. Next to it was the refuse yard. 'No point, the crew will be out. But let's talk to Damien Oxley. He denies seeing the Ellwood paintings but I'm not sure I believe that.' Horton relayed the Southsea address.

Cantelli indicated left at the end of the road and then right, heading south, with the eastern shore of Langstone Harbour on their left. The tide was on its way up and the fresh easterly breeze was causing small ripples on the water. Horton couldn't make out the island where Spender's craft had ended up because it was behind them at the top of the harbour.

'What did you make of Bampton?' Horton said.

'Seems decent and honest.'

'But?'

'I'd say he's not a man to put one over on. If he wants something he'll go all out for it and to hell with the consequences. He could have had the phoneys on his dining room wall and when he saw the originals decided to switch them.'

'And the person who diddled him? What would Bampton's reaction be to whoever deceived him?'

Cantelli considered this for a moment. 'I don't think Bampton would personally resort to violence but the threat of it might be enough to frighten someone. Anther, for instance. Maybe Bampton bought the originals from Anther's Emsworth gallery years ago and on realizing they were forgeries told Anther he was exchanging them. If Anther refused, or let one word of it come out, he'd see him finished.'

That was a possible scenario. 'And where would Catmore fit into this?' Horton mused.

'Maybe nowhere. As we said earlier, he could have had an accident while out metal-detecting and no one's found him yet. Bampton probably knows some heavies who could have persuaded Anther to shut up and clear out. But I can't see why he should have targeted Noel Catmore.'

Horton agreed. 'But Bampton could never display the ones he'd switched, and he said that was the point of owning art.'

'He *said*. And he made a point of talking about sad people who only look at their paintings in their cellars. Maybe he was thinking of himself. Or he could have been playing with us, thinking two dumb coppers wouldn't get the point.'

'You're exceptionally bright this morning, Barney.'

'Must be the thought of escaping to Italy, all that sun, sand and senoritas.'

'Isn't that Spain?'

'Same difference,' Cantelli joked. 'It's all abroad. Nice place.'

'Spain?'

'No, Oxley's house.' Cantelli pulled up in front of a large period property set back off the road. 'Do you think we should use the tradesmen's entrance?' He turned into a sweeping driveway, where a Bentley was parked in front of the portico entrance.

'No, let's be bold and go for the front door.'

CHAPTER TWENTY

They were shown into a large, airy drawing room with two long sash windows overlooking the gardens at the front of the house. Oxley invited them to sit in the opulent room furnished in a modern style that seemed to blend with rather than contradict the age and elegance of the Thomas Ellis Owen house. Seeing Cantelli gazing at the paintings, Oxley said, 'My wife likes challenging modern art. My taste runs to the more traditional scenes displayed in the hall. We have an arrangement — I get to choose what goes up in the hall, my study, bedroom and dressing room, and my wife gets the rest.'

'You must have an awful lot of paintings,' Cantelli replied.

'We do. Not all of them valuable and some are small.'

Horton thought that looking at the house, and what he'd seen of its contents and the car outside, Oxley had indeed sold his air freight business for 'an obscene amount of money', as he had said in the pub on Tuesday evening.

'Do you have children or grandchildren?' Cantelli asked.

'No. Why do you ask?'

'Just wondered if your wife also chooses their paintings or if they get to choose or draw their own.'

He laughed. 'My wife would shudder at the thought of childish scribbles on the walls.'

'I don't know, some modern art looks much like kids' stuff, in fact some of the kids' stuff is better.' Cantelli didn't actually nod at any particular painting on the wall, and neither did his eyes swivel to them, but Oxley knew very well which ones he meant.

His lips twitched as though in a smile but there was a hardness in his eyes that Bampton's had lacked. Of the two men, Horton thought Oxley far more capable of personally inflicting violence or commissioning it than Bampton, although he might not have the heavies at his disposal to do his bidding. But Horton silently corrected himself — he didn't know that for certain. Neither did he know that this display of wealth had all come from the legitimate sale of Oxley's business. Oxley's motive for switching the paintings? The same as Bampton's. Oxley had denied having any Ellwoods in his collection and Bampton had confirmed that, but Oxley could be lying, and how would Bampton know what Oxley had and didn't have?

'So, what can I do for you? I thought I told you everything the other night, Andy.'

'You probably did.' Horton took the seat indicated, again feeling that prickle of irritation at the use of his first name. 'But there are one or two new developments that mean I need to check a few things with you, Damien.' Horton looked for a reaction as he reciprocated the relaxation of formal address. He thought he detected a slight narrowing of nostrils which could have indicated annoyance. On the other hand, perhaps Oxley had an itch. 'First, I need to clarify when you were last in Julian's gallery.' Might as well carry on being informal.

'I told you that while we were having a drink but I'll repeat it.' He smiled, but no hint of it reached those cold grey eyes. 'It was Thursday the twenty-second of April. I also mentioned that Guy Bampton was there.'

'Yes, so he said.'

Oxley's jaw tightened just perceptibly. He clearly didn't like having been checked up on.

'Mr Bampton also told us that he recognized the Michael Ellwood paintings. Did he mention them to you or Julian?'

'No. I knew nothing about them until you and Steve told me in the pub the other night.'

Cantelli chipped in, 'But if you'd known about them, you'd have been keen to buy them.'

'Not if Bampton was after them.'

Cantelli looked bewildered. 'Because you don't think he has taste and you wouldn't want to be seen going after the same style of art, or because he would outbid you?' he asked with studied innocence.

Oxley's chin came up and he crossed his legs. 'He would certainly outbid me, Sergeant Cantelli, I'd make sure of that. I'd have fun pushing up the price at an auction, if it came to that, but as these Ellwoods are fakes, it won't.'

'You've done that in the past?' Cantelli again, pencil poised and with that slightly dumb expression that Horton knew so well, and which often fooled people. It did Oxley, who gave a patronizing smile.

'It's all part of the game, Sergeant.'

'Sounds a bit wacky to me, but each to his own, sir. I guess the artist doesn't mind because he gets more money and so too does the gallery owner.'

'And Maurice Linden, Ellwood's agent. He wins whichever way it goes and whoever sells the painting.'

Was there a slightly more acidic tone to the man's already brittle voice? Horton wondered. Had Oxley and Linden connived in the past to push up prices, with Linden giving Oxley a cut? It might not be much, it depended on how high the price went, though there was a lot of money sloshing around here. Bampton had said Oxley was tight-fisted. Mean men liked to hold on to their money and make more of it in all sorts of ways, sometimes even small amounts that seemed hardly worth it, but Oxley had freely admitted it was fun of a malicious kind, which he obviously revelled in.

'Linden is a very shrewd man,' Oxley said.

'By that you mean dishonest?' asked Horton.

'Depends how you define dishonest, Andy. He has an eye for a deal and is a tough negotiator.'

'Isn't that an agent's job, to get the best for his client?'

'And for himself. He has some powerful connections.'

'As in?' asked Cantelli.

'He mixes with chief executives of large corporates who want art for their boardrooms, politicians, government officials, art connoisseurs, galleries.'

'Again, all part of an agent's job,' said Horton. 'Maurice Linden has to make sure he is in with the right people. How did you meet him? Was it when you worked as an airline pilot?' Horton wasn't quite sure why he had asked that, maybe as an attempt to put Oxley in his place.

'There's no call for art on an aeroplane, and I wasn't in the boardroom,' Oxley replied. 'I met Linden shortly after I started up my own air freight business in 1993. One of our specialisms was the transportation of art, artefacts, antiques and other valuables.'

Was it indeed? Nothing suspicious in that, Horton told himself, except with Oxley he didn't want to believe that. The man's toxic personality was rubbing off on him. He took a silent breath and urged himself to keep an open mind, except that from the start he hadn't liked or trusted the man sitting there in his immaculate clothes in his expensive, tastefully decorated and furnished house with his haughty, vindictive, teasing manner.

Cantelli's voice broke through Horton's thoughts. 'Not your average online shopping stuff then.'

'Hardly, Sergeant. We dealt with many of Linden's clients' artworks, and that included flying Ellwood's paintings.'

'Where to?' Cantelli again.

'Europe, America, South Africa.'

'So Linden helped you kick-start the business.'

'No, we already had an enviable reputation, which was why *he* chose to do business with *us*.'

'We?'

'My partner and I, Dave Middleham. He'd previously worked for an air transport company along similar lines. He had the connections that helped us get started. He's long since gone. Heart attack on his fifty-fifth birthday. I sold the business soon afterwards. Didn't want to end up the same way.'

'Can't say I blame you, all that stress,' Cantelli said. 'What do you do now, sir?'

'I go sailing and I collect art,' Oxley said. He uncrossed his legs and looked pointedly at the clock as it chimed eleven.

Horton said, 'When did you last speak to Julian?'

'Monday evening to make arrangements for the painting for my wife's birthday to be delivered on Saturday morning. I tried him again on Wednesday but got no reply and he's not returned my messages.'

'Have you paid for it?'

'Of course.' Oxley looked baffled.

'Electronically?'

'Yes.' Now he looked concerned. He crossed and uncrossed his legs. 'Why the questions?'

'Can I ask how much?'

'I can't see what business that is of yours. However, it was £875, if you must know.'

Cantelli pressed heavily on his notepad.

Before Horton could break the news about Anther being missing, a woman's voice called out from the hall. 'Damien, whose is that disgusting battered old Ford in front of our house? Oh!' She drew up sharply, a short, heavy-bosomed woman with a great deal of suntanned cleavage on show. She was flashily dressed, in her early fifties, with highlighted fair hair in a shoulder-length bob and enough make-up to delight the shareholders of the cosmetic companies. Her treacle-coloured eyes narrowed and her lipstick covered mouth hardened as she weighed up her visitors.

Horton and Cantelli both rose. Cantelli said solemnly, 'I'm afraid it's mine.'

'These are police officers,' Oxley announced as though, Horton thought, they had come to sweep the chimneys.

'Police! What have you done, Damien? Parked the Bentley where you shouldn't have?' she taunted, not at them, but at Oxley.

He didn't react. Neither did he bother rising. 'This is my wife, Leanne.'

Horton wondered if he wanted to add, 'unfortunately'. On initial impression she seemed as acerbic and scornful as her husband. Perhaps their marriage had made them like that, or perhaps they had originally been drawn to each other because they were of the same ilk.

'I told you that Anther's gallery has been robbed,' Oxley said curtly, as she crossed the room on heels so high that she was tilting forward.

'Did you? I wasn't paying much attention,' she answered with studied vagueness as though goading her husband. Her bracelets jangled as she waved an arm.

'Some original paintings by Michael Ellwood have been switched for forgeries.'

'Poor old Julian, he must be in a right state.' There was a mocking tone in her voice and Horton didn't miss the stress on the word 'old'. Neither did her husband and he was about the same age as Anther. 'They can't be very good forgeries if Anther spotted the switch.' She sat and crossed her stubby legs. Her mobile phone sounded. She glanced but didn't answer it, and waved them back to their seats.

Oxley said, 'Julian didn't spot it. Ellwood's daughter did.'

'Well, she should know.'

'Have you met her, Mrs Oxley?' asked Horton.

'Me? No, why should I have?'

'Do you visit Mr Anther's gallery with your husband?'

'Occasionally. I certainly didn't switch his paintings,' she joked.

No one laughed, or smiled, which caused her brow to pucker. Horton thought it was time he tossed in his grenade and watched for a reaction. 'Mr Anther is missing.'

It took a moment for it to sink in with both the Oxleys. She looked nonplussed then disinterested, while Oxley was clearly taken aback. 'You mean he's run off?' he said with something akin to horror. Probably thinking about the money he'd handed over for that painting, thought Horton.

'That's what we're trying to establish.'

'But you must have some idea, or some lead?' Oxley insisted. Leanne Oxley was now looking amused.

'Do you know of anyone he might have gone to? Any friends or family?' Horton asked, just as he had Bampton.

'Hardly. We're not on those terms.'

'Mrs Oxley?'

'Don't look at me. I've no idea.'

Cantelli said, 'Did he seem depressed when you last spoke to him, Mr Oxley?'

'No. What are you doing about it?' he demanded.

'This,' replied Horton. 'Talking to his clients, and others.'

'Have you checked his bank account?' Oxley snapped.

'Not yet, but we will if we need to. We've put out an alert for his car.'

'He could be miles away by now,' Oxley scoffed, rising and striding to the fireplace. He spun round. 'Did he take his passport?'

'No. There is the chance that Mr Anther might have been so upset over what has happened that he's taken his life.'

Oxley sniffed. Leanne studied her manicured and polished nails. They didn't seem to care. Horton could see that Oxley's main concern was for his money and painting.

'Doesn't Linden know where Anther is?' Oxley said tetchily.

Horton noted that Julian had now become Anther, as though Oxley was already disassociating himself from the gallery owner. He also noted that Oxley had always referred to Linden by his surname. He rose. 'We'll keep you informed, but if either of you hear from Julian Anther, or remember anything that might help us locate him, could you get in touch with Sergeant Cantelli?'

Cantelli put away his notepad and handed across his business card, which Oxley took without glancing at it. 'I'll show you out.'

On the threshold he said, 'The painting I bought and paid for is lawfully mine. The money was cleared through the bank. I want it delivered as arranged on Saturday, and don't say I can't because I certainly can.'

Horton answered. 'We don't have keys to the gallery.'

'But you've already been there. You must have been to discover Anther's gone, so one of your constables can meet me and Macey there tomorrow morning at eleven sharp to open it up or force an entry or whatever you need to do, and he or she can stand over us as I take that painting, for which I can show you the receipt. I have every right to get my property.'

'I'll need to get it cleared with my boss,' said Horton. He didn't, but it was a good enough exit line. He knew what Oxley would do next and said as much to Cantelli.

'He'll call Uckfield.'

'Will the Super let him have access to the gallery?'

'He's off sick. But yes, he will.'

Cantelli smiled and popped a fresh piece of chewing gum in his mouth. He seemed reluctant to get in the car. 'Wonder if they're watching us,' he said, rubbing an imaginary speck of dirt from the windscreen. 'Battered indeed. This Ford's only eleven years old.'

'Mind how you reverse, Barney, don't want you going into Mrs Oxley's Porsche.'

Cantelli took his time and went within an inch of the bonnet before driving off. 'Oxley could have the same motive for switching those paintings as Bampton. He doesn't like Bampton much, does he? Although the feeling seems to be mutual, and I don't think it's because of some paintings. I reckon there's something in their background that has caused the rivalry. Could be woman trouble. There's no love lost between Leanne and her husband. I'd say she can't stand him. Maybe she had an affair with Bampton. But even if she did,

185

and Bampton and Oxley hate each other's guts, I can't see that it has much, if anything, to do with switching the paintings. Unless Leanne did it as a joke or to get back at them. No, I think that's a wild card too,' Cantelli said smiling. 'How about stopping along the seafront for lunch? You can buy a roll and I can eat my sandwiches as we chew it over.'

While they had lunch, Horton called Felice hoping she'd have some news on the forgeries. He was also curious as to why she had told Bampton yesterday about Anther's disappearance. If she didn't answer, he could telephone Jonathan Reed direct at Sotheby's and ask him for his initial findings.

She answered almost immediately and anxiously. 'Is there any news about Julian?'

'No, and Noel Catmore's missing.'

'Oh! Is it to do with the paintings?' she asked, concern in her voice. 'Sorry, I guess that was a stupid question.'

'Not necessarily, the two could be unconnected.'

'Mr Catmore didn't strike me as an art connoisseur. I admit I've only met him once, but I can't see him and Julian being involved in any kind of scam.'

Horton heard an announcement in the background. It sounded as though Felice was at a railway station.

'Have you found Aunt Dorothy or any reference to her?' Felice asked.

'We're hoping Nicola Bolton will have something to report on Monday. Has Jonathan discovered anything on the paintings?'

'He's sending over his initial report to you this morning. I'm on my way back to the island. My father's taken a turn for the worse.'

'I'm sorry to hear that.' It accounted for the anxiety in her voice and, judging by her tone and the background noise, she was making her way down the platform to the railway carriage.

'I hope you don't mind but Jonathan told me last night what he's discovered. I thought I might be able to add to it. I know he should have told you first but—'

'I'll just put this on loudspeaker, Sergeant Cantelli's with me. Go on.'

'The analysis of the pigments and the material suggests all three paintings were executed at the same time, in the mid-1970s to mid-1980s.'

'When your father was painting in Paris,' Horton said, his mind turning this over. This was throwing up a few ideas, speculations and questions, which he shelved as she continued.

'Yes. Jonathan's examined the brushstrokes and use of colour and other techniques and he's certain they were all executed by the same painter. However, trying to identify the artist is difficult, practically impossible. He doesn't recognize it as the work of any known forgers. That doesn't mean to say that the forger is not currently forging other paintings, just that he or she hasn't been caught. Whoever did it could have given up painting, either forgeries or artwork altogether. He or she could be dead.'

Horton expressed one of the ideas that had occurred to him. 'In order to imitate your father's style and work during that period when he was living and working in France means that the forger must have known him well, because, as you and Linden both said, your father wasn't selling many paintings then. He wasn't known in the art world and there would have been no financial incentive for anyone to copy him. So why would someone have done so?'

There was a pause. He caught the sound of people in the background. 'Sorry, just boarded the train. For fun? Or possibly on spec that the future might be bright for my father so the forgeries could have been an investment.'

A pretty far-sighted one, thought Horton. For fun? Maybe. Perhaps the forger had copied many artists and somehow the Ellwoods had found their way to Dorothy.

'Why did you tell Guy Bampton that Julian was missing?'

'Did I? Yes, I did. Wasn't I meant to? It came up in conversation. He said he had seen that Julian had some of my father's paintings in the gallery and he was keen to buy them, only he couldn't get hold of him. He asked if he could have first offer on them. He was very generous, practically hinting I could name my own price. I said there had been a hitch. He asked me what and I told him.'

'How did he take the news?'

'He was stunned. He could have sworn they were genuine, although he admitted he hadn't examined them closely.'

'You could sell him the one you have in your gallery in Cowes.'

'I've withdrawn it.'

'Why?' Horton asked, puzzled.

There was a moment's hesitation. 'It doesn't seem right to sell it with Dad being so ill. But I might have to.'

'Your father's finances are none too healthy?' he asked, picking up on the sorrow and hesitancy in her voice, throwing Cantelli a look. He had already suggested that it might be the case.

'They're not. We rent the house from the National Trust, and we have no other assets. My father hasn't painted for three years.'

'Doesn't he have any savings?' Cantelli asked.

'No. Sotheby's have asked me to go back to work for them. It might be the answer if my father has to go into a nursing home. Maurice has offered to help with fees. He's a very generous man. Hospital must be torture for him, but he insists on seeing my father. They go right back to childhood. I'm not sure how I would have managed without him. I'm sorry, I didn't mean to burden you with my problems, and I apologize if I've said something I shouldn't have to Guy.'

'It's fine, Felice. Let me know how things are with your father.'

She said she would and rang off.

Cantelli said, 'I'd have thought Ellwood would have earned a lot of money over the years. He can't have spent it all.'

'Bampton said Ellwood had a drink problem — perhaps he also liked to gamble or made some unwise investments. Perhaps he'd had some hefty tax bills to pay.'

'She sounded tired and worried. Maybe there is more to her concern than her father's illness.'

'You think she's in this scam for financial reasons? But why would she call me in?'

Cantelli didn't answer but finished off his last sandwich.

Horton said, 'Because she thinks I'll be soft with her. I won't be able to see the obvious if I'm attracted to her.'

'Are you?'

'Yes, and I feel sorry for her, but that won't influence me.' He called Leney, pushing aside his feelings for Felice. He liked her. He had hoped their friendship might develop into something more but that had been before he'd taken off for France and had time to think over so many things. He told Leney they needed his services again, tomorrow morning at eleven at Anther's Art Gallery.

'I think I'll cut you a set of my skeleton keys,' Leney joked.

On their arrival back at the station Walters informed them there was no sign of a metal detector in Catmore's belongings. So the theory that he had gone treasure hunting and been taken ill or had an accident was plausible. Walters said he'd get in touch with the National Council for Metal Detecting to find out if Catmore was a member.

Bliss informed Horton there was no forensic evidence on Farrell's clothes, so they'd had to release him. She'd spoken to ACC Dean, who agreed and, out of courtesy, she'd telephoned Uckfield to tell him. The Superintendent had granted that Farrell couldn't have been involved in Spender's murder. Changed his mind then, thought Horton. He reckoned Uckfield had expressed that view with a reluctant grunt.

Bliss reported that the Préfecture de Police de Paris had no criminal record for Spender. They were currently trying to trace an address and work history for him, so far without success. No one had come forward to say they had been friends with Spender or in a relationship with him.

Horton's mobile rang as he was leaving. It was Uckfield, as Horton had expected.

'Oxley's been on to you,' Horton said. 'Bellyaching about his painting.'

'Yes. And I said he can arrange to have it collected. He'll be there at eleven and so will you and I.'

'Thinking of buying a work of art?' Horton asked, tongue-in-cheek.

'No, I'm thinking I might help clear up that investigation too.'

Horton refrained from saying Uckfield hadn't cleared up the Spender case. It would have fallen on deaf ears.

CHAPTER TWENTY-ONE

Saturday

When Horton's phone rang the next morning, just as he was leaving for Anther's gallery, his heart skipped a beat. He half-expected it to be Catherine cancelling the arrangement for Emma to spend Sunday with him — she had the knack of doing that at the last moment. But with relief he saw it was Cantelli.

'Ellen's been hard at work, most of the night I think, though she swears blind she wasn't. She's been tracing Noel Catmore via the internet and she'd like to report in. She won't tell me what she's found. Fancy a spot of lunch at Isabella's?'

Horton said he did. The seafront café was just a short distance from Anther's gallery. One o'clock should give him plenty of time to oversee Oxley collect his goods.

When Horton pulled into the gallery's backyard, Leney was already there. 'Anther's keys could have been copied,' he told Horton.

'I thought you said they hadn't been.'

'Not the ones he allowed me to examine, but he must have a spare set to his flat and to the gallery. Neither were in the safe, the most logical place for them, but then he might have lost the safe key sometime, so he kept that and his spare keys elsewhere.'

Horton cursed himself for not thinking of that before. He'd need to search the gallery and the flat, something he would do before leaving.

Leney said, 'I can search the back two rooms while you're in the gallery.'

'All right,' Horton agreed.

Leney had the rear door unlocked and open just as Uckfield arrived.

'Pity Farrell didn't confess to murdering Spender,' Uckfield said. 'Nasty manner of death with a boat hook, if you're right.' He nodded a greeting at Leney before marching through to the gallery. Sniffing and glancing slowly round he said, 'Smells expensive. This is Oxley's painting, the one he's been bitching about?' He crossed to the easel where the abstract was displayed. 'Can't think what Leanne sees in it. What's Leney doing?' Uckfield added, as a sound came from Anther's office.

'Searching for Anther's spare keys.'

'Haven't you done that already?'

'Obviously not.'

Uckfield rubbed his nose. 'Just shows how much you miss me.' He peered around at the other paintings. 'Nothing else missing I take it?' he added somewhat sarcastically.

Horton was saved from answering by a toot from the rear. He left Uckfield poking around in the gallery muttering about unearthing the spare keys. Macey's van had drawn to a halt across the entrance on account of not being able to fit into the small yard with Leney's and Uckfield's cars there along with Horton's Harley. Horton was pleased to see that with Macey was Maurice Linden. That saved him a phone call. There were a few questions he'd like to ask him.

'Roy picked me up from the railway station,' Linden explained. 'I'm on my way back over to the island for the weekend to see Michael. Sadly, he's taken a turn for the worse and it looks bad for him.'

'Felice told me. I'm very sorry to hear it.'

'I'd like to be with him. I know there's nothing I can do, but he does have moments of consciousness and I'd like him to know I'm there.'

Horton could see that Linden was genuinely upset. His well-chiselled face was even gaunter than on their first meeting and the sparkle in his eyes behind the spectacles had gone.

Linden added, 'Roy phoned me to say he'd been asked by Oxley to transport and hang the Canning this morning, so I decided to delay my sailing to the island until later. Cecil Canning is one of my artists. Not that I need to make sure Roy does his job without any bungling.' He smiled at the muscular man beside him. 'I've known Roy for many years. He's the best in the business.'

Macey inclined his head in acknowledgement of the compliment. Their conversation had taken them into the building, where Horton introduced Leney but made no comment as to why he was there. He saw the curiosity in both Linden's and Macey's eyes.

Linden continued, 'We've been discussing Julian's disappearance and we're both concerned for him.'

'Is there any news?' Macey asked.

'No. Do you have any idea of where Mr Anther might be, Mr Macey?'

'None.'

'Mr Catmore is also missing.'

Linden looked confused. 'I can't see—'

Horton interrupted. 'Don't you find it strange that both the man who brought in the two originals and the forgery and the gallery owner have gone missing?'

Linden gave a tired smile. 'I'm not a police officer. I expect you find many things strange, and are suspicious of coincidence, but it could be just that.'

They walked through to the gallery, where Horton introduced Uckfield.

'How long have you known Mr Anther?' Horton asked Macey.

'For years. We met in Paris. I worked with him at an art gallery there. Julian was in the sale room, I was in the back, and when I wasn't there, I was out delivering pictures and hanging them.'

'And this was when?'

'Towards the end of 1990. You lose track of the time. Julian left France in 1992 and I came back shortly after him. Two years was enough for me and by then I'd met Jacqueline, my wife. She wasn't French,' Macey quickly added, with a smile. 'She was in Paris on a language course. She came from Portsmouth so I came here and we got married in 1993, and I started my business. It's not completely out of character for Julian to disappear, although not so quickly that he'd leave all this behind, unless—'

'He's gone off with some valuable paintings,' furnished Uckfield, bluntly.

Macey answered. 'No. Julian would never leave this willingly.'

Horton said, 'He hasn't taken his passport.'

'He has two,' Linden replied. 'English and French. He has dual citizenship.'

Horton hadn't found a French passport. 'Does he have an address in France?'

'I don't know. He's never mentioned it to me.'

'Or to me,' Macey added.

Horton was prevented from asking further questions by the gallery bell. He opened the door to admit Oxley, who did a double take.

'I didn't realize it took so many men to oversee the removal of one painting,' he quipped. 'I take it that nothing more has occurred to prevent me from collecting it?'

Uckfield jovially answered. 'Don't mind us, Damien. Inspector Horton is just here to look over the place and try and find out where Julian Anther's gone.'

'And you, Linden?' Oxley asked somewhat sourly.

'On my way over to the Isle of Wight to spend some time with Michael. I stopped off to make sure you're perfectly happy with Cecil's work.'

'Why? It's not a forgery, is it?'

Linden smiled at the joke, but it never touched his eyes. 'Not as far as I know.'

'I thought Ellwood was in hospital.'

'He is. I'll give you a hand, Roy.' Linden left with Macey to retrieve the packaging material from the van.

It was clear to Horton that Linden had no time for Oxley. He wondered who had. He asked Oxley if he had lived in France.

'Why on earth do you wish to know that?'

'Have you?' Horton repeated.

Oxley threw Uckfield a glance, but Uckfield was doing his best blank expression.

After a moment Oxley answered crisply, 'Yes, I have lived in France. When I say "lived", I have a property there. Why?'

'How long have you owned it?'

'Ten years. I can't see what this has got to do with you.'

'Neither can I,' said Uckfield glowering at Horton, but he knew it was an act.

'Did you or Mrs Oxley live in France in the 1980s?' Horton persisted.

'Hardly. I was flying and Leanne was an air hostess,' Oxley snapped.

'Is there anyone at your French property at the moment?'

Oxley looked from Horton to Uckfield and back again. 'No, and if you're implying that Anther has gone there—'

'Has he?'

'Of course not. Don't be ridiculous, Inspector.'

Horton noted his first name had been dropped. Good. That suited him fine. 'Perhaps we could have your French address.'

'No, you cannot. Now, I'd like to get on,' he snapped, as Macey returned with some packaging. Linden wasn't with him.

Horton excused himself, leaving Uckfield to mollify Oxley and Macey to see to the large abstract. Leney shook his head to indicate he'd had no joy in finding any keys. Horton doubted they could be anywhere in the gallery. He said he'd like the flat door opened, if Leney could spare the time. He could. They'd wait until Oxley and the others were off the premises though and could lock up the gallery.

Linden was on the telephone. He rang off when he saw Horton.

'Damien Oxley is not the easiest of men or clients,' Linden said with a sad smile. 'But I shouldn't grumble, he's spent a fair bit of money on the artists I represent and therefore he pays part of my salary. That's probably what irritates him. Not that it comes out of his pocket but the artists'. Oxley thinks I inflate the prices.'

'Do you?'

'Sometimes.' He grinned. Horton thought how it made him look less haggard.

'Did you know that Michael Ellwood is in financial straits? Felice has told me,' Horton said.

'Yes. I only recently discovered that. I obviously know he hasn't been painting since the accident. I tried to encourage him, but he's been suffering from depression.'

'He must have earned a great deal of money in his career. How come he's got through it?'

'You mean does he gamble or drink it away?'

Horton recalled the road accident report. 'He was found with well over the alcohol limit in his bloodstream.'

'Sadly, yes. He, like many artists, probably found that a drink or two released the creative juices. Then it became that he couldn't paint without having a drink, and if he painted in the morning, then out would come the wine or whisky and soon it became an all-day drinking session. He probably told himself that he could stop at any time. Then he found that the drink impaired his artistic ability and he stopped painting altogether.'

'And he went out on his motorbike to end his life?'

'I'm not sure if he was thinking rationally at that stage, probably not. He obviously stopped drinking while in hospital but when he came out, he started up again, trying to keep it from Felice. It's the results of heavy drinking that ails him now rather than the result of his physical injuries from the accident.'

As Bampton had told them.

'He'll get his wish to end it all,' Linden said sorrowfully. 'I wish I could help him or could have helped him. I offered to pay for him to go into a clinic to dry out, but he stubbornly refused.'

Horton considered this. 'Would drink alone have got through Michael's savings?'

'He drank expensively. And Michael was hopeless with money. Both I and his accountant tried to tell him but he wouldn't listen. He stopped answering his phone and emails. I went over to the island in person to plead with him but to no avail. He also had some heavy tax bills to pay and as he had stopped painting, he therefore stopped selling. His income dried up. It's a crying shame the two original paintings have been swapped for forgeries because their sale would have helped Felice and Michael — if he pulls through, but I doubt he will.'

'Sotheby's believe the forgeries were executed between the mid-seventies and eighties, when Michael was living in Europe, firstly Italy and then Paris. Does that suggest anyone to you?'

Linden shook his grey head. 'No. I wasn't Michael's agent then.'

Macey came out carrying the painting carefully wrapped.

Linden said, 'I'd better make sure Oxley's happy, or as happy as that man can ever be. If you need me over the weekend, Inspector, or if you hear any news about Julian, will you let me know? I'll be on the island with Felice. You have my number.' Linden turned to Macey. 'I'll walk over to the hovercraft. Hope all goes well with the hanging.'

'So do I. Let's hope Mrs Oxley likes her birthday present.' Macey grimaced and climbed into the van.

Horton turned back inside, where Linden was taking his leave of Oxley, who was also keen to get home in time to give Macey instructions for the picture hanging. As they left, Leney entered. 'The flat door is open.'

Horton and Uckfield made their way towards it while Leney secured the gallery before following them.

'Why did you ask Oxley about living in France?' Uckfield said, as they climbed the stairs.

'It seems to be cropping up rather frequently, not only in relation to this but to Spender. It's likely he lived in France and probably in Paris for a while.'

'You can't think Oxley and Spender are connected?' Uckfield said incredulously as they came out on the landing.

'No.' But perhaps they were. Could Oxley be Spender's blackmail victim? Had Spender overheard Oxley talking to someone and saying something incriminating when he had been collecting his rubbish? The same went for Anther. Was his gallery and Oxley's house on Spender's round? Could Anther or Oxley have killed Spender?

'A lot of people live in France,' Uckfield grunted. 'I'll do the bedroom and bathroom. Leney, you take the kitchen. Andy, the sitting room.'

Horton didn't elaborate. Ideas were running through his mind but were cut short when within what seemed just a couple of minutes, Leney cried out, 'Eureka!'

Horton went onto the landing, with Uckfield a few seconds behind him, where Leney was flourishing a set of four keys.

'Where did you find them?' Horton asked.

'In a pot at the back of the fridge.'

'What made you look there?'

'First place I usually check.'

'Isn't it where those suffering from dementia usually put their keys?'

'Don't know, haven't got there — yet. This is obviously a spare car key,' Leney said. 'These are the keys to the gallery. These are to this flat. And this one—'

But Leney didn't need to say more because Horton was staring at a duplicate of the key he'd found under Spender's pillow.

CHAPTER TWENTY-TWO

'The keys prove Spender and Anther are connected. Anther must have been Spender's latest blackmail victim. Anther killed Spender and then took off,' Horton insisted when he and Uckfield were sitting in Isabella's café on the seafront. Cantelli and Ellen weren't due for another thirty minutes and Uckfield said he had to get home for one o'clock as Alison had invited her parents for lunch.

The café was busy but their table in the corner was relatively private, most of the customers being outside on the patio taking in the May sunshine and watching the numerous leisure craft on the Solent. The promenade was teeming with strollers, dog walkers and joggers in the bright but blustery day. Horton hoped for the same weather tomorrow. 'Spender must have been collecting the bin from the yard when he overheard Anther talking about switching the paintings and threatened to expose him.'

'But that doesn't explain the key,' Uckfield stressed. 'Why would both Anther and Spender have the same key?'

Horton sat back and swallowed some coffee. It was a question that had bugged him on the way to the café. 'If it's not blackmail, then the key must be to a lock-up where stolen paintings are stashed, not stolen marine equipment as I thought.'

But Uckfield was shaking his head. 'If they'd been stealing works of art, the owners would have been all over us like a rash. And why would Spender have access to such a lock-up? He can hardly be the fence. He wouldn't have the contacts, Anther would. It could be the key to their love nest. Anther and Spender are, or were, lovers. Anther didn't want lover boy in his flat, and he certainly wasn't going to go to Spender's grotty hole for a bit of the other, so they had another place.'

'I just can't see Anther choosing Spender as a lover,' Horton said, although something was tugging at the back of his mind.

Uckfield ploughed on. 'Spender was blackmailing Anther over his sexual proclivities and Anther had had enough. He called Spender last Saturday night and said he wanted to meet up. Spender says, "I'm on my boat about to steal gulls' eggs with a mate, can't it wait?" Anther says no it can't. Spender says, "OK I'll ditch him and meet you on the pontoon next to Southsea Marina." Anther rams the boat hook into Spender's chest, ditches the body overboard and lets the boat drift. When you show up asking questions about this art theft, Anther gets scared that you'll discover his secret, takes his French passport and scuttles over to the continent.'

Horton had to admit that it fitted. He swallowed his coffee. 'We've nothing to say that either Spender or Anther are homosexual.'

'Doesn't mean they aren't.'

'Anther doesn't look as though he'd have the strength to get Spender into the cockpit and toss his body in the water.'

'Rage and fear were driving him. Better check out his blood group. He could be the AB negative we're looking for. Pity we haven't got an address to go with the keys.' Uckfield had given Leney instructions to chase up the manufacturers sharpish on Monday, when Uckfield would also get uniformed officers to go through Anther's apartment and gallery with a fine-tooth comb for any paperwork relating to a possible French address and the location of premises that matched the key. They'd also bag up all his clothes and shoes for forensic examination, as well as revisit every scrap of information on both the Spender case and the art fraud.

Uckfield continued, 'I'll get Trueman to check with the Border Agency on Monday to find out if Anther has left the country. And Trueman and the team can ascertain if Anther bought an airline ticket or caught the ferry or Eurostar to France. His car might be registered in one of the terminal car parks. We'll contact the Paris police to see what they can get on Anther, past and present.'

'Bliss has already asked them to check out Spender.'

'Then I'll leave her to liaise over Anther. Talk to Spender's colleagues again, find out if any of them have ever heard Spender mention Anther.'

'Where does this leave us with Noel Catmore's disappearance?'

Uckfield downed the rest of his coffee. 'Maybe he's also taken off for France unless Anther's disposed of him too. Either that or the poor sod is lying injured or dead with his metal detector by his side.' He rose. 'Let's see what we get on Monday.'

After Uckfield had left, Horton called Maurice Linden. He was expecting his voicemail so was pleased when Linden answered.

'Can I ask, Mr Linden, is Julian Anther homosexual?'

There was a moment's pause. Was that small hesitation because Linden wasn't sure or because he didn't wish to answer?

'Not that I'm aware of — he's never mentioned it, but then there's no reason why he should. I've never known him have a relationship, but our dealings are professional. Why do you ask?'

'I wondered if he might have been in a relationship with a Neil Spender, the man who is missing from his boat. We've found something in Mr Anther's flat that connects the two men.'

'Really! What? Or can't you say, police business and all that?'

Horton caught the sound of voices in the background. He couldn't make them out and had no need to. 'Did Mr Anther have another property in or around Portsmouth?'

'Not as far as I know.'

Horton rang off after thanking Linden for his help, knowing he was curious to ascertain just what they had found. He fetched another coffee and ordered a baguette, exchanging news with Isabella about her family, in particular Johnnie Oslow, her son, who not long ago Cantelli and he had to locate after he'd gone missing from the racing yacht team at the International Cowes Sailing Regatta during Cowes Week. It had been touch-and-go whether they would find him alive. Horton was glad to hear that Johnnie was having a great deal of success racing sailing yachts in America.

Into Horton's head came Harriet Ames's fair, troubled face because she had been sailing during that particular Cowes Week, and it had been that week he'd met Richard Ames for the first time and had become convinced the peer had been involved with Jennifer's disappearance. He'd been right, as it turned out. There was still no news on Ames's yacht and neither Ducale nor Harriet had been in touch with him. Where was Harriet now? Was she sailing in the Solent? Was she on the Isle of Wight at her family's substantial summer house? He could see its location from here, though he couldn't see the property as it bordered an isolated bay. Or was Harriet back at work at The Hague, immersing herself in a case while trying to push aside thoughts of her missing father?

Horton knew that he would have to speak to her again. He couldn't leave it hanging in the air — they might be called upon to work together in the future. Equally, he knew he could never tell her the truth.

The café was doing a brisk trade, and Isabella and her three assistants were rushed off their feet. As Horton bit into his baguette, he looked up to see Cantelli enter with a slender girl dressed fashionably in jeans and a tight-fitting T-shirt showing a slim bare midriff. Her long dark hair was sleek and she was beautifully and carefully made-up. She was carrying a rucksack. He watched as they exchanged greetings and kisses with Isabella, who gestured them into their seats saying she would bring over their order.

Horton rose as they drew near and addressed Ellen. 'It's good of you to come.'

'That's OK. It's about time Dad bought me lunch,' she said brightly with a confidence that surprised Horton. He thought how much she had matured in the last eighteen months. Barney had had a bit of trouble with her then. She had told her parents she was staying overnight with a school friend when she was instead going to a party. That friend and others, Ellen had admitted to her mother and father, had taken drugs but she, scared, had ducked out and got away as soon as she could and run home, for which Barney and Charlotte had been profoundly grateful. Since then, Ellen had focused on her studies, leaving school with a clutch of qualifications at the highest grade and those so-called friends far behind. She seemed to have found her forte in computers.

Cantelli said, 'Well, as you're only having a salad.'

'Got to keep an eye on the figure and you'd do well to remember that,' she jibed at Cantelli, whose wiry frame was by no stretch of the imagination overweight. 'Aunt Isabella's baguettes are huge. It's like eating a loaf of bread with everything in the kitchen stuffed inside it.'

Horton eyed the three quarters remaining of his. 'She's right.'

'You wait until you see what she gives Dad. She thinks everyone needs feeding up.' Ellen withdrew a slim computer from her rucksack. To Horton she said, 'I thought you'd like to see what I've found.'

'I would, but eat your salad first.'

'When it comes.'

Horton could see that she was keen to begin. He exchanged a glance with Cantelli, who slightly raised his eyebrows as his daughter's long nail-varnished fingers slid over the mousepad and screen with an expertise that made Horton feel positively Neolithic.

'I started by looking at the metal-detecting sites, because Dad said Catmore might be an enthusiast. And he's there on two website forums. See?' She swivelled the screen around to show Horton.

'There's no photograph and that's not his name.'

'Isn't it?' she posed smugly.

He listened, intrigued, and Cantelli looked fit to burst with curiosity.

'I had to search through the forums to find someone who talked about metal-detecting in the local area, that being Portsmouth and Portchester, because of the Roman castle there. There's also Hayling Island, where there are remains of two Roman villas, both covered with earth. Then there are the beaches of Hayling and Portsmouth, which are popular areas for metal detectorists.'

Horton was impressed with Ellen's diligence and intelligence. She was prevented from further explanation by the arrival of their drinks, milkshake for Ellen and tea for Cantelli.

'Your food order's just coming,' Isabella said.

Ellen took a long sip of her milkshake. 'I found several men and two women in those areas chatting about their finds, nothing exciting. Obviously, I discounted the women, although there's nothing to stop him from pretending to be one online.'

Horton thought Ellen was sounding more like a police officer with every remark.

'I concentrated on the men. There were two with funny names, so I looked them up and found him. Ezui. That's your man,' she declared triumphantly as her salad and Cantelli's baguette arrived. 'And I'll tell you why,' she added once the waitress had left. Horton could see she was glowing with pride, so too was her dad, but he was also looking puzzled.

Reading Horton's mind Cantelli said, 'This is news to me, she wouldn't tell me. Said she had to explain it to us both at the same time.'

'Fair enough. Go on, Ellen.'

'When I looked up "Ezui", I found that in the time of Edward the Confessor, a Saxon called Ezui held the manor of — guess where?'

Cantelli shook his head.

'I give in,' said Horton.

'Catmore!' She pushed her hand through her hair and a broad smile lit her young face.

'My God, Barney, we need her on the force.'

'Sorry, I'm spoken for. I'm going to work for GCHQ.'

'Since when?' Cantelli's jaw dropped.

'We had this man come to talk to us at college and my tutor singled me out to meet him.'

'He really is from GCHQ?' Cantelli said, worried.

'Of course. I shall be completing my course and then applying to be sponsored by them for further study.'

'You never told me or your mother this.'

She rolled her eyes at her father as though he was dim. 'No, because I've only just heard from them that they would like me. It's OK, Dad, you'll get to see all the papers and confirm it's legit and not a scam. I know scams when I see them, even if they are very, very good. And this is the real stuff.'

Horton said, 'Congratulations. Sounds like a fantastic opportunity.'

'Dad?'

'Yeah, well, as long as it's legit and your mother approves.'

'She will and I'll be eighteen by then anyway.' She didn't need to add, 'So you won't be able to stop me.' Horton knew that Cantelli would be right on to this man at GCHQ and the tutor of the college to confirm the offer's authenticity as soon as he got home.

Cantelli bit into his baguette and Ellen took a mouthful of salad before continuing in a very businesslike manner, only just suppressing her excitement at what she'd discovered.

'The manor of Ezui was destroyed in the Norman Conquest. Catmore is a small village in West Berkshire. And because of its history Ezui is an ideal name for your man,

Catmore, to adopt. Reading his entries on his forum, I discovered he lives in Portsmouth, used to be a coach driver, went on metal-detecting forays and is mainly active around the local area. I then found him on other social media websites and history website forums, not only registered as Ezui, but also as Wild-Cat Lake, it's Old English for Catmore.'

Horton said, 'And this from a man who told us he didn't look up the name Michael Ellwood on the internet because he didn't bother with all of that.'

'Obviously a lie,' said Ellen. 'If I can get hold of his IP address — Internet Provider—' she explained, assuming they were dim — 'I could tell you a lot more about the sites he's visited and who he's communicated with, although it's not legal because he's an individual rather than a business, but the police could probably do it with the right authorization. If I have a bit more time, I could probably locate it anyway.'

Cantelli said, 'I think what you've already discovered is enough. We can check that out.'

Horton said, 'Catmore lied about not using the internet, and he probably lied about not knowing what the paintings were worth, having looked up the artist's name on the website. The passer-by might also be a lie, or it could have been Spender.'

'Eh?'

Horton swiftly told him about finding the key in Anther's flat but no more because of Ellen's presence. 'Does he say where he's going metal-detecting next and when, Ellen?'

'His most recent comment on the forum, on Monday, says he's off to Hayling Island detecting around The Kench.'

That area was at the south-western end of the island and its U-shaped shore faced onto Langstone Harbour. It was close to the Hayling Island ferry to Portsmouth and the harbour master's office. Heading eastwards from the ferry there were a small number of detached houses, then a group of individually owned holiday chalets, some houseboats facing onto the harbour before the shore curved around past the adult holiday camp. Several large properties hugged the shore farther north, some with pontoons.

'I'll take a trip over to Hayling Island and see if Catmore's car is parked near The Kench. You've been a great help,' Horton said to Ellen.

'It was fun. I'll let Dad know if I find anything more.'

Cantelli eyed her daggers. 'You'll take the afternoon off. We're going for a walk along the seafront.'

She didn't seem too pleased about that. Horton left them and took a leisurely ride on his Harley north out of Portsmouth and along the dual carriageway heading east, before turning south and across the bridge onto the small semi-rural Hayling Island. The traffic was heavy with people making for the beach, but he was able to weave in and out of the queue. After arriving opposite the funfair, he turned west towards the Hayling ferry and halted outside a derelict house, which in all his memory had never been anything but derelict and was rumoured to be owned by the Duke of Norfolk. There looked to be no way into it nor the grounds, not unless you wanted to be scratched to death by brambles. A little further on was The Kench.

He rode on and pulled into the car park by the Ferry Boat Inn bordering the harbour entrance. The car park was packed, but there was no sign of Catmore's Ford Fiesta, and neither was it in the public car park that ran adjacent to the shore. Perhaps Catmore had put this location out on the forum as a decoy to deter others from exploring where he had really unearthed his treasure. Or perhaps he had taken off, as Uckfield had suggested.

Horton rode back towards The Kench, where he drew to a halt. He looked across the expanse of Langstone Harbour. His mind turned to thoughts of Spender and his abandoned boat to the far north of the harbour. If Farrell was telling the truth — and Horton believed he was — then how far out of the harbour had Spender got before he'd received the telephone call? Farrell said it was just after they had boarded the boat. So, the real question was how far had Spender gone after Farrell left? Not so far for the boat to have drifted back up the harbour on the incoming tide and wind, unless his killer had piloted it. But how would the killer have got off the boat? The tender had been taken by Farrell.

Who had Spender met? Was it Anther? Ruth Bowen's words seemed to scotch that for Horton — he couldn't see Anther carrying Spender in a fireman's lift. The blood had congealed in the cabin, indicating that the body had lain there for a while before being moved and, as he and Cantelli had discussed, there was the possibility of another person having come on board and disposed of the body, someone strong.

Horton's eyes swept to the left and up along the eastern shores of Portsmouth, where Farrell had abandoned Spender's tender. He could see the incinerator chimney, close to where Spender worked for Jeplie and where Bampton's office was. Bampton was a very strong man. Would he have gone to Anther's aid? Possibly, if he had been promised the original Ellwood paintings as payment. And there was somewhere he could have met Anther on Spender's boat, and it wasn't Southsea.

Horton made his way off the island as quickly as the speed limit and traffic would allow until he was on the dual carriageway heading south along Portsmouth's eastern shore. There, opposite the public open space and golf course, he pulled into a car park overlooking the harbour and silenced the Harley.

Alighting, he walked out onto a square of concrete that was Salterns Lake Quay. At mid and low tides nothing could moor up here because nothing could reach the quay except seagulls and other birds, but at high water, like now, it was perfectly accessible. It was also deserted because there wasn't anything for a sailor to moor up here for — no facilities, no nightlife, not even peace and quiet with the roar of the traffic on the busy dual carriageway behind him. There were no CCTV security cameras save those over the traffic lights some distance away, no pontoons and no passing boat owners. And in the dark, no one to see a moored craft.

As Horton stared out across the harbour to the small RSPB islands to the north, he knew that Spender hadn't travelled far for his rendezvous with death.

CHAPTER TWENTY-THREE

Monday

'I take it by your youthful grin and general good humour that Catherine didn't call off your day with Emma yesterday,' Cantelli said as he drew up at the traffic lights. They were on their way to interview Guy Bampton. Horton had relayed his ideas about Spender's boat mooring up at Salterns Lake Quay to the team, including Uckfield and Bliss, earlier that morning.

'Knowing where he might have met his killer doesn't confirm Anther killed him or that Bampton helped him,' Uckfield had said. He had agreed, however, to ask the traffic-management company for any CCTV footage at the lights, and Taylor was to take scrapings from the quayside to see if they matched any on Spender's boat.

'Are you saying I'm usually a miserable sod?' Horton joked. 'Don't answer that. You're right, she didn't, and it was great.' He and Emma had sailed over to Bembridge on the Isle of Wight, where they had picnicked and eaten ice creams before sailing back. His young daughter was proving to be a very competent sailor and he had so enjoyed teaching her new methods. He'd also revelled in her comments that he was a much better teacher than Grandad, who bossed her about and wouldn't let her try things on her own, and Grandma was always telling her to be careful or she'd fall overboard. And it was much more fun than sitting on Peter's boat, which was 'so boring'. He could have punched the air for joy but that was nothing compared to his feelings after Catherine's news when she collected Emma. He'd been considering it all night and early this morning.

'There's more good news, which makes a change,' he added. 'No, I haven't found anywhere to live, Barney, but I will — because Catherine dropped the bombshell that she is not going to contest my request for increased access to Emma. In fact, she's willing to come to an arrangement without it having to go to the family court.'

'That's great. It's not before time that she's seen sense. What's brought on this miraculous about-face?' Cantelli reached for his packet of chewing gum.

'An enormous and very expensive diamond ring on the third finger of her left hand.' Where once his paltry offering had sat along with the wedding ring.

Cantelli dashed him a concerned glance.

'It's OK, Barney, it doesn't bother me now.'

'Maybe Jarvis has persuaded her it would be better for you to see more of Emma.' Cantelli popped a piece of gum in his mouth and pulled away as the lights changed.

'Yeah, maybe.'

'You don't sound convinced.'

'My cynical copper's brain says that maybe he doesn't want Emma along on his luxurious trips abroad, which he's hoping to increase. We both know that he doesn't need to work, he's a millionaire — probably a multimillionaire — dabbling in investments and start-ups and goodness knows what. Emma's presence might cramp his style, and Catherine's bound to go with Jarvis on his overseas jaunts, staying in his luxury apartments and villas. Her parents are getting older and can't have Emma all the time. It suits Jarvis and Catherine that Emma should spend more time with me, but my fear is that instead of her being a weekday boarder, Catherine might ensure that Emma becomes a full-time boarder at her school, and I'll not get much chance to be with her anyway.'

'Those private schools get a lot of holidays, more than the state school kids, so I doubt if you'll be deprived of her company much if that happens.'

'Catherine said they are getting married just before Christmas, followed by a honeymoon, although she didn't specify where, and I didn't ask. Emma is to spend Christmas with her grandparents but can stay with me after that and over the New Year on the proviso that I find suitable accommodation, not a boat, unless I could conjure up one like Jarvis's superyacht — that's my words not Catherine's. And unless I win the pools or lottery, which I don't do in the first place, it's never going to happen.'

'You'll find somewhere, and you'll still have your boat.'

Horton wasn't convinced about the former. After he had waved his chattering, happy but tired daughter away he'd spent a couple of hours on the internet looking at property websites, which had made his heart sink. He'd despised all he had viewed, seeing, even if it was only in his mind's eyes, the grubby, grotty flats of Spender and Farrell. He'd also looked at houses to rent and had expanded his search area, but nothing had appealed. They were either too small, too claustrophobic, in the wrong neighbourhood or far too expensive in the right ones. He needed to find somewhere before the autumn. Emma could stay on his boat during the summer months. There had to be something, somewhere that would appeal to him.

'Anything further from Ellen on Catmore?' Horton asked.

'Not that she's told me, but she's probably been searching the internet again.'

'She's a very bright girl. You must be proud of her.'

'I am, and scared for her.'

'Aren't we all scared for our children?'

'I guess so. My mum says they're an arm-ache when they're young and heartache when they're old. Charlotte says the GCHQ opportunity sounds good. We read up on it, and it is legitimate.'

'I'm pleased to hear it.'

Cantelli drew into the visitors' parking space outside Bampton's office. He silenced the engine. 'You really think Bampton would have gone to Anther's aid?'

'If the rewards were high enough, maybe.'

'I just can't see Anther falling for Spender. He doesn't seem Anther's type.'

'We've seen stranger couplings.'

'I guess so.'

They found Bampton in the yard talking to one of his drivers beside a skip lorry. Another three lorries were parked in addition to two stacks of skips — one large and one smaller — some rubbish bins, a bicycle shed, a wooden bench, table and seats.

'Hello, Inspector. Back to check up on me?' Bampton joked.

Horton smiled. 'Something like that.'

'Then here's the driver who took me to Anther's gallery and he'll swear blind I never came out with any paintings.' It was said in jest but there was an edge of irritation behind the voice.

'If we could have a word in private?'

Bampton nodded at the burly driver, and they moved away out of earshot.

'Any news on Julian and the forgeries?' Bampton asked.

'Not at the moment. Have you had yours validated?'

'I've got someone coming down from Sotheby's tomorrow to examine them, but I think they're kosher.'

It had been a good guess on Horton's part — he had judged the man well. 'Did you know that Anther had dual citizenship with France?'

'He never said, although I know he's fond of going over there and speaks French fluently.'

'Do you speak it?'

His eyes widened. 'You must be kidding, although I do speak a bit of Spanish. I have a villa in Spain.'

'No property in France?'

'No.'

'Ever lived in France?'

'No.'

'Do you know Neil Spender?'

'The man who's gone missing from his boat? No. I heard about it on the radio. Look, Inspector, I know you have a job to do but I can tell you I have no idea where Anther is or this man, Spender, who I've never met.'

Horton left a moment's pause. Then, 'Where were you on Saturday night between seven thirty and midnight?'

Bampton's eyebrows shot up and he shook his head with a sad smile. 'You're barking up the wrong tree if you think I have anything to do with this man Spender, but if it makes you happy, I'll tell you. I was entertaining at home. My wife and our fourteen guests will all confirm that I didn't slip out, not even for ten minutes, unless you count going for a leak. I'm too large a man not to be missed.'

Horton returned the smile. 'We think Mr Spender could have put into Salterns Lake Quay on Saturday evening on his boat. I wondered if you noticed a boat mooring up there, or heading there on your way home from here?'

'I didn't because one, I don't leave the yard that way, I take the road along the edge of the golf course and past the supermarket to join the dual carriageway north, and two, I wasn't here on Saturday afternoon, and neither was I on my boat. I keep that at Northney Marina on Hayling Island. The marina staff can probably verify that. Now if that's all, I've got work to do.'

Cantelli put away his notebook.

Horton said, 'How was Mr Ellwood?'

Bampton's expression softened. 'He's in a bad way,' he said sorrowfully. 'He wasn't conscious. I don't think it'll be long.'

In the car, Cantelli said, 'Bampton could have arranged for someone to help Anther dispose of the body, except that would make him vulnerable to another person and I don't see Bampton taking that risk.'

'If his alibi for Saturday holds out then he could have assisted Anther before seven thirty, or perhaps he didn't see his first guests until eight or eight thirty, and his wife will swear on all she holds sacred her husband was at home. He could even have gone to Anther's aid after his guests had left.'

Horton's phone rang. 'It's Nicola Bolton.' He expected to hear she had drawn a blank tracing Catmore's Aunt Dorothy.

He listened for a moment. 'We'll be right round. Give me your address. We're practically there now.' Ringing off, he said, 'Nicola's found Dorothy.'

Within fifteen minutes they were shown into the kitchen of the modest semi-detached house by a well-built woman in her mid-fifties with no-nonsense, short brown hair, minimal make-up and modern spectacles on a round, friendly face.

She gestured them into seats around a table on which was a laptop, a folder and a notebook. Beside her, on a chair, a tabby cat eyed them malevolently. Cantelli took the seat next to it and began to stroke it. The look changed to a squint and a soft purr emanated from the animal.

'How sure are you that you've found the Dorothy we're looking for?' Horton asked.

'I'm not, because I can't find any relationship between the Dorothy Massett I've located and Noel or Beryl Catmore. I've charted their family genealogy a fair way back. Dorothy might have been called an aunt when she had no relationship with the late Beryl Catmore and was only a family friend.'

Horton glanced at Cantelli. 'Are you thinking what I am?'

'There is no Aunt Dot. Catmore made her up. He was given the paintings by someone to take into Anther and spin him the tale about an Aunt Dot to see if he, or who-ever is behind Catmore, could get away with selling both the forgeries — using Anther as the fence — and selling the originals, for which Anther had the contacts.'

Nicola said, 'Then I've wasted your time, although Dorothy Massett is interesting.'

'Tell us what you've got.' Horton didn't wish to disappoint her, and he was curious.

'OK. I had no idea of where Dorothy lived but I took the starting point as somewhere in Hampshire because of Mr Catmore's address — that was after looking into his and his wife's family tree and finding no Dorothy. I assumed she might be deceased because of what you told me about Mr Catmore saying she could be elderly. I found Dorothy Stella Massett, born in 1944 in Chichester, died on the fifteenth of May 1993 in The Coach House, Old Bedhampton.'

That was north-east of the city of Portsmouth, a small conurbation gradually being swallowed up by new housing developments.

'How did you find her?' asked Cantelli, who was taking notes, although Horton thought he probably didn't need to.

'From her estate. I examined the bona vacantia list—'

'Eh?' Cantelli's small pencil froze.

'It's a list of unclaimed intestate estates, which is updated every working day and is published online by the Government Legal Department. An estate is added to the list when someone dies without leaving a will and seems to have no next of kin. Probate research is an intensely competitive industry, so the arrival of the updated list is like the starter's gun in a race to probate researchers.'

Horton said, 'Then someone will have been working on Dorothy's estate in 1993 trying to trace a beneficiary?'

'Most certainly. But I don't know who that was. There are some big organizations, as well as freelancers like me, who specialize in this. The family tree of the deceased person will be examined. I have done the same, and from my initial research at the Register of Births, Deaths and Marriages I found no registration of marriage for Dorothy. I also checked the Land Registry for details of the two properties she owned in the hope of locating the solicitor who dealt with her affairs, but the properties aren't registered. It wasn't a legal requirement to do so until 1990 and she bought both before then.'

'How much is the estate worth?' asked Cantelli.

'Combining property, investments and savings, just over two million pounds.'

Cantelli emitted a low whistle. 'That's a huge amount.'

Horton thought so too.

'It's a very substantial estate. And no one has made a claim on it, although there is still time. Claims have to be submitted within thirty years of the date of death so if there is a next of kin, he or she still has time to do so.'

'So what happened to her estate?' asked Horton.

'In Dorothy's case, the rules of intestacy were applied. A search was made for her next of kin by a probate researcher and advertisements were placed in all the local newspapers. You'll find evidence of them on the local newspaper's website, but I've printed them off for you.' She tapped the folder on the table.

'Wouldn't that give the name of the probate researcher?'

'No, only the legal officer in the council department. He's retired but I spoke to my contact at Havant Borough Council, who looked up the file. No one came forward to say they were related or knew her. The council took possession of her estate. Money was subtracted from her estate to cover the cost of a basic funeral. She was cremated and her ashes scattered in the grounds of Portchester Crematorium. Councils get thousands of Freedom of Information requests every year regarding those who have died with no family. While they will usually supply details such as full name, date of death, marital status and last known address, they often withhold the rest — maiden name if married, date of birth and the value of the estate — because of the risk of fraud. I know her age because it was revealed at the inquest. As I am known to the council legal officer and have worked on their behalf, and as I am also engaged by you, the police, I was able to obtain more information. I suggested they could clear it with you, but it wasn't necessary.'

'How did she die?' asked Horton.

'Brain haemorrhage from a fall in her home. No alcohol in her bloodstream. She tripped and fell on a loose stair rod. She lived alone, never married, and as far as I can ascertain had no children. I found some press coverage on her death. I've printed it out for you, although you might find more in your police files. Her death was briefly investigated. The inquest ruled death by misadventure. Her body was discovered by her cleaner, Mrs Ida Tidy, a rather apt name.' She smiled.

'What happened to Dorothy's effects?' Horton was curious despite knowing it wasn't linked to their investigation.

'Valued and auctioned off. The council office can give you a list. The properties were boarded up and remain so to this day. After the thirty-year period, if no one comes forward, they will be sold by auction and the money will go to the Crown, as will the money from her effects, investments and savings.'

'So her properties lay derelict, with no one maintaining them or the grounds?'

'Yes.'

Horton exchanged a glance with Cantelli, who said, 'Catmore?'

Maybe there was a link after all.

'He could have entered one of those properties while on a metal-detecting foray and found the three paintings. But surely the council would have found them?'

'They might have been hidden in the basement and Catmore, with his metal detector, locked on to a piece of metal close by, or on to a case containing them and thought he'd check out the artist on the internet and see if they were worth a few quid. When he saw that Ellwood was a big-shot artist, he thought, "Hey, finders keepers", even though he knows it's against the law. He doesn't think anyone will discover his secret with all those phoney names on his internet profiles. He must have seen part of the name on the case, Dorothy Mass, or the whole name, but chose to ham it up with us.' With growing excitement, Horton addressed Nicola. 'Can you give us the address of the other property Dorothy owned?'

'Yes. Lower Grant Road, Havant.'

Neither the Bedhampton property nor the Havant one were near The Kench on Hayling Island, where Catmore had said on the forum he had gone with his metal detector. But as Horton had previously considered, that might have been to distract anyone else from heading there.

He rose. 'Can you continue researching Dorothy's background and let us know if you find anything more?'

'With pleasure.' She showed them out.

'Let's take The Coach House first, Barney. I'd like to see if Catmore found a way inside, or if there are any outhouses. I'll ask Trueman if he can get an address for Ida Tidy.'

Trueman said he'd send it over when he had it. He also said the case file on Spender's attack had come in, confirming that the assault had taken place at the port of Newhaven and Spender had been on foot, waiting to board the Newhaven to Dieppe ferry. He'd had a single ticket. No one was ever found and charged for it. So, Spender had been returning to France rather than arriving from there. A random attack? Or planned?

* * *

The Coach House was a substantial property, built most probably in the nineteenth century. It was securely boarded with no indication of a breach anywhere and no sign of Catmore's car. The grounds were overgrown and there were no outhouses. A neighbour emerged to ask who they were and what they were doing and seemed reassured after he had scrutinized their warrant cards. Unfortunately, he had not lived there in Dorothy Massett's time and, as far as he was aware, there was no one left in the close who had. He regularly checked over the property, not wanting squatters to move in and reporting any rat infestations to the council, but he'd be glad when the place could be claimed or put on the market and sold. He had a few more years to wait yet.

The second property in Havant fronted onto the Hayling Billy nature trail at the Langstone end of it, closer to Havant railway station than the bridge that crossed to the island. It was a 1930s' detached family house in a short road culminating in a dead end. The dual carriageway flyover was at the end of it. Horton suspected Dorothy had bought it with the aim of letting it. There might have been tenants who had long since moved out. Again, everything was securely boarded up with nothing in the garden in the form of sheds or outhouses, just grass and weeds. Horton couldn't see Catmore coming here or to The Coach House with his metal detector, both being in residential areas. Disappointingly this, like the road, looked like a dead end.

Cantelli eyed the house as he climbed in the car. 'Makes you feel sad. Not for the property but for Dorothy. No one to mourn or remember her.'

Horton agreed. Regrettably, there were quite a few similar cases that he and Barney had come across in their careers.

He told Cantelli to head back to the station, but they hadn't gone far when Horton's phone went. It was Trueman with the address of an Ida Tidy. Horton didn't think it worth talking to her but seeing as they were only a short distance from where she lived, he gave Cantelli instructions to make for it. They might at least be able to rule out this line of enquiry.

CHAPTER TWENTY-FOUR

'Pity you didn't come by police car,' a plump, beaming lady boomed. She ushered them into her small, spick-and-span ground-floor flat on the edge of the sprawling council estate. Her voice was so loud that Horton thought it could have reached the shopping centre some three miles away. 'It would have given the neighbours something to talk about for days,' she bellowed. 'Not that the boys and girls in blue are a rare sight around here. There's a flat across the way and a couple of houses down the road where they're so regular they might as well move in. Dennis, shift your backside, the young men want to sit down.'

For a moment Horton thought she must be talking to her husband although there was no one else in the cramped room except a surly-looking border collie, who took not the slightest bit of notice of his mistress. She reached out a huge, fleshy arm and scooped the animal off one of the two armchairs covered with brightly coloured crocheted blankets. After a look from Cantelli, Horton took the seat vacated by Dennis, resigning himself to his trousers being covered in dog hairs. Still, he'd had worse, a great deal worse. Cantelli sat in the other armchair and Ida Tidy settled her substantial frame on the settee, arranging the folds of her tent-like colourful dress around her. Dennis immediately jumped up beside her.

'Right, so you want to talk about Dorothy,' Ida Tidy said crisply. Horton had made the announcement on the doorstep which, along with a show of their warrant cards, had granted them entry. 'It's taken you long enough to get around to it but better late than never, as they say.'

'You think her death was suspicious?' Horton asked, surprised.

'Must be if you're here.' She stroked the dog with bejewelled stubby fingers, her bracelets jangling like wind chimes. Dennis growled softly.

Horton smiled at her logic. He put her in her early seventies. There was a mischievous and intelligent twinkle in her small, round eyes. Her short white hair suited her forthright manner, and reserves of energy radiated from her which belied her ample proportions. The small flat was crowded with furniture, knick-knacks and photographs of children and grandchildren along with some of an equally corpulent man, whom Horton took to be Mr Tidy. By his lack of presence Horton thought he must be deceased, although he could be out shopping, betting, or down the pub. Then he spied the casket on the top of a cabinet.

Catching him looking, Ida said brightly, 'That's Trevor, my late husband. Died two years ago. If he thought he'd get the better of me by buggering off up there—' she jerked her head heavenwards — 'then he had another think coming.' She laughed. 'Dennis and I like to have a chat with the silly old bugger now and again, don't we boy?'

Dennis yawned and smacked his jaws.

Horton said, 'Could you tell us about Dorothy? I know it's going back a while to 1993, so don't worry if you don't remember much.'

She threw back her head and laughed, a deep throaty sound that could have shaken the paper-thin walls. The neighbours would always know when Ida was at home.

'I'm not in my dotage yet, Inspector. My memory is as sharp as crystal. And I can never forget Dorothy. She was larger than life, and I don't mean large like me but lively, funny, full of energy. Quite a character. Where to begin is the question.' She plumped her hair. 'I worked for Dorothy for three years, from 1990, when she bought the house in Bedhampton, until she died there. She was just a month short of her fiftieth birthday, but you'd never have believed it. Looked and acted more like thirty. A very attractive woman, lots of dark, curly hair, always dressed nice, very fashionable, a good figure, with a zest for life but not overbearing with it. Everyone from the milkman to the postman to the binman fell in love with her. She could have charmed Satan himself if she had wanted to. She never stood on ceremony, not an ounce of snobbishness about her. When we had a power cut and the electricity men had to dig up the road, she was out there giving them tea, cake and chocolate biscuits. Did more talking than digging I think and took twice as long over the job, but Dorothy didn't care, although the neighbours weren't very happy about it. Paid me over the going rate and always a handsome Christmas bonus. A very generous woman.'

'The inquest said her death was accidental, that she fell down the stairs,' Horton said, recalling what Nicola had relayed and what he had read on the way here in the copy of the press coverage she'd given him. 'There was no alcohol found in her system, but did she like a drink?'

'Of course, she did,' Ida declared as though Horton was stupid for asking. 'Red wine and champagne, although not together. But then again, she might have done. She had it delivered from the wine merchant in Emsworth. She was a very wealthy woman, so I was given to understand, although she never talked about money and, as I said. she wasn't mean either, not like some who once they've got hold of a bit of cash hang on to it, as if they can take it to the grave.'

Horton thought of Damien Oxley, but then he had bought that expensive painting for his wife. 'I understand that she wasn't married and hadn't had any children, is that correct?'

'She said she could never be tied down to one man, and kids would cramp her lifestyle, which was obvious to me. I was amazed she'd settled down here. Couldn't see why she should and asked her that. "Trying to cure my itchy feet" she said, "got to settle somewhere", but she didn't settle, she was always popping over to France. She spoke French like a native. Told me she had lived there for a long time and couldn't get it out of her blood. That didn't surprise me in the least.'

But it did Horton, although he tried not to show it. His mind began to race. France certainly seemed to be a common denominator in all this. He exchanged a quick glance with Cantelli, but before either of them could speak, Ida was off again.

'She had an apartment in Paris.'

More surprises. Nicola hadn't discovered that and neither had the council legal department, because if they had the officer would have told Nicola. Perhaps Dorothy had sold it before her death and the funds were in her bank account, hence her large estate. The fact that Paris was also frequently cropping up was intensely interesting — Anther, possibly Spender, Ellwood, Maurice Linden and Roy Macey — but was it significant? He could just hear Uckfield saying, 'A lot of people live in Paris.'

'Did she sell her Paris apartment before she died?' he asked.

'Not that I know of. Leastways, she was there three weeks before she died, and I don't think she could have sold it that quickly.'

'You don't happen to know where in Paris?' he asked but not expectantly.

'No idea. She didn't have any relatives. Told me she was a poor little orphan girl who had run away to the bright lights of gay Paree as soon as she could.' Ida laughed boisterously, almost causing Cantelli to drop his pencil. Even the dog looked startled at the volume. 'She told me she had been an artist's model, posing nude and that sort of thing, and I can well believe it, because as I said she still had a good figure at forty-nine and was very attractive. She must have been stunning as a young woman.'

Even more surprises. Horton's antennae were twitching like mad and he suspected Cantelli's also. It was Cantelli who voiced Horton's next question.

'Do you have a photograph of her?'

'No. But I have a drawing.'

Even better, thought Horton. 'Here?' He gazed around the walls but could see only the bog-standard chain-store prints.

'No. It's in one of my drawers somewhere.'

'Do you think we could see it?'

'Now?'

'In a moment.' He was very keen to see if an artist's name was on it. 'Did she have many paintings?'

'A few. She might have had some in her Paris apartment or at her other properties.'

Properties, plural, Horton thought, amazed and even more intrigued. 'You mean aside from the one at Havant and the Paris apartment?'

'Of course. She had a flat in London and a house on Hayling Island right by the sea. I asked her why there and she said she could keep a boat at the bottom of the garden. I said, "What do you want to do that for?" — "So I can sail into the sunset," she'd say, and she did, not on her boat, but at the bottom of the stairs.'

Nicola and the council officers were obviously oblivious of these properties, so how had they been missed? Cantelli, on the same wavelength, said, 'Did she buy them in her name?'

'Must have done. I didn't hear her use any other. She said her investments in land and properties were for her old age. I said, "You're never going to be old," and I was right, although I wish I hadn't been.'

After a short pause, through which music playing from next door thudded, and a car tooted loudly outside, Horton asked, 'Do you know where on Hayling Island her house was?'

'No. But she said she could look across to the army base and hoped to see some fit, handsome soldiers on manoeuvres.'

That was Thorney Island in Chichester Harbour. It bordered the Emsworth Channel on the opposite side of Hayling Island.

'Her house had a funny name, The Shambles.'

This was valuable news. Could Catmore have discovered it? Horton knew that Cantelli was thinking the same.

'I know she died intestate, but did she ever talk about making a will?' Horton asked.

'No.'

'Don't you think that strange for a smart businesswoman?'

'Some people don't like to do it because they feel it might be tempting fate. She probably thought she had lots of time left. Sadly, that wasn't to be.'

'I'm sorry you had to find her.'

'Someone had to. I was just glad she hadn't been lying there for days.'

'Did anything strike you about her death, anything unusual?'

'Of course. Not that anyone listened to me. I was just a cleaner.'

'Well, we're listening now. Go on,' Horton encouraged, not that he really needed to. He was pleased Ida Tidy was a talker. It made their job so much easier.

'For a start, they said she'd fallen, which was unusual because she was very sure-footed — she'd once been a dancer as well as an artist's model. I wondered if she might have had too much to drink although I'd never seen her drunk or with a hangover. And there were no empties in the kitchen to be put out for the bottle bank and none in the garden or in the bin. There were also no glasses unwashed or in the dishwasher. Then they said that she had tripped over a loose stair rod at the top of the stairs, but I'm telling you, Inspector, there was no loose stair rod when I vacuumed those stairs the day before.'

'And was there on the day you found her?'

'I don't know, checking them was the last thing on my mind what with the poor woman lying there dead.' Her bright eyes penetrated Horton's as though weighing him up. She leaned forward, lowering her voice to loudhailer level. 'I cleaned those stairs twice a week and I polished those ruddy stair rods once a week. God knows why she wanted the stair carpet like that, but she did. It was a new carpet and Dorothy wanted it laid in the old-fashioned style to suit the house, you know, with an edge each side, not fitted but fixed with brass stair rods.'

Cantelli nodded.

'I used to grumble about cleaning them. "They may look nice," I'd say, "and you might think it's all very swish, but I'm the bugger who has to clean them." Dorothy would laugh. I can tell you that stair rod was fixed firmly in place when I cleaned it on the Monday, and I couldn't see how it had come loose between then and when I found her on the Friday.'

'Was this raised at the inquest?'

'It was but no one asked my opinion on it and when I made to say, I was told, "Thank you, Mrs Tidy, that will be all."'

Horton didn't need to look at Cantelli to see that he was thinking along the same lines as him — someone had loosened it. Before or after her fall? he wondered. Who? And why?

Cantelli said, 'Did any of her friends come to the inquest?'

'Not when I was there.'

'Didn't you think that unusual?'

'There's a lot of things I thought unusual but, like I said, no one was listening to me. I guessed they weren't there because they were foreign.'

'Foreign?' Cantelli prompted before Horton could speak.

'French. There was a small, wiry man, a fancy dresser, what you might call dapper, who visited her a couple of times. And a bigger, broader man, good-looking, very charming. They didn't come at the same time, leastways not when

I was there, but when they did, they all jabbered away in French. Dorothy would also speak to someone in French on the phone.'

'And I don't suppose you know what they spoke about?'

'Me! I can just about speak English,' she joked. 'Dorothy asked me if I spoke French and I said, "Not likely."'

So, they could all talk freely without fear of being understood.

'Were they Dorothy's lovers?' Cantelli asked.

'They might have been. Don't know. Didn't act as lovers, and there was none of that kissing on both cheeks like the continentals do. I heard raised voices once between the good-looking one and Dorothy. Might have been a lovers' tiff.'

'Did you tell the police about this?'

'Course not. No one asked. PC Plod showed up, took my name and address, said it looked like an accident and that I'd be asked to make a statement about finding her and could I make myself available for the inquest, but that was it. I'll get you that drawing.'

She hauled herself up and waddled off. The dog hesitated, wondering whether to follow her, then decided he couldn't be bothered, changed position and settled down to snooze.

'Interesting,' mused Cantelli in a low voice, 'and illuminating. Could the smaller, wiry, dapper man have been Julian Anther?'

'Possibly, but who was the other?'

'Guy Bampton?'

'Maybe. The description doesn't fit Oxley, although Dorothy could have been speaking to him on the telephone, and he could have visited her when Ida wasn't cleaning. But that's just speculation, probably because I don't like or trust him. There's nothing to put any of the men with Dorothy, save possibly Anther, but then he's not the only snazzy dresser in the world.'

They were prevented from speculating further by Ida's reappearance. She was clutching a small drawing about eight inches by six. She handed it across to Horton. 'You can see how beautiful Dorothy was.'

Horton agreed. It was a skilfully executed and moving pencil portrait of a vivacious woman in a tutu standing at the barre wearing red ballet shoes. She was in a thoughtful pose but there was a confidence about her, and a mischievous, beguiling look in her eyes. In the right-hand corner were the artist's initials. Cantelli, peering over Horton's shoulder, muttered them aloud. 'M.E.' To Ida he said, 'Did Dorothy tell you who drew this?'

'She might have done, but I can't remember.'

Even if the initials hadn't been on it, Horton would have known instantly who had drawn the picture, because Maurice Linden's words came back to him from when they had first met in Anther's gallery: *Michael started out with drawings in chalk, pencil and wash, of ballet dancers and circus performers.*

He said, 'We'd like to keep this for a while, Mrs Tidy. Sergeant Cantelli will give you a receipt and we will make sure to return it to you in perfect condition. We'll let you have it back as soon as we can, but it will help us with our enquiries.'

'Dorothy's death was no accident then? I was right?' she boomed victoriously. 'It's OK, you don't have to admit it and commit yourself. You keep it as long as you need it, my love. And good luck to you—' She faltered for a moment and looked preoccupied.

'You've remembered something,' Horton said.

'I'm not sure if it is of any help, but talking about those French men and not being able to understand a word they said has jogged my mind. There was one word I understood, the only one, and they said it many times. It made me think of that Shirley Bassey song. I thought it must be the same in French and English.'

Horton's pulse raced. He was already ahead of her, and was certain Cantelli was too. He felt a stab of triumph. 'And what song was that?'

'"Hey Big Spender".'

CHAPTER TWENTY-FIVE

'We now have a firm connection between Dorothy, Neil Spender and Michael Ellwood,' Horton said as they made their way to the north-east of Hayling Island. The traffic was heavy, giving Horton time to check on his phone for the location of The Shambles. He couldn't find it, but that didn't mean it wasn't there. He had speculated that it was in one of two places, the ends of two narrow country lanes that faced east on to the Emsworth Channel of Chichester Harbour. He'd also called Havant Police Station and asked for a request to be put out for any officers who knew the house, or any derelict houses, overlooking the Emsworth Channel.

Cantelli indicated left just after the road bridge that joined the island to the mainland and followed the winding country lane east, past the fields and rows of small semi-detached cottages of North Hayling. 'Strange too that Spender was assaulted in March 1993 and Dorothy died two months later.'

'Or not so strange if both had to be silenced because of their part in criminal activity. Anther was also involved in it judging by Ida's description of the smaller, dapper man, and we know that the key found in his gallery matches the one I found under Spender's pillow. If we put that with Anther's occupation, working in an art gallery in Paris, and Spender's possible time in France from 1976 to 1993, most probably living in Paris, then I'd say we're looking at them and Dorothy being involved in art fraud, which is how she accumulated her wealth.'

Cantelli halted at the farm while some geese took a leisurely stroll across the road to join the cows in the opposite field. 'And Anther is alive and unharmed, and on the run. So maybe he killed Dorothy back in 1993, when he also had Spender beaten up and left for dead. Only Spender survived and resurfaced recently, then threatened Anther that he'd tell all unless he paid up.'

'Sounds possible.'

'Were Ellwood and Roy Macey involved? They lived in Paris.' Cantelli moved off as the geese had reached their destination.

Horton briefly considered this. 'Macey was working there from 1990 to 1993, and Ellwood returned from the States in 1993 when Linden became his agent. But we now know who the forger of those Ellwood paintings was. The hands, Barney. Why were Spender's hands so badly mutilated?' Horton asked excitedly.

Cantelli flashed him a glance before putting his eyes back on the twisting lane. 'Because he was an artist. He was the forger.'

'Yes. That was his role in Paris. He forged paintings,' Horton triumphantly declared. 'And he recognized the Ellwood paintings in Anther's gallery as *his* forgeries. He must have seen them when he was collecting the bins.'

'Catmore found both the originals and the forgeries then?'

Cantelli was right to be puzzled. 'It sounds unlikely, doesn't it? And I can't see Spender having the forgeries because he'd have sold them long ago, passing them off as originals.'

'Not if he didn't know what he had — he'd lost his memory.' Cantelli slowed down behind two horse riders.

'Yes, he had, you're right,' Horton said, his mind scrabbling to pull together the information they'd gleaned. 'And recently he'd got it back because he would surely have black-mailed Anther before now if he had recognized him as his co-conspirator.'

Cantelli turned into a narrow tree-lined lane.

Horton said, 'I'll look for an entrance to The Shambles this side which gives onto the water.'

'What was Dorothy's role in the fraud?' asked Cantelli, driving slowly.

'Connections. Being an artist's model and clever she must have known a lot of people in the art world.'

'Could she have identified which paintings to be forged?'

'Possibly, and she pooled resources with Anther. Perhaps her role was to engage artists capable of forging works of art — Spender, for one. When he wanted out, or he became a risk for some reason, he got a warning to keep his mouth shut.'

Cantelli pulled up at the end of the lane. There was nowhere else for him to go. The road had run out of steam. 'I can't see the same motive applying to Dorothy, threatening to tell all, from Ida's description of her. She'd have had to sacrifice her wealth and liberty, and from what Ida says it seems Dorothy enjoyed both her money and lifestyle. So why was she killed?'

'And she did amass some wealth, although The Shambles doesn't appear to be along this road. Turn round.'

Cantelli began his three-point turn.

Horton continued, 'Someone wanted her out of the way, *if* her death was suspicious, and I think it was. So, who?'

'Anther, because she was blackmailing him over his dodgy past and he was trying to go legit with his gallery in Emsworth.'

'Which according to Bampton he opened in 1993, but he could be wrong, although Trueman said it was in the early nineties.'

'Could Anther have introduced Dorothy to Bampton? He said he had always been interested in art. He could have been the broad, muscular, good-looking one Ida talked about. He's also strong enough to have carried Spender's body off that boat, and he started his business in 1993 — I read it on one of the pictures on the wall in his office. Perhaps he was paid well to see that Dorothy had an "accident" and that Spender was beaten up. The money helped to kick-start his business.' Cantelli's three-point turn had metamorphosed into five points.

'Oxley also started his business in 1993 and acquired some lucrative art freight contracts.'

'A lot seems to have happened that year.'

'Doesn't it just? Ellwood returned from America, a successful artist, Linden became his agent, and Macey started his business. There's one more lane where The Shambles might be. Take the next turning left.'

There they also drew a blank. Horton wondered if The Shambles was a nickname Dorothy had given the house, and perhaps she had lied to Ida about it overlooking the Emsworth Channel.

'I'll ask for Bampton's and Oxley's backgrounds to be checked. Ellwood is beyond interviewing being so ill, but we can talk to Linden — he's on the Isle of Wight — and we can also speak with Macey. Although he was in Paris after the critical time, he's known Anther and Linden a long time and might be able to tell us something. Pull over, Barney. I'll see if I can get his address.'

Cantelli drew into an entrance to a field while Horton called up the internet on his phone. 'His business is based in Havant. He might be there or out on a job. Hang on, let's see where he lives.' Horton searched for Macey's home address. Being a company director it would be listed in the *Directory of Directors*.

'He lives here on Hayling Island, and his house backs on to Langstone Harbour. Let's see if he's at home. If not, we'll try his office.'

Cantelli headed east across the small island and fifteen minutes later pulled into an impressive driveway leading up to a substantial and well-kept art deco house. There were two expensive cars on the driveway, which suggested that Macey was at home. A fair-haired woman in her late forties opened the door. Her eyes were red-rimmed and her expression anxious.

'Mrs Jacqueline Macey?' Cantelli enquired, while Horton mentally calculated that Macey must have married a child. Either that or Mrs Jaqueline Macey, who he had said he married in 1993, had found the answer to eternal youth. Her wary reply explained that she was Mrs Vicky Macey and Jacqueline had died in 2000.

When Cantelli furnished the introductions, Horton thought she was going to faint. Her hand flew to her mouth, and she swayed, deathly white. 'Oh my God, it's Roy. He's . . . he's . . .'

'No, Mrs Macey we haven't come with bad news,' Cantelli quickly assured her.

Well, not that kind, thought Horton, wondering what had occurred and getting a sinking feeling.

'What is it, Mum?' A scrawny, dishevelled boy in his early teens appeared at the end of the wide hall.

'It's the police. They say they haven't come with news about Dad.'

'But we would like to talk to you about him,' Horton said. 'Can we come inside?'

She stepped back.

'Is there somewhere we can sit down?'

She gestured them into a room on their left which looked out over the garden, at the end of which Horton could see a jetty. There was no boat on it. On the walls, here and in the hall, Horton noted some stunning and very valuable-looking paintings — originals, not prints, and probably not forgeries.

All this swiftly crossed Horton's mind as they sat. The boy, who Mrs Macey introduced as Kyle, perched on the arm of his mother's chair.

'I'm sorry we startled you, Mrs Macey. You are clearly very upset. May I ask what's happened?'

'Don't you know? B-But you're here,' she stammered, confused, pushing her shoulder-length hair off her face.

'We're from the Portsmouth police and we're keen to talk to Mr Macey about an investigation.'

'What kind of investigation?' Her brow puckered.

'Some paintings have gone missing from Julian Anther's gallery.'

'I knew there was something wrong,' she declared, wringing her well-manicured hands and flashing a worried glance at her son. 'Roy has been so distracted lately. What does this mean?'

'Where is your husband, Mrs Macey?' Horton asked kindly.

'That's what we'd like to know. We haven't seen him since Saturday when he went out on the boat. I didn't worry when he didn't come home Sunday morning because he said he would be away overnight. But when he didn't return by Sunday night I got concerned. What if he'd had an accident or a heart attack on the boat? I've been trying him all day, and there's been no answer. I called his office, but no one there has seen or heard from him. I tried Julian, but his line is dead. I rang round the marinas on the Isle of Wight, but they haven't seen my husband and the boat hasn't put into any of them. I called the police three hours ago and you turning up, I thought . . .'

Horton rapidly digested this. He knew Cantelli was also considering this development in light of their previous conversation in the car a short while ago. 'Did you give the police a description of your husband and the boat?'

She nodded and fiddled with her bracelet while her son frowned, worried.

'What's the name and make of the boat?'

Kyle answered. '*Wind Drift*, and it's a Bayliner 2858 motor cruiser.'

'And it's usually kept on your private jetty at the end of the premises?'

The boy nodded. Horton rose. 'Can you give the details to Sergeant Cantelli please? I'll just make a call to our marine unit. Could I step out into the garden, Mrs Macey?'

She nodded and Kyle crossed the parquet floor. He pushed open a Crittall door and Horton stepped onto the patio, retrieved his mobile and made his way down the immaculate landscaped garden to the jetty. Cantelli would get all the details and ask further questions.

The sun was shining off the water. It was an hour after high tide.

'Have you had a report of a missing boat owner, Roy Macey, and a boat called *Wind Drift*, a Bayliner 2858?' he asked Elkins when he came on the line.

'About an hour ago. We haven't picked up anything on him.'

Horton briefly explained how he thought Macey's disappearance could be connected with the art thefts and with the Spender murder. 'Mrs Macey says she's tried the marinas on the Isle of Wight, which is where her husband said he was making for, but that could have been a bluff on his part.'

'He could be across to France or the Channel Islands by now,' Elkins said. 'I'll ask for the ports and marinas to be on the lookout.'

'Where are you now?'

'At Oyster Quays.'

'On the RIB or the launch?'

'RIB.'

'Good. Come round to Macey's jetty, Langstone Harbour, Hayling Island. I'll look out for you.'

Horton had an idea he wanted to explore. He returned to the house.

'The marine unit will search for your husband's boat, Mrs Macey, and put out a call for it. I've asked them to pick me up from your jetty, I hope that's OK with you.'

She nodded.

'We'll keep you informed. Meanwhile, if you hear from your husband, contact us immediately. I'd like a quick word with the sergeant.'

Cantelli rose and handed over his card, then followed Horton into the garden. They walked down to the jetty.

'What did you get?' Horton asked.

'Roy Macey doesn't really need to drive the van and collect and deliver paintings or hang them — he has skilled and qualified staff to do that — but he likes to keep his hand in and always likes to work with Anther.'

'Did Mrs Macey ask you why we thought her husband was involved in art theft? She was upset when I mentioned it but there was no denial. It was as though we were confirming her suspicions.'

'She's numb and genuinely anxious, but her reason for not getting on her high horse and claiming her husband is as pure as the driven snow is because Kyle overheard his father speaking to Anther two weeks ago and again on Friday. Yes, we know he was missing by then, so Macey must have another number for Anther. They were talking in French. Mrs Macey doesn't speak the language, but Kyle does, fluently. He's learned it not only from his father but at school. On the first occasion Macey said something about Ellwood's paintings and that it was impossible; Dorothy couldn't have had them. When I asked Kyle if he heard the name Catmore mentioned, he said he did. Then on Friday he heard his dad say to Anther that Catmore was dead.'

Horton was disturbed by that even though he'd come to believe that Catmore had been killed. 'What did he and his mother make of that?'

'They're not sure, and if they're making guesses then they're not saying. Both claim though that Macey has been irritable and preoccupied this last fortnight and unlike his usual self, Kyle says he's snapped his head off for the smallest things. Mrs Macey says there are no business worries, and that it's booming, although he might have told her that and been lying. It sounds as though his worries surfaced when those wretched paintings did.'

Horton agreed. He stared across the sparkling sea of the harbour towards the south, where the small ferry was crossing. His mind was full of the case, pulling together the threads.

Cantelli continued. 'Mrs Macey confirmed that Roy learned his trade in Paris, where he worked with Julian in the 1980s.'

'Are you sure she said 1980s?' Horton asked sharply.

'Positive. Puts rather a different complexion on the matter.'

'He lied to us. Unless he lied to his wife.'

'She said Macey returned to England in 1993 when he married Jacqueline. He met the current Mrs Macey in 2002. She's twenty years younger than him. No children from his first marriage, just Kyle from this one. She and Kyle were away the weekend of the eighth and ninth of May at her sister's in Yeovil. She said her husband had told her he had a big weekend job to oversee in a gallery in London. We can check that with his business colleagues.'

'And when Catmore went missing? Where was Macey then?'

'At home in the evening, at work during the day. I showed them pictures of the Ellwood forgeries, but they've never seen them. Macey could have killed Spender and could have met Catmore somewhere during the day, when he was allegedly at work, and killed him.'

The police RIB came into view. 'I'm going to check the east shore of Hayling with Elkins and Ripley for a derelict jetty or slipway that could belong to The Shambles. Head back to the station and update Bliss and Uckfield. I'll call in if we find anything.'

Cantelli was only too relieved to do so. He was not the world's best sailor.

Horton climbed on board the RIB, donned a life vest and gave instructions to Ripley. He saw Kyle in the garden, watching them as they headed south, and felt sorry for the boy. Whatever the outcome, it didn't look good for him or his mother.

Ripley made out of the harbour and headed east, keeping the Hayling coast on their left. The sound of barking dogs came to them from the beach. A clutch of windsurfers and kitesurfers were making the most of the breeze. As they headed past the small funfair, Horton brought Elkins and Ripley up to date with events and the reason for his search of the coast. Soon they were rounding the south eastern tip of the island and heading up into the Emsworth Channel past the Hayling Sailing Club. A couple of boats were making their way out from the Chichester Channel to the east.

Ripley steadily headed north while Horton and Elkins scoured the shore to their left. It was easy enough for Horton to get his bearings from the country lanes that he and Cantelli had earlier traversed. Elkins had the charts up on the screen and although the house Ida had mentioned could possibly be sited in an inlet by the Hayling Yacht Company, the fact that she had said it faced Thorney Island meant it was farther north on Hayling Island. It was Ripley who spotted it first.

'There!' he cried. It wasn't a crumbling pontoon or dere-lict jetty that he was pointing at but a reasonably sized motor cruiser with a flybridge.

Horton's heart skipped a beat. He swiftly took in the surroundings. The concrete slipway to the left of the boat was covered in sand, grit and ingrained seaweed and the quayside was overgrown with brambles, grass, and bushes. It was clear to Horton that somewhere in the jungle beyond was the late Dorothy Massett's house and within the grounds most prob-ably the body of Noel Catmore.

The make of the boat and the name confirmed it was Macey's. Why hadn't he cleared out? Why come here? Where was he?

Ripley swung the launch towards it. Horton's mind was a swirling torrent of thoughts.

Elkins voiced one of them. 'I hope this isn't going to be a déjà-vu of Spender's boat, only this time with a body on board.'

Horton hoped not too, but he wasn't overly optimistic.

Ripley pulled alongside the craft. *Wind Drift* was roped up stern and aft to two rusting iron rings. Horton and Elkins alighted and made their way to the boat. There was nothing untoward in the cockpit that Horton could initially see. No sign of blood or blood spatter. But the smell was overwhelmingly sickening.

Exchanging a glance with Elkins, Horton steeled himself and boarded the craft. Elkins followed suit, pinching his nostrils.

Horton's gut tightened. He knew that the buzzing of a hundred flies wasn't coming from the undergrowth. Taking a deep breath, he pushed open the cabin door.

Across the table in the middle of the cabin was the slumped, decomposing body of Roy Macey.

CHAPTER TWENTY-SIX

Tuesday

Suicide, Uckfield had proclaimed last night. Macey had killed Spender and Catmore and had then killed himself.

As Horton shaved after a very late night and little sleep, he again considered this, as he had done for much of the night. There had been an empty bottle of whisky on the cabin table and alongside it an empty bottle of tablets. There had been no label on the bottle. The drug, whatever it had been, had probably been bought off the internet rather than prescribed. An analysis of Macey's organs would tell them what he had swallowed. It would have been difficult for any-one to have forced that amount of alcohol and pills down Macey's throat against his will and the doctor had said there were no signs of him being bound. But the police doctor wasn't as expert as Gaye, and the flesh had been infested, so it had been difficult to tell.

Horton wished Gaye was here. She said she'd be back at the end of the week so perhaps the autopsy would be post-poned until then. There had been no suicide note, but that wasn't unusual. And no photographs of his wife and son in front of him, which in Horton's experience was more usual.

Macey had been dead about forty hours, possibly longer, which put his time of death at approximately Saturday late afternoon or evening.

After finding Macey, Ripley had returned to the pontoon at the Portsmouth side of Ferry Road while Horton had called up Uckfield and Taylor. Ripley had then brought Uckfield around on the launch. The Super wouldn't normally have visited a suspected suicide, but this one was different. Ripley had again returned to Portsmouth to pick up the scene of crime team, including Clarke, the photographer. Dusk had fallen and arc lights had been erected. It had been too late to search the grounds but Horton had followed a slightly trampled path until he came upon the ruins of a substantial and heavily overgrown brick-built house. He hadn't entered it and didn't find Noel Catmore in the limited area of the grounds he'd covered. A team was going in this morning along with Walters, who would liaise with the uniformed sergeant in charge of the search.

Walters's enquiries with Spender's crew had revealed they'd never heard Spender mention Anther, but they had confirmed the bin route took in the rear of Anther's gallery and that Spender did that side of the road while Reams ran ahead to do the back of the retail units in the yard at the end of the service road.

Cantelli, accompanied by a woman police officer, had the sad and distressing task of informing Mrs Macey and her son of the tragic news, saying that it appeared her husband had taken his own life. They would be making a full investigation and would keep her informed. It meant they would need to search her husband's belongings and his office, and take away his computer, clothes and shoes for examination. Horton hadn't found a mobile phone on the boat. He suspected Macey had thrown it overboard. Trueman would apply to the phone company for access to a log of Macey's calls.

Cantelli had reported back saying that Vicky and Kyle Macey had shown little surprise at the news because they'd almost resigned themselves to some kind of tragedy having taken place. But they all knew that shock. Anger and grief would follow along with a myriad of questions, some of which the police would be able to answer and some they still were seeking answers to. Cantelli had gotten confirmation of Macey's blood group from Mrs Macey — it was AB negative, which seemed to support the theory that Macey had been on board Spender's boat and was his killer. The pathologist would look for a cut on Macey's body that had caused the limited bloodshed.

Cantelli had shown Mrs Macey the photographs of the Ellwood paintings that Catmore had taken to Anther's gallery, but neither she nor Kyle had seen them before. If Macey had owned the forgeries and switched them for the originals, then he must have kept the forgeries out of his family's sight. Cantelli and two uniformed officers were returning to Mrs Macey's this morning and were going through her husband's belongings and papers, for which she'd given permission. Two other officers from Havant police were to go into Macey's business premises. There was the possibility he had kept the forgeries there and had had no idea they were fakes until the originals had shown up. If that were so then Horton thought Macey must have displayed the paintings at work, because why hide them if he believed them to be genuine?

Taylor's examination of the boat in situ at The Shambles hadn't revealed anything startling except that there were several prints and hairs that didn't match the dead man's. They'd need Mrs Macey's and her son's prints for elimination purposes, which an officer, with Cantelli, would obtain. Elkins had taken the boat round to the secure compound at the port, where it would be more thoroughly examined if needed later.

As Horton showered, he revisited the facts of the case, looking for answers to the tragic series of deaths. It was obvious that Macey, Spender, Anther and Dorothy had all been involved in art fraud in Paris in the late seventies and throughout the eighties. They ceased when they returned to the UK in the early nineties, and that could have been because the Paris police were beginning to suspect them. They had divided up the money they'd made from the crime, enough for Anther to open up a gallery in Emsworth, Macey to start his picture-hanging business, and Spender to — what? Spend, it seemed, while Dorothy invested in property, three of which had been missed off her estate: the Hayling Island house and the London and Paris apartments. Uckfield had demanded to know how the legal officer at the council could have overlooked them but Cantelli, who had spoken to Nicola Bolton, had explained that it was easy to miss land and property when there was no will and if it had been bought before the legal requirement for purchases to be registered with the Land Registry, which was what had happened in this case. Sometimes registered property could be overlooked too, even if the deceased had made a will, if he or she had died before it could be included and a sloppy solicitor or executor didn't look for it.

It would be difficult trying to find Dorothy's missing properties in London and Paris, although Trueman had said if they caught up with Anther in France they might have some luck. They had confirmed that he had sailed on the Brittany ferry from Portsmouth to Cherbourg on Tuesday night. But where he went after that no one knew. Bliss was liaising with the Gendarmerie Nationale, who covered motorway and coastal patrols, and with the Préfecture de Police de Paris, who were assisting in the search for an apartment owned by Anther or Dorothy Massett. Bliss spoke fluent French, a fact that astounded them all. She'd never given any hint of it before and Horton wondered if she had property there.

He locked up the boat with only a third of his mind on what he was doing while the other two thirds considered what must have happened in 1993 when Spender was attacked, and then two months after, when Dorothy had died. It was Horton's bet that Spender had rapidly burned through his share of the money and asked the others for more. They all had more to lose than him, and he'd begun his blackmail racket, but one of the gang wasn't going to have that — Macey. Macey tried to kill Spender and failed. But as Spender had lost his memory as a result of the attack, they were all safe.

But why kill Dorothy? Maybe that *was* an accident. Or perhaps Dorothy had threatened to go to the police, but not the Dorothy that Ida Tidy had painted a picture of.

Horton pulled in on the seafront and stared across the Solent. The southerly wind was getting up steam and already creating rollercoaster waves. He could barely make out the hills of the Isle of Wight in the distance. He didn't think Anther capable of killing Dorothy, although Cantelli had suggested that maybe Anther had killed her by accident, then loosened the stair rod. Anther and Macey then agreed to forget the whole matter and get on with their lives, which is what they did until Spender got his memory back and recognized his paintings.

And there was Ruth Bowen's evidence about the blood pooling and congealing: *This pool of blood would, over time, congeal and solidify, which is precisely what has happened here.* Spender's body had been lifted and carried off the boat, which Macey was perfectly capable of doing and had done — but he hadn't done it immediately after killing Spender. As Horton had pointed out and Ruth had confirmed, there wouldn't have been pooling in the cabin deck and there would be more bloodstains in the cockpit. It seemed likely therefore that Anther had killed Spender and then summoned Macey to help him dispose of the body and cast the boat adrift.

So, who had Spender been blackmailing after leaving Southern and before taking the job with Jeplie? He had got that money to buy his designer clothes and the boat from somewhere. It was a thought that had occupied Horton most of the night. And in the early hours of the morning, he had realized the answer.

Horton headed for the Wightlink car ferry. Twenty minutes later he was on board drinking a coffee, and an hour later he was at St Mary's Hospital.

Felice looked up as he entered the single-bedded room. Her face was gaunt, her eyes red-rimmed and every inch of her body registered exhaustion as she sat beside the motionless man in the bed. There was little left of the vivacious woman he'd met in April. His heart went out to her. She didn't seem surprised to see him.

'You know, don't you?' she said wearily.

'Not all of it.'

She rose. 'Let's talk outside.'

They didn't speak until they were in the hospital grounds and some distance from the main entrance. There Horton began to voice his thoughts.

'There was no swap,' he said. 'You knew the paintings Catmore took into Anther's galleries were forgeries the moment you saw them.'

'Yes.' She pushed her hand through her hair and turned an anguished face on him. 'If I had known it would lead to all these deaths, I'd never have done it. That wasn't my intention. I just wanted to find out . . . to establish . . .'

'Who had forged your father's paintings, who had been blackmailing him before his motorbike accident, and why?'

Her head whipped round. 'How did you know about the blackmail?'

'Let's take that seat.' He indicated a wooden bench in the far corner of the grounds that had just been vacated by an elderly couple whose taxi had turned up. It was one of a few set around a circular raised flower bed, protecting them from the traffic pollution and sound on the dual carriageway beyond.

'The accident your father had two years ago on his motorbike was no accident. That's what really drove you to lie, when you learned that. You wanted to know who had bled your father so dry and tormented him so much that he went out with the deliberate intention of killing himself.'

She peered into the distance with haunted eyes. Horton remained silent.

Finally, she spoke. 'When he was hospitalized after the accident I had to go through the accounts. I soon realized something was very wrong.' She turned to study him, her tone earnest. 'Money had been pouring out at an alarming rate. He'd been taking out large sums of cash and had stopped painting. I was living and working on the other side of the world at the time and had no idea of this,' she said anguished, full of guilt.

'So, you saw a way of getting some money from these forgeries that had turned up.'

'No!'

Her denial seemed genuine, but Horton let it go for now.

'The first two paintings you authenticated were forgeries,' he continued, 'as was the third, which you identified as a forgery. Nothing much would have come of it, if you had said that right at the beginning. Yes, you could have reported it to the police, and yes, the Arts and Antiques Unit would have logged it and possibly made an investigation into it because of your father's standing and his reputation, but you needed a much more thorough investigation than that. You needed to know who had blackmailed your father. Maybe at that stage you didn't even stop to think that, by doing so, it would expose your father's shady past.'

'I couldn't believe that my father could be involved in anything that warranted blackmail. I thought he must be protecting someone. I confronted him over it, but he refused to tell me where the money had gone. I tried many times to get it from him but it only made matters worse, so I stopped asking. He recovered sufficiently from the accident to be sent home with my care. I encouraged him to try and paint but he wasn't interested. He was drinking heavily, even though he tried to hide that from me. I had put things right with the bank and others. I opened the gallery with Maurice's help and tried to put it behind me. It was done. I had control of our finances and could look after us both. I begged my father to get help for his alcoholism and get back to painting. Maurice also tried but nothing worked. My father grew more and more depressed. The drink and his injuries from the accident meant his health deteriorated. When those paintings turned up out of the blue, I knew they must have been copied when my father had lived in Paris, and I knew they were forgeries. I began to wonder. I needed to know who had painted them. Would they lead me to the person who had driven my father to attempt suicide and was even now still killing him?' Her mouth hardened and her eyes flashed with anger.

'I told Julian the first two paintings were originals. I didn't know then a third would be taken in by Mr Catmore. I said I needed to go through my father's paperwork to find a reference to them, and I wished to show my father photographs of the paintings, thinking he might recall them. He might tell me who had executed them and why, and I might get to the truth, although I didn't know if they had anything to do with who he was protecting. I had to wait until my father was conscious, which was becoming increasingly rare, but there came a moment when he looked at them and the pain in his eyes tore at my heart.' She took a gulp of air that was almost a sob.

Horton reached out and grasped her hand. Her eyes were full of sorrow and pain as she squeezed it.

'My father said nothing, he just shook his head. But I knew it was what lay at the bottom of his wretchedness. I had to know who had done those forgeries, Andy, and why. I thought . . . that perhaps I could ease my father's pain.' She sighed. 'I was naive, but we all believe and hope.' She gave a weary, sad smile.

Horton also had believed and hoped for many a long year as a child that his mother would return and rescue him from the children's homes. More recently on his quest to discover the truth about Jennifer he had believed and hoped he would at first find her alive and, when that hope had died, that he would unravel the truth behind her disappearance. He'd got there in the end, and wished he hadn't, and his obsession had resulted in death, just as Felice's had. In his case, that of one of the Ames brothers, even though a body hadn't been found. He released Felice's hand and watched as she composed herself.

'Then Julian called me again to say he had a third painting and would I return to examine it. He sent me a picture of it because I was in Wales conducting a valuation. I wondered how many more paintings were going to turn up. I returned home on Thursday and asked Maurice about it when he came over to the island on Friday. On my second visit to Anther's gallery on the following Monday with Maurice, I declared, as you know, that the third painting was a fake and said the two originals had been swapped for forgeries. I said I would telephone you because of our recent contact, and that you were very thorough and an inspector with Portsmouth CID. I wanted you to be involved because I knew I could trust you. I was confident you would find out what was going on and that you might discover who had been blackmailing my father and why.'

He had. Neil Spender. Perhaps her remark about trusting him was genuine, or perhaps she had hoped his attraction to her would override any suspicion.

He said, 'Anther knew from the start the paintings were forgeries. He also knew who had executed them and when.'

'He did? But he didn't say! Why didn't he?' she declared, baffled.

'Greed got the better of him when you claimed them to be originals. He couldn't understand how they had been found and by a man claiming to be a relative of Dorothy when he knew, as did Roy Macey, that Dorothy didn't have any relatives.'

'Then she did exist. I didn't know that.'

But she did. He could see it on her face and hear it in her voice.

'The fact that Julian called you in to authenticate the pictures puzzled me, even more so as we got deeper into the investigation and unravelled the past fraud. Why did Anther send for you? Why didn't he keep silent about the paintings? But then, in order to do so, Noel Catmore would also have had to be silenced for the paintings to then be passed off as originals. Anther didn't have the stomach for murder, so he pushed that aside and concentrated on how he could turn the find to his financial advantage. He was stupid to do so. We all make mistakes, although his cost lives.'

Horton paused as a couple walked past talking loudly. 'Anther knew the paintings would fetch a huge sum of money. His commission would be substantial. And with Maurice Linden terminally ill, Anther wouldn't have to wait very long before putting them up for auction and bypassing Linden. Also, with your father seriously ill, Anther thought, he could grab more of the proceeds. He was also aware that your father was in dire financial straits and if he recovered from his illness that he would need care, which costs a considerable amount of money.' Just as Cantelli had suggested right at the beginning when Horton hadn't like to contemplate Felice's duplicity in the case.

He continued, 'Anther thought even if you proclaimed them to be forgeries on first sight, you might still be persuaded to say they were originals for the sake of your father being able to afford top-quality nursing care. Or if your father died then you would inherit, and you needed the money.'

'That never crossed my mind,' she vehemently declared. 'I don't care about the money. I just wanted to know who had blackmailed my father.'

'Anther must have been delighted when you declared the first two pictures as originals. He rubbed his hands in glee. You — not only an art expert but the artist's daughter — had accepted them at face value, even though you knew they were forgeries. Then he had a shock when you declared the originals had been swapped for forgeries, not the first shock, the third one in fact. The paintings surfacing at all had been the first jolt to him and the second was that before you returned to authenticate that third painting, something happened. Neil Spender saw the paintings. He knew they were forgeries and confronted Anther. Spender had to be dealt with but Anther couldn't do it, so he turned to you.'

'No! I didn't kill him. Andy, you must believe me, I haven't killed anyone.'

He'd heard that before, many times. Was it the truth? 'You knew Spender had a boat because your father had paid for it. You'd traced the financial transaction. Easy enough to discover where he kept it, especially for a person who sails, as you do. You telephoned Spender and asked him to meet you at Salterns Lake Quay, where you drove a boat hook through his chest, hauled his body overboard and cast his boat adrift. Did you then persuade Catmore to tell you where he had found the paintings and meet him in the grounds of The Shambles on Hayling Island — a property belonging to the late Dorothy Massett — and kill him? Did you tell Roy Macey what you had done because you knew he had been involved in the art fraud in the 1980s? He killed himself. Or did you help him on his way?'

She was staring at him wide-eyed and pale, shaking her head. 'No! I didn't do any of that! I don't know Spender. Is Roy . . . But he can't be! How is that possible? He didn't know . . . Oh my God, please say it's not true?'

He studied her for a long minute. 'Why did you lie to me about Maurice being here at the hospital?'

'I didn't, he was here . . .' She looked down.

'Where will I find him, Felice?'

She remained silent. But Horton already knew. Not at Felice's house, but on her boat in East Cowes Marina.

'Will he still be there when I reach your boat?'

Her tortured expression tore at his heart. She made to speak but couldn't. He reached out a hand and touched her shoulder. She grasped it. 'I'm so sorry.'

Horton made his way across the island to East Cowes Marina. His heart was heavy with sorrow for her and her father but mingled with it was anger and frustration. If she hadn't lied, Anther wouldn't have panicked and set off the deadly chain of events. If Catmore hadn't found the paintings, if he hadn't taken them to Anther's gallery, if Spender hadn't seen and recognized them. But, as he had thought so many times in investigations, 'if' was a pointless road down which to travel. Spender had been a crook, but he hadn't deserved to die. Neither had Roy Macey and Noel Catmore.

Horton got the pontoon number and name of the boat from the marina staff. Linden was in the cockpit of the sturdy yacht looking out for him. Felice had obviously phoned him. His face was drawn and grey, his cheeks hollowed, and the weight seemed to have oozed off his frame since Horton had last seen him.

'Come on board, Inspector.'

As they stepped down into the cabin, Horton knew that Linden could reach for a knife or a boat hook and stab him, but he didn't think he would. The marina was too public a place for him to try anything, and besides, he'd done all he'd set out to do.

But Horton was wrong. Only a soft movement gave warning before something struck him violently on the back of the head.

He stumbled. He tried to right himself but couldn't. He hit the ground.

Then darkness.

CHAPTER TWENTY-SEVEN

It was the noise he first registered, a deep throb that seemed to vibrate through his whole body and thud in his head. He heard a groan — his. A glimmer of light. He blinked. It hurt. He blinked again and after a moment peeled open his eyes.

It took some seconds for him to focus. He was on the floor of the cabin and his hands were restrained behind his back. He pulled at them, but they remained firmly secured.

'I'm sorry, Inspector,' a voice came to him from above. Horton shifted slightly to see Linden peering down at him from the helm. 'I hope I haven't caused too serious an injury, that was not my intention. If you bear with me a moment, I'll join you.' He made it sound as though they were about to partake of cocktails.

Horton concentrated on getting his full vision back and on ignoring his pounding head. He cursed his stupidity for underestimating a dying man. In fact, he had underestimated Linden from the word go, a mistake that could cost him his life. Linden might be terminally ill — and of that Horton was certain, he could see it etched in every pore of his gaunt frame — but he still might wish to eliminate the one person who could expose him. And Linden would certainly want his last days on earth to be spent in freedom.

Horton wasn't sure how long the boat continued to travel, and he couldn't see where they were headed. There was a swell but nothing to give him the direction. He shuffled back to lean against the locker and gradually pulled himself up so that he was sitting on the bench seat. Glancing out of the porthole all he could see was the sea. The craft swung to the right and Horton made out the chine and downs. They looked to be off the South West coast of the Isle of Wight.

He rose and swayed a little, not with the movement of the boat, but because of his head. His vision blurred, then cleared. He was about to go up on deck when the engine ceased. The movement of the boat above the rocking caused by the waves told him that Linden was letting down the anchor. What now? he wondered, swiftly registering his surroundings. There was a grey flask on the table, nothing else.

Linden stepped down into the cabin. 'Once again, I apologize for the rough stuff and hope I haven't caused any lasting damage.'

'Fortunately, I have a thick skull, or so I've been told. It's happened to me before,' Horton replied a little cynically, resuming his seat.

Linden gave a small smile. 'I can't untie you or offer you refreshment, I'm afraid. But I'm not going to harm you. I hoped you'd come alone. And seeing that you had done so, I didn't want you calling up reinforcements and arresting me. There is no need for that. I haven't got long.' He sat to the left of the table, opposite Horton on the other side of the cabin. 'We're just off Brook Bay, on the Isle of Wight, alone. No one will disturb us here. Michael is dead. Felice called to say he passed away while you were talking to her.'

Horton's heart wrenched. It so often happened. People could spend all day and night at a loved one's bedside, and the moment they stepped outside, the loved one slipped away. Felice would probably never forgive herself — or him — for not being there.

'Michael killed Dorothy,' Linden said in a matter-of-fact tone.

Horton started with surprise. Was this a bluff? Was Linden trying to shift the blame? But no, he seemed in earnest.

'I can tell you this because now he's dead it doesn't matter anymore. In fact, nothing matters.'

'Then untie me and let's go back to the island.'

'You know I can't do that. And I'm sure you would like to hear the full story.'

'About Dorothy Massett, who knew you all in Paris, even though you lied to me about living there with Michael in the 1980s?'

'I didn't lie. I just never volunteered that information and you never asked me directly. I said Michael and I were at school together and that we went back a very long way. I'm surprised you managed to trace Dorothy, and so quickly.'

'We also traced her derelict property on Hayling Island and found Macey's body.'

'Felice told me. But how did you discover the Hayling property? Did Catmore tell you he'd been metal-detecting there?'

'No. We talked to Dorothy's cleaning lady.'

Linden frowned. 'How did she know?'

'Dorothy told her, although not exactly where the property was. But Catmore told *you* before you killed him.'

'Yes. I called on him on Tuesday evening, having got the address from Julian. I told him I was Ellwood's agent and that the paintings were worth a fortune and that I had switched the originals for forgeries because I didn't trust Anther, who was trying to swindle him. I said that if he showed me where they had been found, we might find others and we might be able to find documentation that could authenticate them. I knew what to look for. And I would make sure he got the full value of the originals when I sold them discreetly to collectors, minus my commission of course. We drove to Hayling and he parked the car along the country lane. We walked down a footpath to the shore, headed east and then north along the shore until we came to the quayside. I had no idea about Dorothy's Hayling Island property or that she had kept some paintings there.'

Horton thought it a shame that the woman living opposite Catmore hadn't seen another man with him. Or perhaps she had and had forgotten to say.

'Were there other paintings?'

'A few. They no longer exist.'

'Forgeries by Spender or by Michael?'

'Both. Catmore found the first two in one of those metal briefcases that were popular in the 1980s, along with the fragment of a letter with the words "Dorothy Masse" remaining. He looked up the artist's name on the internet, saw that Michael Ellwood was a very renowned artist, and took the paintings to Anther's gallery.' Linden gave a twisted smile. 'A quirk of fate when you think he could have taken them to any other gallery in Portsmouth, although there aren't that many in the city and Anther's was the nearest to where he lived.'

'The passer-by who he said told him to get them valued didn't exist?'

'No. He embellished his tales, as I think he liked to do in other matters. After Anther said he would need to get the two paintings examined, Catmore returned to Hayling to Dorothy's house on Friday the twenty-third of April to look for more.'

'Why did he go there in the first place?'

'He was metal-detecting along the shore. As you probably know it is very private around that part of the island with no right of way for the public and no vehicular access. The land above the mean high-water line is private, but Catmore wasn't bothered by that. He was looking for Roman remains. There are very few houses backing on to the shore on that side of the island, it's practically deserted. He saw the old quay and decided to explore inland, found the house and wondered if there might be some rich pickings in there and in the grounds that he wouldn't have to declare as treasure. He didn't need anyone's permission to trample over the land because it was clear it had been abandoned. On his second visit, he found the third painting in a steel archival box. The ones I found when I went back with him were in a large art archival case, leather. They had deteriorated but I still destroyed them.' He stalled, sucked in his breath and took a drink from the flask. His emaciated face was twisted with pain.

'You need medical help,' Horton said, worried.

'Too late for that, Inspector. I need to confess, and you are to hear my confession, which I am sure you have no objection to. To get back to Dorothy. Michael was so upset and furious with Dorothy for having had Neil beaten up.'

'They were Dorothy's orders?' Horton asked, again shocked at this revelation, although perhaps he shouldn't have been from what Ida had said about her employer's past lifestyle and her wealth.

'Dorothy was the boss and Dorothy always got her own way, whether it was money, crime or sex.'

'You were Dorothy's lover?'

'Briefly. We all were, including Michael and Neil. Oh, except Anther. Even Dorothy drew the line there. She knew that Anther could never satisfy her. Roy superseded me and lasted the longest. It seems he was much better at pleasing Dorothy than I, or any of us, was. When Michael found out how seriously injured Neil was, he confronted Dorothy. I don't know exactly what happened but as Michael told it, she told him to grow up and heed it as a lesson that the same would happen to him if he so much as breathed a word about the art fraud. Then she laughed and said she knew he wouldn't say anything because he was making a name for himself in the art world and wouldn't want his sordid past of forging valuable paintings being exposed. He lost control. He put his hands around her throat and began to choke the life out of her. When he realized what he was doing, repulsed, he pushed her away. They were at the top of the stairs. She had her back to him. The push caused her to topple and down she went. She was dead by the time she reached the bottom. He called me.'

'And you went to his aid.'

'We've always looked after each other, even at school. The only time I couldn't look out for him was when he went out on that damn motorbike and tried to kill himself. But we'll come to that in a moment.' Linden took a drink from the flask. He winced. Not from the drink, whatever it was, but in pain.

'I told Michael to stay put at Dorothy's and not to do or touch anything until I got there. That wasn't difficult for him because when I arrived an hour later, he was just sitting in a trance on the floor close to the body. I made sure there was nothing in the house that linked with us. There were no paintings by Michael or copies by Spender.'

'You missed one by Michael.'

'Really? How?'

'Dorothy had given one to her cleaning lady. A drawing of Dorothy at the barre in her ballet dress.'

'Ah. I made a mistake by overlooking the cleaning lady. I didn't find anything on the purchase of the Hayling Island property in Dorothy's house. I found documents on the apartment in Paris and the one in London, which I took away. I didn't want the police, or anyone else, to find them. There was no will. Dorothy would never countenance her death. I wanted as little known about Dorothy as was possible. I certainly didn't want her crooked past coming out—'

'And yours, Michael's, Anther's and Macey's. Was Guy Bampton involved?'

'Guy, no! What made you think that? Because he's an avid collector, I suppose. No.'

'And Oxley?'

Linden gave a cruel smile. 'I only wish he were, and I could point the finger at him. Prison would do him good.'

He took another drink. 'After Dorothy's death, I had to check out her apartments in London and Paris. There could have been documents of Michael's time as a forger or paintings he'd copied. I needed to make sure the trail was clean. I visited both and made certain there was no evidence linking back to any of us. I took over the London apartment and Julian the Paris one. We all swore never to talk of Dorothy. Spender wouldn't because his memory was shot to pieces. Julian had been terrified of her and was heartily relieved when she died. Roy had been sick of Dorothy for some time, but he couldn't get out of her grasp as her lover, even after he married Jacqueline. He didn't love Dorothy. He thought his marriage would bring him release but Dorothy wouldn't let him go. She enjoyed having power over people, particularly men, and she knew how to get it, how to keep hold of it and how to wield it. I think he was the only one she really loved, if her voracious sexual appetite could be called love. She threatened to tell Jacqueline, saying no woman would believe a man could make love to another woman against his will, and that was true to an extent. Roy both hated Dorothy and needed her. I told Julian and Roy that I had killed Dorothy, that it had been an accident, but the police would never believe that when they probed deeper. No one knew the truth, except me and Michael.'

Which meant that Ellwood was even more in Linden's debt. He could never have escaped him if he had wanted to.

'When Dorothy died,' Linden continued, 'I made sure to visit her two houses, the one in Bedhampton and in Havant, to remove any valuable paintings. Fortunately, there was no tenant at Havant, and no paintings, but I had to check. There were however some very valuable paintings in The Coach House at Bedhampton, originals for which there was provenance. Even if there hadn't been, Julian, Roy and I knew those who would pay privately to acquire them. I set Julian up in the gallery at Emsworth and through it we gradually sold the paintings. We shared the money from the sale between us. It gave Julian enough to continue the gallery, Roy to start and grow his business in the UK, me to expand my agency, and Michael to paint, except that Michael wouldn't touch the money. So, I kept hold of his share and bought one of his paintings with it for insurance later, should he need money from the sale of it.'

'Which you gave to Felice to sell in the gallery.'

'Yes. I told her that Michael had given it to me years ago. I didn't need the money and it would help him get specialist nursing care, which he no longer needs.'

'But she withdrew it because, after seeing the forgeries in Julian's gallery, she was doubtful about its provenance and scared it was a forgery. She told me that she said Spender's forgeries were originals when they weren't. She was trying to find out who had blackmailed her father and rendered him practically penniless. So you didn't take care of Michael then,' Horton said scathingly.

'He should have come to me. But he didn't.'

And Horton knew why. 'Because he was afraid you would see to it that Spender was silenced and, although he wanted Spender off his back, he couldn't countenance murder. He also didn't wish to be beholden to you even more than he already was. Just as Dorothy had influence over you all, you had the same over Michael — there was a toxic emotional attachment, which was hard for him to sever.'

'I can assure you it was nothing like that,' Linden said waspishly. 'Michael was always oversensitive, and useless with money and practical matters. He was one of life's natural victims, a sucker. He needed protecting. When I arrived in Paris, I looked out for him. If Lisa hadn't done the same in New York soon after Michael had arrived there, God alone knows what would have happened to him. When she died, he would have gone to pieces if it hadn't been for me.'

'That's one way of looking at it.' And Michael could have accepted and been grateful for Linden's help, or was too lazy, too timid or too bereaved to fight against it. Bampton had said Maurice Linden had been a tower of strength to Michael, that they'd been friends since their school days, but Linden could never replace Lisa. Horton quickly pulled together what he had learned with what he had heard today and what his experience both as a police officer and as a child growing up in children's homes had taught him. Bampton's description of Michael Ellwood had been that he was gentle, reflective, considerate and sensitive. He felt things deeply. Oxley had described Ellwood as weak and timid. And those eyes in the picture on the crime board Horton had stared at had a hint of uneasiness and shyness behind them. Yes,

Michael Ellwood was a very great artist, but he needed someone with force and character to support him.

He said, 'Michael needed your strength, charm, wit, intelligence and devilment. It was the opposite of how he saw himself. His art was one way out, a form of expressing how he felt, but even then, you took that away from him in Paris, when he copied others' works. You needed adoration and control and Dorothy's murder gave you that over Michael.'

'I didn't know you were a psychoanalyst,' Linden said cuttingly.

'No, just a police officer, and sometimes they amount to being the same.'

Linden shrugged as though to say, 'Please yourself' and swallowed more of the liquid.

'Michael tried hard to break the hold you had over him when he was a young man. He dropped out of school to escape you and ran away to Paris, but five years later, with a degree in Art History, you found him. You also met Dorothy, a clever, attractive, sensual young woman with a quick brain, charm, a yearning for wealth and adventure, a careless disregard for danger and a voracious appetite for sex. Her wildness and her extreme sexual magnetism attracted you and together you hatched the art fraud plan.'

'She really was a remarkable woman,' Linden said, 'but callous. I'll save you speculating, Inspector. I introduced Michael and Neil to Dorothy. By then the two of them were starving in the proverbial garret trying to sell their paintings. Neil was a dreadful painter when it came to style and originality, but he was an excellent forger, as you've seen. Michael was extremely talented, a good copyist, and they both needed money. We were all young and thought it would be a laugh and one in the eye for the art establishment. It was easy to identify who owned original paintings of value.'

'Your job or Anther's?'

'All four of us — me, Dorothy, Roy and Julian, but Dorothy was the ringmaster, or mistress if you prefer. Roy was working for the same gallery as Julian, as you know.'

'Yes, and he lied about the dates when he lived in Paris.'

Linden gave him a 'So what?' look. 'Roy was involved in transporting artworks and learning how to display them, so he came across many owners. Dorothy moved in both the art and criminal world. She had contacts who would pay vast sums for original artworks. Julian knew the gallery owners and auctioneers. Either she or Julian would get the names and addresses of who had bought what. I, or Dorothy, depending on the individual purchaser, would make contact and charm our way into their properties and confidences, suss out the lie of the land and engineer the switch.'

'And this wasn't just in Paris?'

'No, it was across the continent, although mainly France and Italy — nationals of both those countries appreciate fine art. We made a very good living for ten years, all through the loads-of-money eighties.'

'What went wrong?'

'Do you need to ask?'

No, thought Horton. 'Dorothy got bored, Anther got nervous, Spender started drinking and Michael left for America without telling any of you, which must have annoyed and hurt you.'

'We carried on for a while without him,' Linden said, ignoring the jibe and grimacing in pain. He swallowed some more drink. His eyes were growing cloudy and there were pinpricks of sweat on his forehead. 'But you're correct. Spender was drinking heavily and making mistakes. We were nearly caught. We had to get out. We all returned to the UK, except for Michael, who had found love in New York and then fame.'

'Were you jealous?' Horton asked, curious to know.

'No.'

It was a lie. 'You were annoyed that Michael had managed to achieve fame on his own without you being there to hold his hand,' Horton taunted. He saw from the tightening of Linden's jaw that he'd struck a nerve. He wriggled his hands behind his back and flexed his fingers to release his bonds, but the tie was too strong.

'Not without Lisa, he wouldn't have.'

'And when she died you capitalized on his grief and stepped in to become his agent, something he probably didn't want but was powerless to prevent. Not only did you know about his past, but he needed your strength and business acumen, which Lisa had provided in your absence. He retreated further into his own world, leaving you to handle everything. Felice was working miles away. Ellwood's paintings, thanks to your efforts, became even more highly sought after. Then just over three years ago something happened that resulted in Spender blackmailing him.'

CHAPTER TWENTY-EIGHT

Linden removed a handkerchief from his pocket and wiped his brow. His hand was shaking. The boat rocked and bucked with the roll of the waves and wind. Horton could hear it whistling through the mast. He strained for the sound of approaching boats but even if there were any, they wouldn't stop, and they wouldn't hear his shouts above the weather and the sea.

When Linden didn't speak, Horton continued. 'Michael saw Spender on the train.' He registered Linden's surprise that he had guessed correctly. 'Spender worked on the train presentation team, cleaning them. He was invisible to most people, he overheard conversations, saw things that could be used for blackmail. He also spoke French. Did he hear Michael speaking to you in French on the phone? Did that prompt something in his memory?'

'You're almost right. Congratulations, Inspector, for getting so far. Michael was travelling home to the Isle of Wight from an exhibition of his paintings in London. He usually travelled from Waterloo to Portsmouth on the South Western trains but this time, because of where his exhibition had been in London, he went from Victoria to Portsmouth on the Southern train, which terminates, as you know, at

Portsmouth Hard, where the cleaning crew go on board. But Spender didn't overhear anything and no, he wasn't invisible to Michael, quite the opposite. Before Michael could prevent himself, he recognized Spender and made himself known to him. Spender at first didn't recognize him, or know what he was talking about, but Michael was insistent that they meet. He felt sorry for Neil and guilt-ridden over what had happened to him and that each of us save Michael had benefited financially from Dorothy's death in the selling of her paintings. Michael thought that Spender was entitled to his share, the share that Michael had waived.

'Spender's memory was very bad — the head injury had made it disjointed — but with regular prompting he began to recall Michael and their time in Paris. He didn't remember being an artist or a forger, but Michael foolishly persisted. He thought he was helping Neil to recover his memory by carefully coaching him. And he succeeded, unfortunately. He invited Neil over to the Isle of Wight. They spent time together. Michael tried to help Neil get his appetite for art back. He saw it as therapy. Felice was on the other side of the world. Michael said nothing to me because he knew what I would do. Michael would also meet Neil on his day off on Southsea seafront. They would go for a walk, a drink and talk. Spender's memory began to clear little by little. Michael bought a small studio in Portsmouth for Spender to try to resume his art.'

'The key Spender kept under his pillow.'

'Did he?'

'Yes, and you got the one Michael had. Michael told you where it was, or you found it while searching his studio and gave it to Anther. That was a mistake.'

'I passed it to him on the Monday when I first met you in his gallery. I'd been on the island, if you remember, visiting Michael in hospital and came over with Felice. I told Julian to go to the studio and make sure there was nothing in it to show it had been used as an art studio and that there was nothing to incriminate Michael or any of us, and nothing to link us with Spender.'

'Where is the studio?'

'In the lanes adjacent to Portsmouth Football Club. It's an old stable building with an upper loft area and good roof light. Julian said there were no artists' materials, only marine equipment, stolen no doubt. Spender had always been dishonest.'

Horton let that go. He pulled at his restraints. Did they ease a little?

Linden swallowed some more from the flask and wiped his forehead. His skin was the colour of gunmetal. Concerned, Horton said, 'Untie me, Linden. I'll take you back and get you help.'

'I'm beyond that, as I've already said.' Linden was fighting to control his pain. 'Spender realized he was onto a good thing. He asked for more money and Michael gave it to him, then it became more and soon Michael was hooked as a blackmail victim. We both know that it never stops, not until either the blackmailer or the victim is dead or dried out. Michael thought he could handle it alone. He couldn't. When he could stand it no longer, he went out on his motorbike, and you know what happened next.'

Michael Ellwood had chosen to destroy himself rather than go to his lifelong friend and agent and ask for help. It bore out what Horton suspected: Ellwood hated the emotional grip Linden had on him. He hated the fact that he both loved and despised Linden, and he was consumed with guilt over his part in the art fraud and the killing of Dorothy. Horton wondered if Linden had played on the latter over the years, accentuating the fact that it was far from an accident and that Michael had committed manslaughter. Perhaps he'd even convinced Michael that he would be convicted of murder.

'Why didn't Spender turn to blackmailing Anther and Macey after Michael's money dried up?'

'Because Michael never mentioned them to him, nor did he mention my name. He told Neil they had shared a flat in Paris and had painted together. There were huge gaps in

Neil's memory. The brain is a funny thing. Spender retained all his fluency in French but not that he had been an artist or a forger. When Michael willingly gave Spender money, Spender was grateful and then curious. He pushed to see just how far Michael would go, and he went a long way. Slowly Spender's memory cleared and gradually Michael let out what had occurred in Paris without mentioning any of us, although he did talk about Dorothy. She was dead, so Michael felt it was safe to do so. He thought he was helping Spender when in reality he was providing the bait for more blackmail demands.' Linden struggled to get his breath.

Horton said, 'Michael attempted suicide, and as a result of his terrible injuries, Spender's money was cut off.'

Linden nodded. 'Michael was pretty much cleaned out by then anyway.'

'Spender kept hold of the boat and the expensive clothes bought with the blackmail money. He kept the studio and used it to store stolen items, as you said. I take it that he had no interest in resuming his art, either original or forged?'

'None. He just played along with Michael to get money, without really realizing how big the fraud had been. If he had known, or even stopped to think about it, he might have sold the story to the media and earned himself another tidy sum. But then Spender wasn't very bright to begin with and the head injury had made him even less so.'

Horton took up the tale. 'When the money dried up, and after Michael's accident, Spender had to give up the flat and get a job. Then eighteen months later, Noel Catmore showed up with the Ellwood forgeries. Was it at Anther's gallery that Spender recognized them or in Catmore's house?'

Linden took a breath before answering. 'At the gallery. It was one of those chance happenings. Who would have thought it could trigger more of Spender's memory, but Michael had inadvertently been helping that. Better than paying for therapy, eh?' He said with bitterness. 'And, of course, Spender spoke fluent French, as do I, Julian and Roy.'

'He overheard Julian on the phone talking to you.'

Linden drained the flask and nodded. He blinked several times and seemed to sway a little but took control of himself, clearly with an effort. He gave a twisted, tortured smile that was almost a grimace. 'Spender was collecting the bins from the yard. It was Wednesday the twenty-eighth of April after Catmore had come in with the third painting the day before. The back door was open. The cleaner asked Spender to hold on, there was something she needed to put in the bin, and she went into the gallery to fetch it. Spender was curious and keen to take a peek in the gallery because of Michael's insistence about him trying to paint again. The door to Julian's office was also open, and the third painting was facing out. He recognized it immediately as one of Michael's — after all, he'd been to his studio enough times and Michael had shown him photographs of his work. But it was more than that. It jogged a long dormant memory. I've read that it can sometimes happen — an accident, shock, word or phrase, a sighting of someone or something and the memory can suddenly return as though a curtain has been pulled back to reveal daylight. He knew he must have painted it. Maybe Michael had told him they used to imitate each other's artworks. He also heard Julian puzzling over the provenance of the paintings from Catmore's "Aunt Dorothy", when he knew Dorothy Massett to be dead with no family. Spender knew about Dorothy as Michael had told him about her. Spender said nothing but went away and thought about it.'

'He went off sick from work, allegedly with a migraine, but instead he caught the ferry to the island and visited Michael in hospital,' Horton added. One of Spender's crew members had said Spender had gone off sick on Friday and Saturday.

'Yes, and Michael, who wasn't as heavily sedated then but knew his time on this earth was limited, foolishly told him everything. Spender became his confessor, just as you're mine, Inspector.' Linden took a breath, which turned into a contortion of pain.

Horton rapidly put himself in Spender's shoes and thought what he would have done next. It didn't take much of a leap of imagination. 'On the Saturday morning, after visiting Michael in hospital on Friday, Spender entered the gallery dressed in his designer clothes, not looking at all like a refuse collector.'

Linden's words began to come in short, soft gasps. 'Julian didn't recognize him, neither did he recognize him as the refuse collector, even given his scarred face and gnarled hands. But then who looks at the binmen?'

Mademoiselle Dufrés had said as much.

Linden continued with difficulty, 'When Spender mentioned he was interested in Michael Ellwood's paintings, and that he knew Julian had some, Julian idiotically showed him the ones Catmore had brought in. Then Spender dropped the bombshell. He said that Julian, Roy and I owed him. While he'd suffered and lived in poverty, we had all gone on to make money. He'd keep quiet about the past in return for financial compensation, enough to allow him to quit his job.'

Mademoiselle Dufrés's words confirmed this. *You won't be seeing me anymore after today . . . He said, 'I've hit the jackpot.'*

'Michael told Felice nothing of this?' Horton asked.

'No . . . wanted to protect her . . . and her memory of him. Michael had no idea Felice had told Julian that the first two paintings, the only ones she'd seen at that time, were originals. Neither did I know, not then. When Neil tried to blackmail Julian, me and Roy . . . Michael had given him our names and told him who we were, it was not difficult to find us . . . Julian told me about the first two paintings and Felice's authentication.' Linden tried to take a breath, which turned into a gasp.

Horton, deeply concerned, pressed once again for him to take Linden back to the shore but Linden ignored him or didn't hear. He had to get his story out. With a supreme effort, he continued. 'I'm used to clearing up other people's mess. Roy was frantic with worry that his crooked past would be revealed and his business and marriage wrecked. We planned to dispense with Spender. Roy called Neil on the following Saturday evening, the eighth of May, and asked to meet him.

Spender said he was on board his boat. Roy told him to motor over to Salterns Lake Quay. Spender thought he was meeting Roy, so he was surprised when I showed up, but not worried. He should have been. I pushed the boat hook into his chest. It was dark . . . car park and quay deserted.'

'But you couldn't have thrown his body overboard. That would have taken some considerable strength.'

'Roy.'

'You took the boat across the harbour to Roy's jetty. Vicky and Kyle were away. The tide was up. Roy got Spender out of the cabin and into the sea. He cut himself doing so.'

'Did he?' Linden's voice was slurred.

'Roy's wife has confirmed that he was a rare blood group, so we know he was on board.'

Linden seemed not to hear.

'You threw the boat hook overboard and Roy cast the boat adrift. It was dark, the tide was rushing in, it was windy. Roy drove you back to Salterns Lake Quay, where you had parked Anther's car, which you'd borrowed.'

Linden nodded. Horton wasn't sure he could hear him. He carried on regardless.

'You returned to Anther's gallery and told him the deed had been done, which left Noel Catmore. When Macey knew you'd killed Catmore, he killed himself because he was unable to live with the guilt, or did you arrange to meet him on Dorothy's derelict quayside and end it for him by lacing the whisky with morphine? That is morphine in your flask, isn't it?'

'It was . . . be joining them all very soon.'

'Not Anther.'

'Even him . . . massive stroke . . . telephoned him at apartment . . . concierge told me . . . died yesterday.' Linden's voice was slurred. Horton was struggling to understand him. If he could just reach his phone —

He rose and crossed to Linden. 'Untie me. I'll get help.'

'Too late, Inspector.' Linden fell heavily onto the table, the flask sliding off and crashing onto the deck.

Horton, twisting his hands, managed to place a finger on Linden's neck. There was no pulse.

He went up on deck and swiftly took stock. There were no boats in sight and the day had grown overcast. His phone went but he was unable to reach it inside his leather jacket. Felice would have flares on board, but even if he found them in one of the lockers, he'd be unable to prise open the water-tight canister and let them off. However, there was a fixed VHF radio at the helm, which was just what he needed. He leaned forward and, with his teeth, lifted off the receiver by the flex. It clattered onto the top of the shelf of the helm.

Turning round and cricking his neck to look back at the radio, he slowly but successfully punched in the marine police channel and waited. With relief he heard Ripley answer.

Bending down, with his fingers, he switched on the receiver and spoke into it. 'This is *Sunlight Streaming*, Andy Horton speaking. I'm on board with Maurice Linden. I think it's too late for medical help but get a paramedic on standby at Shepherds Wharf, Cowes. Oh, and Ripley, if you're not doing anything can you and Elkins get over to Brook Bay right away? I'm rather tied up at the moment. Out.'

CHAPTER TWENTY-NINE

The police launch arrived soon after Horton's radio message. After Elkins had freed Horton's hands, Horton piloted Felice's boat to West Cowes, where a paramedic was waiting. He confirmed what Horton knew, that Linden was dead. As Elkins made arrangements for Linden's body to be taken to the mortuary, Horton rang Uckfield and gave a swift update, but it wasn't until he was in the incident suite some four hours later that he brought the team up to speed with all that had happened. He also handed over Linden's will and a written confession, which he had found in the cabin. Linden had confessed to the murders of Dorothy, Spender, Catmore and Macey. There were also two photographs, one of Linden and Ellwood as boys on an Isle of Wight beach, the other as young men in Paris with their arms entwined around each other, smiling into camera. Horton would have liked to think that Ellwood looked wary and shy and Linden confident and powerful, but it was just a picture of two happy young boys and two carefree young men, so perhaps he had been wrong about Michael wanting to free himself of Linden.

He'd called Felice when he had returned her boat to its berth at East Cowes Marina, and twice on the car ferry. She hadn't answered. He'd left a message on the first call to say her boat was secure on her berth, and the keys were with the marina office staff. He'd also relayed the fact that Linden was dead. He felt for her. She would need to make a statement. Horton would leave it to Uckfield to decide whether or not to press charges against her for misleading them and withholding information. Horton thought it unlikely though, given that her father had been a victim of blackmail.

He had said nothing to Uckfield about Linden's verbal confession to him that Michael Ellwood had killed Dorothy. There was no need when Linden had signed a written confession that he had killed her. Horton knew it was a lie. Linden had done that so the police wouldn't probe any further into Dorothy's death. Not that they would have come up with Ellwood if they had, but to the last Linden was protecting Michael as well as his daughter, who had inherited Linden's estate and was named as his executor. Linden's London flat would be searched, as would Anther's in Paris. Bliss confirmed Linden's claim that Anther was dead, and all of those who had taken part in that art fraud in the 1980s were now gone.

It wasn't until the following day that Walters's team found Catmore's body in a particularly dense patch of undergrowth of bracken, branches and earth. Spender was still missing. Horton wondered if his body would ever surface.

The day was filled with completing reports, sadly bringing Mrs Macey up to date with the tragic, sordid tale. It would all come out at the inquest anyway. The autopsy on Macey found that he had overdosed on morphine, which Linden had administered by spiking the whisky. Horton was angry at that. Why had Linden done that when he and Michael would soon be dead? But Macey had known that Ellwood had killed Dorothy, and Linden could never countenance the fact he might tell, even when Michael was dead.

Macey's laptop had shown emails from him to Anther but nothing incriminating. If it hadn't been for Ida Tidy they would never have found out about the Hayling Island house, The Shambles. Macey's boat would have been discovered though and a search might have been made of the grounds, so Catmore might have been found. Linden had arranged that rendezvous and had crossed to it using Felice's boat on which he'd been staying, not in Ellwood's studio.

Horton had tried Felice's phone a couple more times. He'd said he was sorry for her loss and if she needed to talk to him, he would be happy to hear from her. He knew that she would need time, a great deal of it.

It was just on seven when he reached for his leather jacket and helmet to go home. His mobile rang as he was about to climb on the Harley. He thought it might be Felice, but with a lift of his heart and a quickening pulse he saw it was Gaye.

'Has your corpse surfaced?'

'Not yet. Where are you?'

'Back in good old Pompey.'

'Then I'll buy you dinner.'

'Fine, but I'm warning you, Andy, you'll have to expect me as I am, having just got home after a horrendous journey, which I won't bore you with. I'm not dressed for anywhere posh.'

'Then we won't go anywhere posh, and for all I care you can come dressed in your mortuary garb, just as long as you do come, Gaye.'

'You sound a tad desperate,' she teased.

'I am.'

'To tell me about your missing corpse?'

For a moment, Richard Ames flashed into his head, not Spender. 'No, to see you,' he said, meaning it.

'Missing my mortuary wit, no doubt.'

That and more, he thought but didn't say.

'Has it been that bad without me?'

'Awful.'

She laughed. How good it was to hear that again and her voice.

'I'll pick you up on the Harley.'

'No thanks.'

'Where's your spirit of adventure?'

'On the M1. *I'll* pick *you* up, but I'm warning you, I'm not driving far to eat.'

'Then we'll eat in the marina restaurant, they do a mean curry.'

'Perfect. See you in twenty minutes.'

'Make it ten.' And with a smile Horton climbed on his Harley and made for his yacht.

THE END

ACKNOWLEDGEMENTS

With grateful thanks to Jonathan Smith, senior forensic scientist, who assisted with blood pattern analysis; Dr Carolyn Lovell, who assisted with crime scene management; and Wez Smith, Solent Manager for the Royal Society for the Protection of Birds (RSPB), who assisted with all things avian.

ALSO BY PAULINE ROWSON

THE SOLENT MURDER MYSTERIES
Book 1: THE PORTSMOUTH MURDERS
Book 2: THE LANGSTONE HARBOUR MURDERS
Book 3: THE HORSEA MARINA MURDERS
Book 4: THE ROYAL HOTEL MURDERS
Book 5: THE ISLE OF WIGHT MURDERS
Book 6: THE PORTCHESTER CASTLE MURDERS
Book 7: THE CHALE BAY MURDERS
Book 8: THE FARLINGTON MARSH MURDERS
Book 9: THE OYSTER QUAYS MURDERS
Book 10: THE COWES WEEK MURDERS
Book 11: THE BOATHOUSE MURDERS
Book 12: THE THORNEY ISLAND MURDERS
Book 13: THE GUERNSEY FERRY MURDERS
Book 14: THE RAT ISLAND MURDERS
Book 15: THE LUCCOMBE BAY MURDERS
Book 16: THE SOUTH BINNESS MURDERS

Thank you for reading this book.

If you enjoyed it please leave feedback on Amazon or Goodreads, and if there is anything we missed or you have a question about, then please get in touch. We appreciate you choosing our book.

Founded in 2014 in Shoreditch, London, we at Joffe Books pride ourselves on our history of innovative publishing. We were thrilled to be shortlisted for Independent Publisher of the Year at the British Book Awards.

www.joffebooks.com

We're very grateful to eagle-eyed readers who take the time to contact us. Please send any errors you find to corrections@joffebooks.com. We'll get them fixed ASAP.

Printed in the USA
CPSIA information can be obtained
at www.ICGtesting.com
LVHW042016260724
786517LV00005B/1028